The Snare

Rafael Sabatini

The Snare

The present edition is a reproduction of previous publication of this classic work. Minor typographical errors may have been corrected without note; however, for an authentic reading experience the spelling, punctuation, and capitalization have been retained from the original text.

ISBN: 978-1-63637-522-9

CONTENTS

CHAPTER I

THE AFFAIR AT TAVORA

It is established beyond doubt that Mr. Butler was drunk at the time. This rests upon the evidence of Sergeant Flanagan and the troopers who accompanied him, and it rests upon Mr. Butler's own word, as we shall see. And let me add here and now that however wild and irresponsible a rascal he may have been, yet by his own lights he was a man of honour, incapable of falsehood, even though it were calculated to save his skin. I do not deny that Sir Thomas Picton has described him as a "thieving blackguard." But I am sure that this was merely the downright, rather extravagant manner, of censure peculiar to that distinguished general, and that those who have taken the expression at its purely literal value have been lacking at once in charity and in knowledge of the caustic, uncompromising terms of speech of General Picton whom Lord Wellington, you will remember, called a rough, foulmouthed devil.

In further extenuation it may truthfully be urged that the whole hideous and odious affair was the result of a misapprehension; although I cannot go so far as one of Lieutenant Butler's apologists and accept the view that he was the victim of a deliberate plot on the part of his too-genial host at Regoa. That is a misconception easily explained. This host's name happened to be Souza, and the apologist in question has very rashly leapt at the conclusion that he was a member of that notoriously intriguing family, of which the chief members were the Principal Souza, of the Council of Regency at Lisbon, and the Chevalier Souza, Portuguese minister to the Court of St. James's. Unacquainted with Portugal, our apologist was evidently in ignorance of the fact that the name of Souza is almost as common in that country as the name of Smith in this. He may also have been misled by the fact that Principal Souza did not neglect to make the utmost capital out of the affair, thereby increasing the difficulties with which Lord Wellington was already contending as a result of incompetence and deliberate malice on the part both of the ministry at home and of the administration in Lisbon.

Indeed, but for these factors it is unlikely that the affair could ever have taken place at all. If there had been more energy on the part of Mr. Perceval and the members of the Cabinet, if there had been less bad faith and self-seeking on the part of the Opposition, Lord Wellington's campaign would not have been starved as it was;

and if there had been less bad faith and self-seeking of an even more stupid and flagrant kind on the part of the Portuguese Council of Regency, the British Expeditionary Force would not have been left without the stipulated supplies and otherwise hindered at every step.

Lord Wellington might have experienced the mental agony of Sir John Moore under similar circumstances fifteen months earlier. That he did suffer, and was to suffer yet more, his correspondence shows. But his iron will prevented that suffering from disturbing the equanimity of his mind. The Council of Regency, in its concern to court popularity with the aristocracy of Portugal, might balk his measures by its deliberate supineness; echoes might reach him of the voices at St. Stephen's that loudly dubbed his dispositions rash, presumptuous and silly; catch-halfpenny journalists at home and men of the stamp of Lord Grey might exploit their abysmal military ignorance in reckless criticism and censure of his operations; he knew what a passionate storm of anger and denunciation had arisen from the Opposition when he had been raised to the peerage some months earlier, after the glorious victory of Talavera, and how, that victory notwithstanding, it had been proclaimed that his conduct of the campaign was so incompetent as to deserve, not reward, but punishment; and he was aware of the growing unpopularity of the war in England, knew that the Government—ignorant of what he was so laboriously preparing—was chafing at his inactivity of the past few months, so that a member of the Cabinet wrote to him exasperatedly, incredibly and fatuously—"for God's sake do something—anything so that blood be spilt."

A heart less stout might have been broken, a genius less mighty stifled in this evil tangle of stupidity, incompetence and malignity that sprang up and flourished about him on every hand. A man less single-minded must have succumbed to exasperation, thrown up his command and taken ship for home, inviting some of his innumerable critics to take his place at the head of the troops, and give free rein to the military genius that inspired their critical dissertations. Wellington, however, has been rightly termed of iron, and never did he show himself more of iron than in those trying days of 1810. Stern, but with a passionless sternness, he pursued his way towards the goal he had set himself, allowing no criticism, no censure, no invective so much as to give him pause in his majestic progress.

Unfortunately the lofty calm of the Commander-in-Chief was not shared by his lieutenants. The Light Division was quartered along the River Agueda, watching the Spanish frontier, beyond which Marshal Ney was demonstrating against Ciudad Rodrigo, and for lack of funds its fiery-tempered commander, Sir Robert Craufurd, found himself at last unable to feed his troops. Exasperated by these circumstances, Sir Robert was betrayed into an act of rashness. He seized some church plate at Pinhel that he might convert it into rations. It was an act which, considering the general state of public feeling in the country at the time, might have had the gravest consequences, and Sir Robert was subsequently forced to do penance and afford redress. That, however, is another story. I but mention the incident here because the affair of Tavora with which I am concerned may be taken to have arisen directly out of it, and Sir Robert's behaviour may be construed as setting an example and thus as affording yet another extenuation of Lieutenant Butler's offence.

Our lieutenant was sent upon a foraging expedition into the valley of the Upper Douro, at the head of a half-troop of the 8th Dragoons, two squadrons of which were attached at the time to the Light Division. To be more precise, he was to purchase and bring into Pinhel a hundred head of cattle, intended some for slaughter and some for draught. His instructions were to proceed as far as Regoa and there report himself to one Bartholomew Bearsley, a prosperous and influential English wine-grower, whose father had acquired considerable vineyards in the Douro. He was reminded of the almost hostile disposition of the peasantry in certain districts; warned to handle them with tact and to suffer no straggling on the part of his troopers; and advised to place himself in the hands of Mr. Bearsley for all that related to the purchase of the cattle. Let it be admitted at once that had Sir Robert Craufurd been acquainted with Mr. Butler's feather-brained, irresponsible nature, he would have selected any officer rather than our lieutenant to command that expedition. But the Irish Dragoons had only lately come to Pinhel, and the general himself was not immediately concerned.

Lieutenant Butler set out on a blustering day of March at the head of his troopers, accompanied by Cornet O'Rourke and two sergeants, and at Pesqueira he was further reinforced by a Portuguese guide. They found quarters that night at Ervedoza, and early on the morrow they were in the saddle again, riding along the heights above the Cachao da Valleria, through which the yellow, swollen river swirled and foamed along its rocky way. The prospect, formidable even in the full bloom of fruitful and luxuriant summer, was forbidding and menacing now as some imagined gorge of the nether regions. The towering granite heights across the turgid stream were shrouded in mist and sweeping rain, and from the leaden heavens overhead the downpour was of a sullen and merciless steadiness, starting at every step a miniature torrent to go

3

swell the roaring waters in the gorge, and drenching the troop alike in body and in spirit. Ahead, swathed to the chin in his blue cavalry cloak, the water streaming from his leather helmet, rode Lieutenant Butler, cursing the weather, the country; the Light Division, and everything else that occurred to him as contributing to his present discomfort. Beside him, astride of a mule, rode the Portuguese guide in a caped cloak of thatched straw, which made him look for all the world like a bottle of his native wine in its straw sheath. Conversation between the two was out of the question, for the guide spoke no English and the lieutenant's knowledge of Portuguese was very far from conversational.

Presently the ground sloped, and the troop descended from the heights by a road flanked with dripping pinewoods, black and melancholy, that for a while screened them off from the remainder of the sodden world. Thence they emerged near the head of the bridge that spanned the swollen river and led them directly into the town of Regoa. Through the mud and clay of the deserted, narrow, unpaved streets the dragoons squelched their way, under a super-deluge, for the rain was now reinforced by steady and overwhelming sheets of water descending on either side from the gutter-shaped tiles that roofed the houses.

Inquisitive faces showed here and there behind blurred windows; odd doors were opened that a peasant family might stare in questioning wonder—and perhaps in some concern—at the sodden pageant that was passing. But in the streets themselves the troopers met no living thing, all the world having scurried to shelter from the pitiless downpour.

Beyond the town they were brought by their guide to a walled garden, and halted at a gateway. Beyond this could be seen a fair white house set in the foreground of the vineyards that rose in terraces up the hillside until they were lost from sight in the lowering veils of mist. Carved on the granite lintel of that gateway, the lieutenant beheld the inscription, "BARTHOLOMEU BEARSLEY, 1744," and knew himself at his destination, at the gates of the son or grandson—he knew not which, nor cared—of the original tenant of that wine farm.

Mr. Bearsley, however, was from home. The lieutenant was informed of this by Mr. Bearsley's steward, a portly, genial, rather priestly gentleman in smooth black broadcloth, whose name was Souza—a name which, as I have said, has given rise to some misconceptions. Mr. Bearsley himself had lately left for England, there to wait until the disturbed state of Portugal should be happily repaired. He had been a considerable sufferer from the French invasion under Soult, and none may blame him for wishing to avoid a repetition of what already he had undergone, especially now that it was rumoured that the Emperor in person would lead the army gathering for conquest on the frontiers.

But had Mr. Bearsley been at home the dragoons could have received no warmer welcome than that which was extended to them by Fernando Souza. Greeting the lieutenant in intelligible English, he implored him, in the florid manner of the Peninsula, to count the house and all within it his own property, and to command whatever he might desire.

The troopers found accommodation in the kitchen and in the spacious hall, where great fires of pine logs were piled up for their comfort; and for the remainder of the day they abode there in various states of nakedness, relieved by blankets and straw capotes, what time the house was filled with the steam and stench of their drying garments. Rations had been short of late on the Agueda, and, in addition, their weary ride through the rain had made the men sharp-set. Abundance of food was placed before them by the solicitude of Fernando Souza, and they feasted, as they had not feasted for many months, upon roast kid, boiled rice and golden maize bread, washed down by a copious supply of a rough and not too heady wine that the discreet and discriminating steward judged appropriate to their palates and capable of supporting some abuse.

Akin to the treatment of the troopers in hall and kitchen, but on a nobler scale, was the treatment of Lieutenant Butler and Cornet O'Rourke in the dining-room. For them a well-roasted turkey took the place of kid, and Souza went down himself to explore the cellars for a well-sunned, time-ripened Douro table wine which he vowed—and our dragoons agreed with him—would put the noblest Burgundy to shame; and then with the dessert there was a Port the like of which Mr. Butler—who was always of a nice taste in wine, and who was coming into some knowledge of Port from his residence in the country—had never dreamed existed.

For four and twenty hours the dragoons abode at Mr. Bearsley's quinta, thanking God for the discomforts that had brought them to such comfort, feasting in this land of plenty as only those can feast who have kept a rigid Lent. Nor was this all. The benign Souza was determined that the sojourn there of these representatives of his country's deliverers should be a complete rest and holiday. Not for Mr. Butler to journey to the uplands in this matter of a herd of bullocks. Fernando Souza had at command a regiment of labourers, who were idle at this time of year, and whom his good nature would engage on behalf of his English guests. Let the lieutenant do no more than provide the necessary money for the

5

cattle, and the rest should happen as by enchantment—and Souza himself would see to it that the price was fair and proper.

The lieutenant asked no better. He had no great opinion of himself either as cattle dealer or cattle drover, nor did his ambitions beget in him any desire to excel as one or the other. So he was well content that his host should have the bullocks fetched to Regoa for him. The herd was driven in on the following afternoon, by when the rain had ceased, and our lieutenant had every reason to be pleased when he beheld the solid beasts procured. Having disbursed the amount demanded—an amount more reasonable far than he had been prepared to pay—Mr. Butler would have set out forthwith to return to Pinhel, knowing how urgent was the need of the division and with what impatience the choleric General Craufurd would be awaiting him.

"Why, so you shall, so you shall," said the priestly, soothing Souza. "But first you'll dine. There is good dinner—ah, but what good dinner!—that I have order. And there is a wine—ah, but you shall give me news of that wine."

Lieutenant Butler hesitated. Cornet O'Rourke watched him anxiously, praying that he might succumb to the temptation, and attempted suasion in the form of a murmured blessing upon Souza's hospitality.

"Sir Robert will be impatient," demurred the lieutenant.

"But half-hour," protested Souza. "What is half-hour? And in half-hour you will have dine."

"True," ventured the cornet; "and it's the devil himself knows when we may dine again."

"And the dinner is ready. It can be serve this instant. It shall," said Souza with finality, and pulled the bell-rope.

Mr. Butler, never dreaming—as indeed how could he?—that Fate was taking a hand in this business, gave way, and they sat down to dinner. Henceforth you see him the sport of pitiless circumstance.

They dined within the half-hour, as Souza had promised, and they dined exceedingly well. If yesterday the steward had been able without warning of their coming to spread at short notice so excellent a feast, conceive what had been accomplished now by preparation. Emptying his fourth and final bumper of rich red Douro, Mr. Butler paid his host the compliment of a sigh and pushed back his chair.

But Souza detained him, waving a hand that trembled with anxiety, and with anxiety stamped upon his benignly rotund and shaven countenance.

"An instant yet," he implored. "Mr. Bearsley would never

pardon me did I let you go without what he call a stirrup-cup to keep you from the ills that lurk in the wind of the Serra. A glass—but one—of that Port you tasted yesterday. I say but a glass, yet I hope you will do honour to the bottle. But a glass at least, at least!" He implored it almost with tears. Mr. Butler had reached that state of delicious torpor in which to take the road is the last agony; but duty was duty, and Sir Robert Craufurd had the fiend's own temper. Torn thus between consciousness of duty and the weakness of the flesh, he looked at O'Rourke. O'Rourke, a cherubic fellow, who had for his years a very pretty taste in wine, returned the glance with a moist eye, and licked his lips.

"In your place I should let myself be tempted," says he. "It's an elegant wine, and ten minutes more or less is no great matter."

The lieutenant discovered a middle way which permitted him to take a prompt decision creditable to his military instincts, but revealing a disgraceful though quite characteristic selfishness.

"Very well," he said. "Leave Sergeant Flanagan and ten men to wait for me, O'Rourke, and do you set out at once with the rest of the troop. And take the cattle with you. I shall overtake you before you have gone very far."

O'Rourke's crestfallen air stirred the sympathetic Souza's pity.

"But, Captain," he besought, "will you not allow the lieutenant—"

Mr. Butler cut him short. "Duty," said he sententiously, "is duty. Be off, O'Rourke."

And O'Rourke, clicking his heels viciously, saluted and departed.

Came presently the bottles in a basket—not one, as Souza had said, but three; and when the first was done Butler reflected that since O'Rourke and the cattle were already well upon the road there need no longer be any hurry about his own departure. A herd of bullocks does not travel very quickly, and even with a few hours' start in a forty-mile journey is easily over-taken by a troop of horse travelling without encumbrance.

You understand, then, how easily our lieutenant yielded himself to the luxurious circumstances, and disposed himself to savour the second bottle of that nectar distilled from the very sunshine of the Douro—the phrase is his own. The steward produced a box of very choice cigars, and although the lieutenant was not an habitual smoker, he permitted himself on this exceptional occasion to be further tempted. Stretched in a deep chair beside the roaring fire of pine logs, he sipped and smoked and drowsed away the greater par of that wintry afternoon. Soon the third bottle had gone the way of the second, and Mr. Bearsley's

7

steward being a man of extremely temperate habit, it follows that most of the wine had found its way down the lieutenant's thirsty gullet.

It was perhaps a more potent vintage than he had at first suspected, and as the torpor produced by the dinner and the earlier, fuller wine was wearing off, it was succeeded by an exhilaration that played havoc with the few wits that Mr. Butler could call his own.

The steward was deeply learned in wines and wine growing and in very little besides; consequently the talk was almost confined to that subject in its many branches, and he could be interesting enough, like all enthusiasts. To a fresh burst of praise from Butler of the ruby vintage to which he had been introduced, the steward presently responded with a sigh:

"Indeed, as you say, Captain, a great wine. But we had a greater."

"Impossible, by God," swore Butler, with a hiccup.

"You may say so; but it is the truth. We had a greater; a wonderful, clear vintage it was, of the year 1798—a famous year on the Douro, the quite most famous year that we have ever known. Mr. Bearsley sell some pipes to the monks at Tavora, who have bottle it and keep it. I beg him at the time not to sell, knowing the value it must come to have one day. But he sell all the same. Ah, meu Deus!" The steward clasped his hands and raised rather prominent eyes to the ceiling, protesting to his Maker against his master's folly. "He say we have plenty, and now"—he spread fat hands in a gesture of despair—"and now we have none. Some sons of dogs of French who came with Marshal Soult happen this way on a forage they discover the wine and they guzzle it like pigs." He swore, and his benignity was eclipsed by wrathful memory. He heaved himself up in a passion.

"Think of that so priceless vintage drink like hogwash, as Mr. Bearsley say, by those god-dammed French swine, not a drop—not a spoonful remain. But the monks at Tavora still have much of what they buy, I am told. They treasure it for they know good wine. All priests know good wine. Ah yes! Goddam!" He fell into deep reflection.

Lieutenant Butler stirred, and became sympathetic.

"'San infern'l shame," said he indignantly. "I'll no forgerrit when I... meet the French." Then he too fell into reflection.

He was a good Catholic, and, moreover, a Catholic who did not take things for granted. The sloth and self-indulgence of the clergy in Portugal, being his first glimpse of conventuals in Latin countries, had deeply shocked him. The vows of a monastic poverty that was kept carefully beyond the walls of the monastery offended his sense of propriety. That men who had vowed themselves to pauperism, who wore coarse garments and went barefoot, should batten upon rich food and store up wines that gold could not purchase, struck him as a hideous incongruity.

"And the monks drink this nectar?" he said aloud, and laughed sneeringly. "I know the breed—the fair found belly wi' fat capon lined. Tha's your poverty stricken Capuchin."

Souza looked at him in sudden alarm, bethinking himself that all Englishmen were heretics, and knowing nothing of subtle distinctions between English and Irish. In silence Butler finished the third and last bottle, and his thoughts fixed themselves with increasing insistence upon a wine reputed better than this of which there was great store in the cellars of the convent of Tavora.

Abruptly he asked: "Where's Tavora?" He was thinking perhaps of the comfort that such wine would bring to a company of war-worn soldiers in the valley of the Agueda.

"Some ten leagues from here," answered Souza, and pointed to a map that hung upon the wall.

The lieutenant rose, and rolled a thought unsteadily across the room. He was a tall, loose-limbed fellow, blue-eyed, fair-complexioned, with a thatch of fiery red hair excellently suited to his temperament. He halted before the map, and with legs wide apart, to afford him the steadying support of a broad basis, he traced with his finger the course of the Douro, fumbled about the district of Regoa, and finally hit upon the place he sought.

"Why," he said, "seems to me 'sif we should ha' come that way. I's shorrer road to Pesqueira than by the river."

"As the bird fly," said Souza. "But the roads be bad—just mule tracks, while by the river the road is tolerable good."

"Yet," said the lieutenant, "I think I shall go back tha' way."

The fumes of the wine were mounting steadily to addle his indifferent brains. Every moment he was seeing things in proportions more and more false. His resentment against priests who, sworn to self-abnegation, hoarded good wine, whilst soldiers sent to keep harm from priests' fat carcasses were left to suffer cold and even hunger, was increasing with every moment. He would sample that wine at Tavora; and he would bear some of it away that his brother officers at Pinhel might sample it. He would buy it. Oh yes! There should be no plundering, no irregularity, no disregard of general orders. He would buy the wine and pay for it—but himself he would fix the price, and see that the monks of Tavora made no profit out of their defenders.

Thus he thought as he considered the map. Presently, when having taken leave of Fernando Souza—that prince of hosts—Mr.

Butler was riding down through the town with Sergeant Flanagan and ten troopers at his heels, his purpose deepened and became more fierce. I think the change of temperature must have been to blame. It was a chill, bleak evening. Overhead, across a background of faded blue, scudded ragged banks of clouds, the lingering flotsam of the shattered rainstorm of yesterday: and a cavalry cloak afforded but indifferent protection against the wind that blew hard and sharp from the Atlantic.

Coming from the genial warmth of Mr. Souza's parlour into this, the evaporation of the wine within him was quickened, its fumes mounted now overwhelmingly to his brain, and from comfortably intoxicated that he had been hitherto, the lieutenant now became furiously drunk; and the transition was a very rapid one. It was now that he looked upon the business he had in hand in the light of a crusade; a sort of religious fanaticism began to actuate him.

The souls of these wretched monks must be saved; the temptation to self-indulgence, which spelt perdition for them, must be removed from their midst. It was a Christian duty. He no longer thought of buying the wine and paying for it. His one aim now was to obtain possession of it not merely a part of it, but all of it—and carry it off, thereby accomplishing two equally praiseworthy ends: to rescue a conventful of monks from damnation, and to regale the much-enduring, half-starved campaigners of the Agueda.

Thus reasoned Mr. Butler with admirable, if drunken, logic. And reasoning thus he led the way over the bridge, and kept straight on when he had crossed it, much to the dismay of Sergeant Flanagan, who, perceiving the lieutenant's condition, conceived that he was missing his way. This the sergeant ventured to point out, reminding his officer that they had come by the road along the river.

"So we did," said Butler shortly. "Bu' we go back by way of Tavora."

They had no guide. The one who had conducted them to Regoa had returned with O'Rourke, and although Souza had urged upon the lieutenant at parting that he should take one of the men from the quinta, Butler, with wit enough to see that this was not desirable under the circumstances, had preferred to find his way alone.

His confused mind strove now to revisualise the map which he had consulted in Souza's parlour. He discovered, naturally enough, that the task was altogether beyond his powers. Meanwhile night was descending. They were, however, upon the mule track,

10

which went up and round the shoulder of a hill, and by this they came at dark upon a hamlet.

Sergeant Flanagan was a shrewd fellow and perhaps the most sober man in the troop—for the wine had run very freely in Souza's kitchen, too, and the men, whilst awaiting their commander's pleasure, had taken the fullest advantage of an opportunity that was all too rare upon that campaign. Now Sergeant Flanagan began to grow anxious. He knew the Peninsula from the days of Sir John Moore, and he knew as much of the ways of the peasantry of Portugal as any man. He knew of the brutal ferocity of which that peasantry was capable. He had seen evidence more than once of the unspeakable fate of French stragglers from the retreating army of Marshal Soult. He knew of crucifixions, mutilations and hideous abominations practised upon them in these remote hill districts by the merciless men into whose hands they happened to fall, and he knew that it was not upon French soldiers alone—that these abominations had been practised. Some of those fierce peasants had been unable to discriminate between invader and deliverer; to them a foreigner was a foreigner and no more. Others, who were capable of discriminating, were in the position of having come to look upon French and English with almost equal execration.

It is true that whilst the Emperor's troops made war on the maxim that an army must support itself upon the country it traverses, thereby achieving a greater mobility, since it was thus permitted to travel comparatively light, the British law was that all things requisitioned must be paid for. Wellington maintained this law in spite of all difficulties at all times with an unrelaxing rigidity, and punished with the utmost vigour those who offended against it. Nevertheless breaches were continual; men broke out here and there, often, be it said, under stress of circumstances for which the Portuguese were themselves responsible; plunder and outrage took place and provoked indiscriminating rancour with consequences at times as terrible to stragglers from the British army of deliverance as to those from the French army of oppressors. Then, too, there was the Portuguese Militia Act recently enforced by Wellington—acting through the Portuguese Government—deeply resented by the peasantry upon whom it bore, and rendering them disposed to avenge it upon such stray British soldiers as might fall into their hands.

Knowing all this, Sergeant Flanagan did not at all relish this night excursion into the hill fastnesses, where at any moment, as it seemed to him, they might miss their way. After all, they were but twelve men all told, and he accounted it a stupid thing to attempt to take a short cut across the hills for the purpose of overtaking an

11

encumbered troop that must of necessity be moving at a very much slower pace. This was the way not to overtake but to outdistance. Yet since it was not for him to remonstrate with the lieutenant, he kept his peace and hoped anxiously for the best.

At the mean wine-shop of that hamlet Mr. Butler inquired his way by the simple expedient of shouting "Tavora?" with a strong interrogative inflection. The vintner made it plain by gestures—accompanied by a rattling musketry of incomprehensible speech that their way lay straight ahead. And straight ahead they went, following that mule track for some five or six miles until it began to slope gently towards the plain again. Below them they presently beheld a cluster of twinkling lights to advertise a township. They dropped swiftly down, and in the outskirts overtook a belated bullock-cart, whose ungreased axle was arousing the hillside echoes with its plangent wail.

Of the vigorous young woman who marched barefoot beside it, shouldering her goad as if it were a pikestaff, Mr. Butler inquired—by his usual method—if this were Tavora, to receive an answer which, though voluble, was unmistakably affirmative.

"Covento Dominicano?" was his next inquiry, made after they had gone some little way.

The woman pointed with her goad to a massive, dark building, flanked by a little church, which stood just across the square they were entering.

A moment later the sergeant, by Mr. Butler's orders, was knocking upon the iron-studded main door. They waited awhile in vain. None came to answer the knock; no light showed anywhere upon the dark face of the convent. The sergeant knocked again, more vigorously than before. Presently came timid, shuffling steps; a shutter opened in the door, and the grille thus disclosed was pierced by a shaft of feeble yellow light. A quavering, aged voice demanded to know who knocked.

"English soldiers," answered the lieutenant in Portuguese. "Open!"

A faint exclamation suggestive of dismay was the answer, the shutter closed again with a snap, the shuffling steps retreated and unbroken silence followed.

"Now wharra devil may this mean?" growled Mr. Butler. Drugged wits, like stupid ones, are readily suspicious. "Wharra they hatching in here that they are afraid of lerring Bri'ish soldiers see? Knock again, Flanagan. Louder, man!"

The sergeant beat the door with the butt of his carbine. The blows gave out a hollow echo, but evoked no more answer than if they had fallen upon the door of a mausoleum. Mr. Butler

12

completely lost his temper. "Seems to me that we've stumbled upon a hotbed o' treason. Hotbed o' treason!" he repeated, as if pleased with the phrase. "That's wharrit is." And he added peremptorily: "Break down the door."

"But, sir," began the sergeant in protest, greatly daring.

"Break down the door," repeated Mr. Butler. "Lerrus be after seeing wha' these monks are afraid of showing us. I've a notion they're hiding more'n their wine."

Some of the troopers carried axes precisely against such an emergency as this. Dismounting, they fell upon the door with a will. But the oak was stout, fortified by bands of iron and great iron studs; and it resisted long. The thud of the axes and the crash of rending timbers could be heard from one end of Tavora to the other, yet from the convent it evoked no slightest response. But presently, as the door began to yield to the onslaught, there came another sound to arouse the town. From the belfry of the little church a bell suddenly gave tongue upon a frantic, hurried note that spoke unmistakably of alarm. Ding-ding-ding-ding it went, a tocsin summoning the assistance of all true sons of Mother Church.

Mr. Butler, however, paid little heed to it. The door was down at last, and followed by his troopers he rode under the massive gateway into the spacious close. Dismounting there, and leaving the woefully anxious sergeant and a couple of men to guard the horses, the lieutenant led the way along the cloisters, faintly revealed by a new-risen moon, towards a gaping doorway whence a feeble light was gleaming. He stumbled over the step into a hall dimly lighted by a lantern swinging from the ceiling. He found a chair, mounted it, and cut the lantern down, then led the way again along an endless corridor, stone-flagged and flanked on either side by rows of cells. Many of the doors stood open, as if in silent token of the tenants' hurried flight, showing what a panic had been spread by the sudden advent of this troop.

Mr. Butler became more and more deeply intrigued, more and more deeply suspicious that here all was not well. Why should a community of loyal monks take flight in this fashion from British soldiers?

"Bad luck to them!" he growled, as he stumbled on. "They may hide as they will, but it's myself 'll run the shavelings to earth."

They were brought up short at the end of that long, chill gallery by closed double doors. Beyond these an organ was pealing, and overhead the clapper of the alarm bell was beating more furiously than ever. All realised that they stood upon the threshold of the chapel and that the conventuals had taken refuge there.

13

Mr. Butler checked upon a sudden suspicion. "Maybe, after all, they've taken us for French," said he.

A trooper ventured to answer him. "Best let them see we're not before we have the whole village about our ears."

"Damn that bell," said the lieutenant, and added: "Put your shoulders to the door."

Its fastenings were but crazy ones, and it yielded almost instantly to their pressure—yielded so suddenly that Mr. Butler, who himself had been foremost in straining against it, shot forward half-a-dozen yards into the chapel and measured his length upon its cold flags.

Simultaneously from the chancel came a great cry: "Libera nos, Domine!" followed by a shuddering murmur of prayer.

The lieutenant picked himself up, recovered the lantern that had rolled from his grasp, and lurched forward round the angle that hid the chancel from his view. There, huddled before the main altar like a flock of scared and stupid sheep, he beheld the conventuals—some two score of them perhaps and in the dim light of the heavy altar lamp above them he could make out the black and white habit of the order of St. Dominic.

He came to a halt, raised his lantern aloft, and called to them peremptorily:

"Ho, there!"

The organ ceased abruptly, but the bell overhead went clattering on.

Mr. Butler addressed them in the best French he could command: "What do you fear? Why do you flee? We are friends—English soldiers, seeking quarters for the night."

A vague alarm was stirring in him. It began to penetrate his obfuscated mind that perhaps he had been rash, that this forcible rape of a convent was a serious matter. Therefore he attempted this peaceful explanation.

From that huddled group a figure rose, and advanced with a solemn, stately grace. There was a faint swish of robes, the faint rattle of rosary beads. Something about that figure caught the lieutenant's attention sharply. He craned forward, half sobered by the sudden fear that clutched him, his eyes bulging in his face.

"I had thought," said a gentle, melancholy woman's voice, "that the seals of a nunnery were sacred to British soldiers."

For a moment Mr. Butler seemed to be labouring for breath. Fully sobered now, understanding of his ghastly error reached him at the gallop.

"My God!" he gasped, and incontinently turned to flee.

But as he fled in horror of his sacrilege, he still kept his head turned, staring over his shoulder at the stately figure of the abbess, either in fascination or with some lingering doubt of what he had seen and heard. Running thus, he crashed headlong into a pillar, and, stunned by the blow, he reeled and sank unconscious to the ground.

This the troopers had not seen, for they had not lingered. Understanding on their own part the horrible blunder, they had turned even as their leader turned, and they had raced madly back the way they had come, conceiving that he followed. And there was reason for their haste other than their anxiety to set a term to the sacrilege of their presence. From the cloistered garden of the convent uproar reached them, and the metallic voice of Sergeant Flanagan calling loudly for help.

The alarm bell of the convent had done its work. The villagers were up, enraged by the outrage, and armed with sticks and scythes and bill-hooks, an army of them was charging to avenge this infamy. The troopers reached the close no more than in time. Sergeant Flanagan, only half understanding the reason for so much anger, but understanding that this anger was very real and very dangerous, was desperately defending the horses with his two companions against the vanguard of the assailants. There was a swift rush of the dragoons and in an instant they were in the saddle, all but the lieutenant, of whose absence they were suddenly made conscious. Flanagan would have gone back for him, and he had in fact begun to issue an order with that object when a sudden surge of the swelling, roaring crowd cut off the dragoons from the door through which they had emerged. Sitting their horses, the little troop came together, their sabres drawn, solid as a rock in that angry human sea that surged about them. The moon riding now clear overhead irradiated that scene of impending strife.

Flanagan, standing in his stirrups, attempted to harangue the mob. But he was at a loss what to say that would appease them, nor able to speak a language they could understand. An angry peasant made a slash at him with a billhook. He parried the blow on his sabre, and with the flat of it knocked his assailant senseless.

Then the storm burst, and the mob flung itself upon the dragoons.

"Bad cess to you!" cried Flanagan. "Will ye listen to me, ye murthering villains." Then in despair "Char-r-r-ge!" he roared, and headed for the gateway.

The troopers attempted in vain to reach it. The mob hemmed them about too closely, and then a horrid hand-to-hand fight began, under the cold light of the moon, in that garden consecrated to peace and piety. Two saddles had been emptied, and the exasperated troopers were slashing now at their assailants with the edge, intent upon cutting a way out of that murderous press. It is doubtful if a man of them would have survived, for the odds were fully ten to one against them. To their aid came now the abbess. She stood on a balcony above, and called upon the people to desist, and hear her. Thence she harangued them for some moments, commanding them to allow the soldiers to depart. They obeyed with obvious reluctance, and at last a lane was opened in that solid, seething mass of angry clods.

But Flanagan hesitated to pass down this lane and so depart. Three of his troopers were down by now, and his lieutenant was missing. He was exercised to resolve where his duty lay. Behind him the mob was solid, cutting off the dragoons from their fallen comrades. An attempt to go back might be misunderstood and resisted, leading to a renewal of the combat, and surely in vain, for he could not doubt but that the fallen troopers had been finished outright.

Similarly the mob stood as solid between him and the door that led to the interior of the convent, where Mr. Butler was lingering alive or dead. A number of peasants had already invaded the actual building, so that in that connection too the sergeant concluded that there was little reason to hope that the lieutenant should have escaped the fate his own rashness had invoked. He had his remaining seven men to think of, and he concluded that it was his duty under all the circumstances to bring these off alive, and not procure their massacre by attempting fruitless quixotries.

So "Forward!" roared the voice of Sergeant Flanagan, and forward went the seven through the passage that had opened out before them in that hooting, angry mob.

Beyond the convent walls they found fresh assailants awaiting them, enemies these, who had not been soothed by the gentle, reassuring voice of the abbess. But here there was more room to manoeuvre.

"Trot!" the sergeant commanded, and soon that trot became a gallop. A shower of stones followed them as they thundered out of Tavora, and the sergeant himself had a lump as large as a duck-egg on the middle of his head when next day he reported himself at Pesqueira to Cornet O'Rourke, whom he overtook there.

When eventually Sir Robert Craufurd heard the story of the affair, he was as angry as only Sir Robert could be. To have lost four dragoons and to have set a match to a train that might end in a conflagration was reason and to spare.

"How came such a mistake to be made?" he inquired, a scowl upon his full red countenance.

Mr. O'Rourke had been investigating and was primed with knowledge.

"It appears, sir, that at Tavora there is a convent of Dominican nuns as well as a monastery of Dominican friars. Mr. Butler will have used the word 'convento,' which more particularly applies to the nunnery, and so he was directed to the wrong house."

"And you say the sergeant has reason to believe that Mr. Butler did not survive his folly?"

"I am afraid there can be no hope, sir."

"It's perhaps just as well," said Sir Robert. "For Lord Wellington would certainly have had him shot."

And there you have the true account of the stupid affair of Tavora, which was to produce, as we shall see, such far-reaching effects upon persons nowise concerned in it.

CHAPTER II

THE ULTIMATUM

News of the affair at Tavora reached Sir Terence O'Moy, the Adjutant-General at Lisbon, about a week later in dispatches from headquarters. These informed him that in the course of the humble apology and explanation of the regrettable occurrence offered by the Colonel of the 8th Dragoons in person to the Mother Abbess, it had transpired that Lieutenant Butler had left the convent alive, but that nevertheless he continued absent from his regiment.

Those dispatches contained other unpleasant matters of a totally different nature, with which Sir Terence must proceed to deal at once; but their gravity was completely outweighed in the adjutant's mind by this deplorable affair of Lieutenant Butler's. Without wishing to convey an impression that the blunt and downright O'Moy was gifted with any undue measure of shrewdness, it must nevertheless be said that he was quick to perceive what fresh thorns the occurrence was likely to throw in a path that was already thorny enough in all conscience, what a semblance of justification it must give to the hostility of the intriguers on the Council of Regency, what a formidable weapon it must place in the hands of Principal Souza and his partisans. In itself this was enough to trouble a man in O'Moy's position. But there was more. Lieutenant Butler happened to be his brother-in-law, own brother to O'Moy's lovely, frivolous wife. Irresponsibility ran strongly in that branch of the Butler family.

For the sake of the young wife whom he loved with a passionate and fearful jealousy such as is not uncommon in a man of O'Moy's temperament when at his age—he was approaching his forty-sixth birthday—he marries a girl of half his years, the adjutant had pulled his brother-in-law out of many a difficulty; shielded him on many an occasion from the proper consequences of his incurable rashness.

This affair of the convent, however, transcended anything that had gone before and proved altogether too much for O'Moy. It angered him as much as it afflicted him. Yet when he took his head in his hands and groaned, it was only his sorrow that he was expressing, and it was a sorrow entirely concerned with his wife.

The groan attracted the attention of his military secretary, Captain Tremayne, of Fletcher's Engineers, who sat at work at a littered writing-table placed in the window recess. He looked up sharply, sudden concern in the strong young face and the steady grey eyes he bent upon his chief. The sight of O'Moy's hunched attitude brought him instantly to his feet.

"Whatever is the matter, sir?"

"It's that damned fool Richard," growled O'Moy. "He's broken out again."

The captain looked relieved. "And is that all?"

O'Moy looked at him, white-faced, and in his blue eyes a blaze of that swift passion that had made his name a byword in the army.

"All?" he roared. "You'll say it's enough, by God, when you hear what the fool's been at this time. Violation of a nunnery, no less." And he brought his massive fist down with a crash upon the document that had conveyed the information. "With a detachment of dragoons he broke into the convent of the Dominican nuns at Tavora one night a week ago. The alarm bell was sounded, and the village turned out to avenge the outrage. Consequences: three troopers killed, five peasants sabred to death and seven other casualties, Dick himself missing and reported to have escaped from the convent, but understood to remain in hiding—so that he adds desertion to the other crime, as if that in itself were not enough to hang him. That's all, as you say, and I hope you consider it enough even for Dick Butler—bad luck to him."

"My God!" said Captain Tremayne.

"I'm glad that you agree with me."

Captain Tremayne stared at his chief, the utmost dismay upon his fine young face. "But surely, sir, surely—I mean, sir, if this report is correct some explanation—" He broke down, utterly at fault.

"To be sure, there's an explanation. You may always depend upon a most elegant explanation for anything that Dick Butler does. His life is made up of mistakes and explanations." He spoke bitterly, "He broke into the nunnery under a misapprehension, according to the account of the sergeant who accompanied him," and Sir Terence read out that part of the report. "But how is that to help him, and at such a time as this, with public feeling as it is, and Wellington in his present temper about it? The provost's men are beating the country for the blackguard. When they find him it's a firing party he'll have to face."

Tremayne turned slowly to the window and looked down the fair prospect of the hillside over a forest of cork oaks alive with fresh green shoots to the silver sheen of the river a mile away. The storms of the preceding week had spent their fury—the travail that had attended the birth of Spring—and the day was as fair as a day of June in England. Weaned forth by the generous sunshine, the burgeoning of vine and fig, of olive and cork went on apace, and the skeletons of trees which a fortnight since had stood gaunt and bare were already fleshed in tender green.

From the window of this fine conventual house on the heights of Monsanto, above the suburb of Alcantara, where the Adjutant-General had taken up his quarters, Captain Tremayne stood a moment considering the panorama spread to his gaze, from the red-brown roofs of Lisbon on his left—that city which boasted with Rome that it was built upon a cluster of seven hills—to the lines of embarkation that were building about the fort of St. Julian on his left. Then he turned, facing again the spacious, handsome room with its heavy, semi-ecclesiastical furniture, and Sir Terence, who, hunched in his chair at the ponderously carved black writing-table, scowled fiercely at nothing.

"What are you going to do, sir?" he inquired.

Sir Terence shrugged impatiently and heaved himself up in his chair.

"Nothing," he growled.

"Nothing?"

The interrogation, which seemed almost to cover a reproach, irritated the adjutant.

"And what the devil can I do?" he rapped.

"You've pulled Dick out of scrapes before now."

"I have. That seems to have been my principal occupation ever since I married his sister. But this time he's gone too far. What can I do?"

"Lord Wellington is fond of you," suggested Captain Tremayne. He was your imperturbable young man, and he remained as calm now as O'Moy was excited. Although by some twenty years the adjutant's junior, there was between O'Moy and himself, as well as between Tremayne and the Butler family, with which he was remotely connected, a strong friendship, which was largely responsible for the captain's present appointment as Sir Terence's military secretary.

O'Moy looked at him, and looked away. "Yes," he agreed. "But he's still fonder of law and order and military discipline, and I should only be imperilling our friendship by pleading with him for this young blackguard."

"The young blackguard is your brother-in-law," Tremayne reminded him.

"Bad luck to you, Tremayne, don't I know it? Besides, what is there I can do?" he asked again, and ended testily: "Faith, man, I don't know what you're thinking of."

"I'm thinking of Una," said Captain Tremayne in that

20

composed way of his, and the words fell like cold water upon the hot iron of O'Moy's anger.

The man who can receive with patience a reproach, implicit or explicit, of being wanting in consideration towards his wife is comparatively rare, and never a man of O'Moy's temperament and circumstances. Tremayne's reminder stung him sharply, and the more sharply because of the strong friendship that existed between Tremayne and Lady O'Moy. That friendship had in the past been a thorn in O'Moy's flesh. In the days of his courtship he had known a fierce jealousy of Tremayne, beholding in him for a time a rival who, with the strong advantage of youth, must in the end prevail. But when O'Moy, putting his fortunes to the test, had declared himself and been accepted by Una Butler, there had been an end to the jealousy, and the old relations of cordial friendship between the men had been resumed.

O'Moy had conceived that jealousy of his to have been slain. But there had been times when from its faint, uneasy stirrings he should have taken warning that it did no more than slumber. Like most warm hearted, generous, big-natured men, O'Moy was of a singular humility where women were concerned, and this humility of his would often breathe a doubt lest in choosing between himself and Tremayne Una might have been guided by her head rather than her heart, by ambition rather than affection, and that in taking himself she had taken the man who could give her by far the more assured and affluent position.

He had crushed down such thoughts as disloyal to his young wife, as ungrateful and unworthy; and at such times he would fall into self-contempt for having entertained them. Then Una herself had revived those doubts three months ago, when she had suggested that Ned Tremayne, who was then at Torres Vedras with Colonel Fletcher, was the very man to fill the vacant place of military secretary to the adjutant, if he would accept it. In the reaction of self-contempt, and in a curious surge of pride almost as perverse as his humility, O'Moy had adopted her suggestion, and thereafter—in the past-three months, that is to say—the unreasonable devil of O'Moy's jealousy had slept, almost forgotten. Now, by a chance remark whose indiscretion Tremayne could not realise, since he did not so much as suspect the existence of that devil, he had suddenly prodded him into wakefulness. That Tremayne should show himself tender of Lady O'Moy's feelings in a matter in which O'Moy himself must seem neglectful of them was gall and wormwood to the adjutant. He dissembled it, however, out of a natural disinclination to appear in the ridiculous role of the jealous husband.

"That," he said, "is a matter that you may safely leave to me," and his lips closed tightly upon the words when they were uttered.

"Oh, quite so," said Tremayne, no whit abashed. He persisted nevertheless. "You know Una's feelings for Dick."

"When I married Una," the adjutant cut in sharply, "I did not marry the entire Butler family." It hardened him unreasonably against Dick to have the family cause pleaded in this way. "It's sick to death I am of Master Richard and his escapades. He can get himself out of this mess, or he can stay in it."

"You mean that you'll not lift a hand to help him."

"Devil a finger," said O'Moy.

And Tremayne, looking straight into the adjutant's faintly smouldering blue eyes, beheld there a fierce and rancorous determination which he was at a loss to understand, but which he attributed to something outside his own knowledge that must lie between O'Moy and his brother-in-law.

"I am sorry," he said gravely. "Since that is how you feel, it is to be hoped that Dick Butler may not survive to be taken. The alternative would weigh so cruelly upon Una that I do not care to contemplate it."

"And who the devil asks you to contemplate it?" snapped O'Moy. "I am not aware that it is any concern of yours at all."

"My dear O'Moy!" It was an exclamation of protest, something between pain and indignation, under the stress of which Tremayne stepped entirely outside of the official relations that prevailed between himself and the adjutant. And the exclamation was accompanied by such a look of dismay and wounded sensibilities that O'Moy, meeting this, and noting the honest manliness of Tremayne's bearing and countenance; was there and then the victim of reaction. His warm-hearted and impulsive nature made him at once profoundly ashamed of himself. He stood up, a tall, martial figure, and his ruggedly handsome, shaven countenance reddened under its tan. He held out a hand to Tremayne.

"My dear boy, I beg your pardon. It's so utterly annoyed I am that the savage in me will be breaking out. Sure, it isn't as if it were only this affair of Dick's. That is almost the least part of the unpleasantness contained in this dispatch. Here! In God's name, read it for yourself, and judge for yourself whether it's in human nature to be patient under so much."

With a shrug and a smile to show that he was entirely mollified, Captain Tremayne took the papers to his desk and sat down to con them. As he did so his face grew more and more grave. Before he had reached the end there was a tap at the door. An orderly entered with the announcement that Dom Miguel Forjas had just driven up to Monsanto to wait upon the adjutant-general.

"Ha!" said O'Moy shortly, and exchanged a glance with his secretary. "Show the gentleman up."

As the orderly withdrew, Tremayne came over and placed the dispatch on the adjutant's desk. "He arrives very opportunely," he said.

"So opportunely as to be suspicious, bedad!" said O'Moy. He had brightened suddenly, his Irish blood quickening at the immediate prospect of strife which this visit boded. "May the devil admire me, but there's a warm morning in store for Mr. Forjas, Ned."

"Shall I leave you?"

"By no means."

The door opened, and the orderly admitted Miguel Forjas, the Portuguese Secretary of State. He was a slight, dapper gentleman, all in black, from his silk stockings and steel-buckled shoes to his satin stock. His keen aquiline face was swarthy, and the razor had left his chin and cheeks blue-black. His sleek hair was iron-grey. A portentous gravity invested him this morning as he bowed with profound deference first to the adjutant and then to the secretary.

"Your Excellencies," he said—he spoke an English that was smooth and fluent for all its foreign accent "Your Excellencies, this is a terrible affair."

"To what affair will your Excellency be alluding?" wondered O'Moy.

"Have you not received news of what has happened at Tavora? Of the violation of a convent by a party of British soldiers? Of the fight that took place between these soldiers and the peasants who went to succour the nuns?"

"Oh, and is that all?" said O'Moy. "For a moment I imagined your Excellency referred to other matters. I have news of more terrible affairs than the convent business with which to entertain you this morning."

"That, if you will pardon me, Sir Terence, is quite impossible."

"You may think so. But you shall judge, bedad. A chair, Dom Miguel."

The Secretary of State sat down, crossed his knees and placed his hat in his lap. The other two resumed their seats, O'Moy leaning forward, his elbows on the writing-table, immediately facing Senhor Forjas.

"First, however," he said, "to deal with this affair of Tavora. The Council of Regency will, no doubt, have been informed of all the circumstances. You will be aware, therefore, that this very

23

deplorable business was the result of a misapprehension, and that the nuns of Tavora might very well have avoided all this trouble had they behaved in a sensible, reasonable manner. If instead of shutting themselves up in the chapel and ringing the alarm bell the Mother-Abbess or one of the sisters had gone to the wicket and answered the demand of admittance from the officer commanding the detachment, he would instantly have realised his mistake and withdrawn."

"What does your Excellency suggest was this mistake?" inquired the Secretary.

"You have had your report, sir, and surely it was complete. You must know that he conceived himself to be knocking at the gates of the monastery of the Dominican fathers."

"Can your Excellency tell me what was this officer's business at the monastery of the Dominican fathers?" quoth the Secretary, his manner frostily hostile.

"I am without information on that point," O'Moy admitted; "no doubt because the officer in question is missing, as you will also have been informed. But I have no reason to doubt that, whatever his business may have been, it was concerned with the interests which are common alike to the British and the Portuguese nation."

"That is a charitable assumption, Sir Terence."

"Perhaps you will inform me, Dom Miguel, of the uncharitable assumption which the Principal Souza prefers," snapped O'Moy, whose temper began to simmer.

A faint colour kindled in the cheeks of the Portuguese minister, but his manner remained unruffled.

"I speak, sir, not with the voice of Principal Souza, but with that of the entire Council of Regency; and the Council has formed the opinion, which your own words confirm, that his Excellency Lord Wellington is skilled in finding excuses for the misdemeanours of the troops under his command."

"That," said O'Moy, who would never have kept his temper in control but for the pleasant consciousness that he held a hand of trumps with which he would presently overwhelm this representative of the Portuguese Government, "that is an opinion for which the Council may presently like to apologise, admitting its entire falsehood."

Senhor Forjas started as if he had been stung. He uncrossed his black silk legs and made as if to rise.

"Falsehood, sir?" he cried in a scandalised voice.

"It is as well that we should be plain, so as to be avoiding all misconceptions," said O'Moy. "You must know, sir, and your Council must know, that wherever armies move there must be reason for complaint. The British army does not claim in this respect to be superior to others—although I don't say, mark me, that it might not claim it with perfect justice. But we do claim for ourselves that our laws against plunder and outrage are as strict as they well can be, and that where these things take place punishment inevitably follows. Out of your own knowledge, sir, you must admit that what I say is true."

"True, certainly, where the offenders are men from the ranks. But in this case, where the offender is an officer, it does not transpire that justice has been administered with the same impartial hand." "That, sir," answered O'Moy sharply, testily, "is because he is missing."

The Secretary's thin lips permitted themselves to curve into the faintest ghost of a smile. "Precisely," he said.

For answer O'Moy, red in the face, thrust forward the dispatch he had received relating to the affair.

"Read, sir—read for yourself, that you may report exactly to the Council of Regency the terms of the report that has just reached me from headquarters. You will be able to announce that diligent search is being made for the offender."

Forjas perused the document carefully, and returned it.

"That is very good," he said, "and the Council will be glad to hear of it. It will enable us to appease the popular resentment in some degree. But it does not say here that when taken this officer will not be excused upon the grounds which yourself you have urged to me."

"It does not. But considering that he has since been guilty of desertion, there can be no doubt—all else apart—that the finding of a court martial will result in his being shot."

"Very well," said Forjas. "I will accept your assurance, and the Council will be relieved to hear of it." He rose to take his leave. "I am desired by the Council to express to Lord Wellington the hope that he will take measures to preserve better order among his troops and to avoid the recurrence of such extremely painful incidents."

"A moment," said O'Moy, and rising waved his guest back into his chair, then resumed his own seat. Under a more or less calm exterior he was a seething cauldron of passion. "The matter is not quite at an end, as your Excellency supposes. From your last observation, and from a variety of other evidence, I infer that the Council is far from satisfied with Lord Wellington's conduct of the campaign."

"That is an inference which I cannot venture to contradict. You will understand, General, that I do not speak for myself, but for the Council, when I say that many of his measures seem to us not merely unnecessary, but detrimental. The power having been placed in the hands of Lord Wellington, the Council hardly feels itself able to interfere with his dispositions. But it nevertheless deplores the destruction of the mills and the devastation of the country recommended and insisted upon by his lordship. It feels that this is not warfare as the Council understands warfare, and the people share the feelings of the Council. It is felt that it would be worthier and more commendable if Lord Wellington were to measure himself in battle with the French, making a definite attempt to stem the tide of invasion on the frontiers."

"Quite so," said O'Moy, his hand clenching and unclenching, and Tremayne, who watched him, wondered how long it would be before the storm burst. "Quite so. And because the Council disapproves of the very measures which at Lord Wellington's instigation it has publicly recommended, it does not trouble to see that those measures are carried out. As you say, it does not feel itself able to interfere with his dispositions. But it does not scruple to mark its disapproval by passively hindering him at every turn. Magistrates are left to neglect these enactments, and because," he added with bitter sarcasm, "Portuguese valour is so red-hot and so devilish set on battle the Militia Acts calling all men to the colours are forgotten as soon as published. There is no one either to compel the recalcitrant to take up arms, or to punish the desertions of those who have been driven into taking them up. Yet you want battles, you want your frontiers defended. A moment, sir! there is no need for heat, no need for any words. The matter may be said to be at an end." He smiled—a thought viciously, be it confessed—and then played his trump card, hurled his bombshell. "Since the views of your Council are in such utter opposition to the views of the Commander-in-Chief, you will no doubt welcome Lord Wellington's proposal to withdraw from this country and to advise his Majesty's Government to withdraw the assistance which it is affording you."

There followed a long spell of silence, O'Moy sitting back in his chair, his chin in his hand, to observe the result of his words. Nor was he in the least disappointed. Dom Miguel's mouth fell open; the colour slowly ebbed from his cheeks, leaving them an ivory-yellow; his eyes dilated and protruded. He was consternation incarnate.

"My God!" he contrived to gasp at last, and his shaking hands clutched at the carved arms of his chair.

"Ye don't seem as pleased as I expected," ventured O'Moy.

"But, General, surely... surely his Excellency cannot mean to take so... so terrible a step?"

"Terrible to whom, sir?" wondered O'Moy.

"Terrible to us all." Forjas rose in his agitation. He came to lean upon O'Moy's writing-table, facing the adjutant. "Surely, sir, our interests—England's interests and Portugal's—are one in this."

"To be sure. But England's interests can be defended elsewhere than in Portugal, and it is Lord Wellington's view that they shall be. He has already warned the Council of Regency that, since his Majesty and the Prince Regent have entrusted him with the command of the British and Portuguese armies, he will not suffer the Council or any of its members to interfere with his conduct of the military operations, or suffer any criticism or suggestion of theirs to alter system formed upon mature consideration. But when, finding their criticisms fail, the members of the Council, in their wrongheadedness, in their anxiety to allow private interest to triumph over public duty, go the length of thwarting the measures of which they do not approve, the end of Lord Wellington's patience has been reached. I am giving your Excellency his own words. He feels that it is futile to remain in a country whose Government is determined to undermine his every endeavour to bring this campaign to a successful issue.

"Yourself, sir, you appear to be distressed. But the Council of Regency will no doubt take a different view. It will rejoice in the departure of a man whose military operations it finds so detestable. You will no doubt discover this when you come to lay Lord Wellington's decision before the Council, as I now invite you to do."

Bewildered and undecided, Forjas stood there for a moment, vainly seeking words. Finally:

"Is this really Lord Wellington's last word?" he asked in tones of profoundest consternation.

"There is one alternative—one only," said O'Moy slowly.

"And that?" Instantly Forjas was all eagerness.

O'Moy considered him. "Faith, I hesitate to state it."

"No, no. Please, please."

"I feel that it is idle."

"Let the Council judge. I implore you, General, let the Council judge."

"Very well." O'Moy shrugged, and took up a sheet of the dispatch which lay before him. "You will admit, sir, I think, that the beginning of these troubles coincided with the advent of the Principal Souza upon the Council of Regency." He waited in vain for a reply. Forjas, the diplomat, preserved an uncompromising silence, in which presently O'Moy proceeded: "From this, and from other evidence, of which indeed there is no lack, Lord Wellington has come to the conclusion that all the resistance, passive and active, which he has encountered, results from the Principal Souza's

27

influence upon the Council. You will not, I think, trouble to deny it, sir."

Forjas spread his hands. "You will remember, General," he answered, in tones of conciliatory regret, "that the Principal Souza represents a class upon whom Lord Wellington's measures bear in a manner peculiarly hard."

"You mean that he represents the Portuguese nobility and landed gentry, who, putting their own interests above those of the State, have determined to oppose and resist the devastation of the country which Lord Wellington recommends."

"You put it very bluntly," Forjas admitted.

"You will find Lord Wellington's own words even more blunt," said O'Moy, with a grim smile, and turned to the dispatch he held. "Let me read you exactly what he writes:

"'As for Principal Souza, I beg you to tell him from me that as I have had no satisfaction in transacting the business of this country since he has become a member of the Government, no power on earth shall induce me to remain in the Peninsula if he is either to remain a member of the Government or to continue in Lisbon. Either he must quit the country, or I will do so, and this immediately after I have obtained his Majesty's permission to resign my charge.'"

The adjutant put down the letter and looked expectantly at the Secretary of State, who returned the look with one of utter dismay. Never in all his career had the diplomat been so completely dumbfounded as he was now by the simple directness of the man of action. In himself Dom Miguel Forjas was both shrewd and honest. He was shrewd enough to apprehend to the full the military genius of the British Commander-in-Chief, fruits of which he had already witnessed. He knew that the withdrawal of Junot's army from Lisbon two years ago resulted mainly from the operations of Sir Arthur Wellesley—as he was then—before his supersession in the supreme command of that first expedition, and he more than suspected that but for that supersession the defeat of the first French army of invasion might have been even more signal. He had witnessed the masterly campaign of 1809, the battle of the Douro and the relentless operations which had culminated in hurling the shattered fragments of Soult's magnificent army over the Portuguese frontier, thus liberating that country for the second time from the thrall of the mighty French invader. And he knew that unless this man and the troops under his command remained in Portugal and enjoyed complete liberty of action there could be no hope of stemming the third invasion for which Massena—the ablest of all the Emperor's marshals was now gathering his divisions in the north. If Wellington were to execute his threat and withdraw with his army, Forjas beheld nothing but ruin for his country. The irresistible French would sweep forward in devastating conquest, and Portuguese independence would be ground to dust under the heel of the terrible Emperor.

All this the clear-sighted Dom Miguel Forjas now perceived. To do him full justice, he had feared for some time that the unreasonable conduct of his Government might ultimately bring about some such desperate situation. But it was not for him to voice those fears. He was the servant of that Government, the "mere instrument and mouthpiece of the Council of Regency.

"This," he said at length in a voice that was awed, "is an ultimatum."

"It is that," O'Moy admitted readily.

Forjas sighed, shook his dark head and drew himself up like a man who has chosen his part. Being shrewd, he saw the immediate necessity of choosing, and, being honest, he chose honestly.

"Perhaps it is as well," he said.

"That Lord Wellington should go?" cried O'Moy.

"That Lord Wellington should announce intentions of going," Forjas explained. And having admitted so much, he now stripped off the official mask completely. He spoke with his own voice and not with that of the Council whose mouthpiece he was. "Of course it will never be permitted. Lord Wellington has been entrusted with the defence of the country by the Prince Regent; consequently it is the duty of every Portuguese to ensure that at all costs he shall continue in that office."

O'Moy was mystified. Only a knowledge of the minister's inmost thoughts could have explained this oddly sudden change of manner.

"But your Excellency understands the terms—the only terms upon which his lordship will so continue?"

"Perfectly. I shall hasten to convey those terms to the Council. It is also quite clear—is it not?—that I may convey to my Government and indeed publish your complete assurance that the officer responsible for the raid on the convent at Tavora will be shot when taken?"

Looking intently into O'Moy's face, Dom Miguel saw the clear blue eyes flicker under his gaze, he beheld a grey shadow slowly overspreading the adjutant's ruddy cheek. Knowing nothing of the relationship between O'Moy and the offender, unable to guess the sources of the hesitation of which he now beheld such unmistakable signs, the minister naturally misunderstood it.

"There must be no flinching in this, General," he cried. "Let me speak to you for a moment quite frankly and in confidence, not as the Secretary of State of the Council of Regency, but as a Portuguese patriot who places his country and his country's welfare above every other consideration. You have issued your ultimatum. It may be harsh, it may be arbitrary; with that I have no concern. The interests, the feelings of Principal Souza or of any other individual, however high-placed, are without weight when the interests of the nation hang against them in the balance. Better that an injustice be done to one man than that the whole country should suffer. Therefore I do not argue with you upon the rights and wrongs of Lord Wellington's ultimatum. That is a matter apart. Lord Wellington demands the removal of Principal Souza from the Government, or, in the alternative, proposes himself to withdraw from Portugal. In the national interest the Government can come to only one decision. I am frank with you, General. Myself I shall stand ranged on the side of the national interest, and what my influence in the Council can do it shall do. But if you know Principal Souza at all, you must know that he will not relinquish his position without a fight. He has friends and influence—the Patriarch of Lisbon and many of the nobility will be on his side. I warn you solemnly against leaving any weapon in his hands."

He paused impressively. But O'Moy, grey-faced now and haggard, waited in silence for him to continue.

"From the message I brought you," Forjas resumed, "you will have perceived how Principal Souza has fastened upon this business at Tavora to support his general censure of Lord Wellington's conduct of the campaign. That is the weapon to which my warning refers. You must—if we who place the national interest supreme are to prevail—you must disarm him by the assurance that I ask for. You will perceive that I am disloyal to a member of my Council so that I may be loyal to my country. But I repeat, I speak to you in confidence. This officer has committed a gross outrage, which must bring the British army into odium with the people, unless we have your assurance that the British army is the first to censure and to punish the offender with the utmost rigour. Give me now, that I may publish everywhere, your official assurance that this man will be shot, and on my side I assure you that Principal Souza, thus deprived of his stoutest weapon, must succumb in the struggle that awaits us."

"I hope," said O'Moy slowly, his head bowed, his voice dull and even unsteady, "I hope that I am not behind you in placing public duty above private consideration. You may publish my official assurance that the officer in question will be... shot when taken."

"General, I thank you. My country thanks you. You may be confident of this issue." He bowed gravely to O'Moy and then to Tremayne. "Your Excellencies, I have the honour to wish you good-day." He was shown out by the orderly who had admitted him, and he departed well satisfied in his patriotic heart that the crisis which he had always known to be inevitable should have been reached at last. Yet, as he went, he wondered why the Adjutant-General had looked so downcast, why his voice had broken when he pledged his word that justice should be done upon the offending British officer. That, however, was no concern of Dom Miguel's, and there was more than enough to engage his thoughts when he came to consider the ultimatum to his Government with which he was charged.

CHAPTER III

LADY O'MOY

Across the frontier in the northwest was gathering the third army of invasion, some sixty thousand strong, commanded by Marshal Massena, Prince of Esslingen, the most skilful and fortunate of all Napoleon's generals, a leader who, because he had never known defeat, had come to be surnamed by his Emperor "the dear child of Victory."

Wellington, at the head of a British force of little more than one third of the French host, watched and waited, maturing his stupendous strategic plan, which those in whose interests it had been conceived had done so much to thwart. That plan was inspired by and based upon the Emperor's maxim that war should support itself; that an army on the march must not be hampered and immobilised by its commissariat, but that it must draw its supplies from the country it is invading; that it must, in short, live upon that country.

Behind the British army and immediately to the north of Lisbon, in an arc some thirty miles long, following the inflection of the hills from the sea at the mouth of the Zizandre to the broad waters of the Tagus at Alhandra, the lines of Torres Vedras were being constructed under the direction of Colonel Fletcher and this so secretly and with such careful measures as to remain unknown to British and Portuguese alike. Even those employed upon the works knew of nothing save the section upon which they happened to be engaged, and had no conception of the stupendous and impregnable whole that was preparing.

To these lines it was the British commander's plan to effect a slow retreat before the French flood when it should sweep forward, thus luring the enemy onward into a country which he had commanded should be laid relentlessly waste, that there that enemy might fast be starved and afterwards destroyed. To this end had his proclamations gone forth, commanding that all the land lying between the rivers Tagus and Mondego, in short, the whole of the country between Beira and Torres Vedras, should be stripped naked, converted into a desert as stark and empty as the Sahara. Not a head of cattle, not a grain of corn, not a skin of wine, not a flask of oil, not a crumb of anything affording nourishment should be left behind. The very mills were to be rendered useless, bridges were to be broken down, the houses emptied of all property, which the refugees were to carry away with them from the line of invasion.

Such was his terrible demand upon the country for its own salvation. But such, as we have seen, was not war as Principal Souza and some of his adherents understood it. They had not the foresight to perceive the inevitable result of this strategic plan if effectively and thoroughly executed. They did not even realise that the devastation had better be effected by the British in this defensive— and in its results at the same time overwhelmingly offensive— manner than by the French in the course of a conquering onslaught. They did not realise these things partly because they did not enjoy Wellington's full confidence, and in a greater measure because they were blinded by self-interest, because, as O'Moy told Forjas, they placed private considerations above public duty. The northern nobles whose lands must suffer opposed the measure violently; they even opposed the withdrawal of labour from those lands which the Militia Act had rendered necessary. And Antonio de Souza made himself their champion until he was broken by Wellington's ultimatum to the Council. For broken he was. The nation had come to a parting of the ways. It had been brought to the necessity of choosing, and however much the Principal, voicing the outcry of his party, might argue that the British plan was as detestable and ruinous as a French invasion, the nation preferred to place its confidence in the conqueror of Vimeiro and the Douro.

Souza quitted the Government and the capital as had been demanded. But if Wellington hoped that he would quit intriguing, he misjudged his man. He was a fellow of monstrous vanity, pride and self-sufficiency, of the sort than which there is none more dangerous to offend. His wounded pride demanded a salve to be procured at any cost. The wound had been administered by Wellington, and must be returned with interest. So that he ruined Wellington it mattered nothing to Antonio de Souza that he should ruin himself and his own country at the same time. He was like some blinded, ferocious and unreasoning beast, ready, even eager, to sacrifice its own life so that in dying it can destroy its enemy and slake its blood-thirst.

In that mood he passes out of the councils of the Portuguese Government into a brooding and secretly active retirement, of which the fruits shall presently be shown. With his departure the Council of Regency, rudely shaken by the ultimatum which had driven him forth, became more docile and active, and for a season the measures enjoined by the Commander-in-Chief were pursued with some show of earnestness.

As a result of all this life at Monsanto became easier, and

O'Moy was able to breathe more freely, and to devote more of his time to matters concerning the fortifications which Wellington had left largely in his charge. Then, too, as the weeks passed, the shadow overhanging him with regard to Richard Butler gradually lifted. No further word had there been of the missing lieutenant, and by the end of May both O'Moy and Tremayne had come to the conclusion that he must have fallen into the hands of some of the ferocious mountaineers to whom a soldier—whether his uniform were British or French—was a thing to be done to death.

For his wife's sake O'Moy came thankfully to that conclusion. Under the circumstances it was the best possible termination to the episode. She must be told of her brother's death presently, when evidence of it was forthcoming; she would mourn him passionately, no doubt, for her attachment to him was deep—extraordinarily deep for so shallow a woman—but at least she would be spared the pain and shame she must inevitably have felt had he been taken and, shot.

Meanwhile, however, the lack of news from him, in another sense, would have to be explained to Una sooner or later for a fitful correspondence was maintained between brother and sister—and O'Moy dreaded the moment when this explanation must be made. Lacking invention, he applied to Tremayne for assistance, and Tremayne glumly supplied him with the necessary lie that should meet Lady O'Moy's inquiries when they came.

In the end, however, he was spared the necessity of falsehood. For the truth itself reached Lady O'Moy in an unexpected manner. It came about a month after that day when O'Moy had first received news of the escapade at Tavora. It was a resplendent morning of early June, and the adjutant was detained a few moments from breakfast by the arrival of a mail-bag from headquarters, now established at Vizeu. Leaving Captain Tremayne to deal with it, Sir Terence went down to breakfast, bearing with him only a few letters of a personal character which had reached him from friends on the frontier.

The architecture of the house at Monsanto was of a semiclaustral character; three sides of it enclosed a sheltered luxuriant garden, whilst on the fourth side a connecting corridor, completing the quadrangle, spanned bridgewise the spacious archway through which admittance was gained directly from the parklands that sloped gently to Alcantara. This archway, closed at night by enormous wooden doors, opened wide during the day upon a grassy terrace bounded by a baluster of white marble that gleamed now in the brilliant sunshine. It was O'Moy's practice to breakfast out-of-doors in that genial climate, and during April, before the sun had reached its present intensity, the table had been spread out there upon the terrace. Now, however, it was wiser, even in the early morning, to seek the shade, and breakfast was served within the quadrangle, under a trellis of vine supported in the Portuguese manner by rough-hewn granite columns. It was a delicious spot, cool and fragrant, secluded without being enclosed, since through the broad archway it commanded a view of the Tagus and the hills of Alemtejo.

Here O'Moy found himself impatiently awaited that morning by his wife and her cousin, Sylvia Armytage, more recently arrived from England.

"You are very late," Lady O'Moy greeted him petulantly. Since she spent her life in keeping other people waiting, it naturally fretted her to discover unpunctuality in others.

Her portrait, by Raeburn, which now adorns the National Gallery, had been painted in the previous year. You will have seen it, or at least you will have seen one of its numerous replicas, and you will have remarked its singular, delicate, rose-petal loveliness—the gleaming golden head, the flawless outline of face and feature, the immaculate skin, the dark blue eyes with their look of innocence awakening.

Thus was she now in her artfully simple gown of flowered muslin with its white fichu folded across her neck that was but a shade less white; thus was she, just as Raeburn had painted her, saving, of course, that her expression, matching her words, was petulant.

"I was detained by the arrival of a mail-bag from Vizeu," Sir Terence excused himself, as he took the chair which Mullins, the elderly, pontifical butler, drew out for him. "Ned is attending to it, and will be kept for a few moments yet."

Lady O'Moy's expression quickened. "Are there no letters for me?"

"None, my dear, I believe."

"No word from Dick?" Again there was that note of ever ready petulance. "It is too provoking. He should know that he must make me anxious by his silence. Dick is so thoughtless—so careless of other people's feelings. I shall write to him severely."

The adjutant paused in the act of unfolding his napkin. The prepared explanation trembled on his lips; but its falsehood, repellent to him, was not uttered.

"I should certainly do so, my dear," was all he said, and addressed himself to his breakfast.

"What news from headquarters?" Miss Armytage asked him. "Are things going well?"

"Much better now that Principal Souza's influence is at an end. Cotton reports that the destruction of the mills in the Mondego valley is being carried out systematically."

Miss Armytage's dark, thoughtful eyes became wistful.

"Do you know, Terence," she said, "that I am not without some sympathy for the Portuguese resistance to Lord Wellington's decrees. They must bear so terribly hard upon the people. To be compelled with their own hands to destroy their homes and lay waste the lands upon which they have laboured—what could be more cruel?"

"War can never be anything but cruel," he answered gravely. "God help the people over whose lands it sweeps. Devastation is often the least of the horrors marching in its train."

"Why must war be?" she asked him, in intelligent rebellion against that most monstrous and infamous of all human madnesses.

O'Moy proceeded to do his best to explain the unexplainable, and since, himself a professional soldier, he could not take the sane view of his sane young questioner, hot argument ensued between them, to the infinite weariness of Lady O'Moy, who out of self-protection gave herself to the study of the latest fashion plates from London and the consideration of a gown for the ball which the Count of Redondo was giving in the following week.

It was thus in all things, for these cousins represented the two poles of womanhood. Miss Armytage without any of Lady O'Moy's insistent and excessive femininity, was nevertheless feminine to the core. But hers was the Diana type of womanliness. She was tall and of a clean-limbed, supple grace, now emphasised by the riding-habit which she was wearing—for she had been in the saddle during the hour which Lady O'Moy had consecrated to the rites of toilet and devotions done before her mirror. Dark-haired, dark-eyed, vivacity and intelligence lent her countenance an attraction very different from the allurement of her cousin's delicate loveliness. And because her countenance was a true mirror of her mind, she argued shrewdly now, so shrewdly that she drove O'Moy to entrench himself behind generalisations.

"My dear Sylvia, war is most merciful where it is most merciless," he assured her with the Irish gift for paradox. "At home in the Government itself there are plenty who argue as you argue, and who are wondering when we shall embark for England. That is because they are intellectuals, and war is a thing beyond the understanding of intellectuals. It is not intellect but brute instinct and brute force that will help humanity in such a crisis as the present. Therefore, let me tell you, my child, that a government of

36

intellectual men is the worst possible government for a nation engaged in a war."

This was far from satisfying Miss Armytage. Lord Wellington himself was an intellectual, she objected. Nobody could deny it. There was the work he had done as Irish Secretary, and there was the calculating genius he had displayed at Vimeiro, at Oporto, at Talavera.

And then, observing her husband to be in distress, Lady O'Moy put down her fashion plate and brought up her heavy artillery to relieve him.

"Sylvia, dear," she interpolated, "I wonder that you will for ever be arguing about things you don't understand."

Miss Armytage laughed good-humouredly. She was not easily put out of countenance. "What woman doesn't?" she asked.

"I don't, and I am a woman, surely."

"Ah, but an exceptional woman," her cousin rallied her affectionately, tapping the shapely white arm that protruded from a foam of lace. And Lady O'Moy, to whom words never had any but a literal meaning, set herself to purr precisely as one would have expected. Complacently she discoursed upon the perfection of her own endowments, appealing ever and anon to her husband for confirmation, and O'Moy, who loved her with all the passionate reverence which Nature working inscrutably to her ends so often inspires in just such strong, essentially masculine men for just such fragile and excessively feminine women, afforded this confirmation with all the enthusiasm of sincere conviction.

Thus until Mullins broke in upon them with the announcement of a visit from Count Samoval, an announcement more welcome to Lady O'Moy than to either of her companions.

The Portuguese nobleman was introduced. He had attained to a degree of familiarity in the adjutant's household that permitted of his being received without ceremony there at that breakfast-table spread in the open. He was a slender, handsome, swarthy man of thirty, scrupulously dressed, as graceful and elegant in his movements as a fencing master, which indeed he might have been; for his skill with the foils was a matter of pride to himself and notoriety to all the world. Nor was it by any means the only skill he might have boasted, for Jeronymo de Samoval was in many things, a very subtle, supple gentleman. His friendship with the O'Moys, now some three months old, had been considerably strengthened of late by the fact that he had unexpectedly become one of the most hostile critics of the Council of Regency as lately constituted, and one of the most ardent supporters of the Wellingtonian policy.

He bowed with supremest grace to the ladies, ventured to kiss

37

the fair, smooth hand of his hostess, undeterred by the frosty stare of O'Moy's blue eyes whose approval of all men was in inverse proportion to their approval of his wife—and finally proffered her the armful of early roses that he brought.

"These poor roses of Portugal to their sister from England," said his softly caressing tenor voice.

"Ye're a poet," said O'Moy tartly.

"Having found Castalia here," said, the Count, "shall I not drink its limpid waters?"

"Not, I hope, while there's an agreeable vintage of Port on the table. A morning whet, Samoval?" O'Moy invited him, taking up the decanter.

"Two fingers, then—no more. It is not my custom in the morning. But here—to drink your lady's health, and yours, Miss Armytage." With a graceful flourish of his glass he pledged them both and sipped delicately, then took the chair that O'Moy was proffering.

"Good news, I hear, General. Antonio de Souza's removal from the Government is already bearing fruit. The mills in the valley of the Mondego are being effectively destroyed at last."

"Ye're very well informed," grunted O'Moy, who himself had but received the news. "As well informed, indeed, as I am myself." There was a note almost of suspicion in the words, and he was vexed that matters which it was desirable be kept screened as much as possible from general knowledge should so soon be put abroad.

"Naturally, and with reason," was the answer, delivered with a rueful smile. "Am I not interested? Is not some of my property in question?" Samoval sighed. "But I bow to the necessities of war. At least it cannot be said of me, as was said of those whose interests Souza represented, that I put private considerations above public duty—that is the phrase, I think. The individual must suffer that the nation may triumph. A Roman maxim, my dear General."

"And a British one," said O'Moy, to whom Britain was a second Rome.

"Oh, admitted," replied the amiable Samoval. "You proved it by your uncompromising firmness in the affair of Tavora."

"What was that?" inquired Miss Armytage.

"Have you not heard?" cried Samoval in astonishment.

"Of course not," snapped O'Moy, who had broken into a cold perspiration. "Hardly a subject for the ladies, Count."

Rebuked for his intention, Samoval submitted instantly.

"Perhaps not; perhaps not," he agreed, as if dismissing it, whereupon O'Moy recovered from his momentary breathlessness.

"But in your own interests, my dear General, I trust there will be no weakening when this Lieutenant Butler is caught, and—"

"Who?"

Sharp and stridently came that single word from her ladyship.

Desperately O'Moy sought to defend the breach.

"Nothing to do with Dick, my dear. A fellow named Philip Butler, who—"

But the too-well-informed Samoval corrected him. "Not Philip, General—Richard Butler. I had the name but yesterday from Forjas."

In the scared hush that followed the Count perceived that he had stumbled headlong into a mystery. He saw Lady O'Moy's face turn whiter and whiter, saw her sapphire eyes dilating as they regarded him.

"Richard Butler!" she echoed. "What of Richard Butler? Tell me. Tell me at once."

Hesitating before such signs of distress, Samoval looked at O'Moy, to meet a dejected scowl.

Lady O'Moy turned to her husband. "What is it?" she demanded. "You know something about Dick and you are keeping it from me. Dick is in trouble?"

"He is," O'Moy admitted. "In great trouble."

"What has he done? You spoke of an affair at Evora or Tavora, which is not to be mentioned before ladies. I demand to know." Her affection and anxiety for her brother invested her for a moment with a certain dignity, lent her a force that was but rarely displayed by her.

Seeing the men stricken speechless, Samoval from bewildered astonishment, O'Moy from distress, she jumped to the conclusion, after what had been said, that motives of modesty accounted for their silence.

"Leave us, Sylvia, please," she said. "Forgive me, dear. But you see they will not mention these things while you are present." She made a piteous little figure as she stood trembling there, her fingers tearing in agitation at one of Samoval's roses.

She waited until the obedient and discreet Miss Armytage had passed from view into the wing that contained the adjutant's private quarters, then sinking limp and nerveless to her chair:

"Now," she bade them, "please tell me."

And O'Moy, with a sigh of regret for the lie so laboriously concocted which would never now be uttered, delivered himself huskily of the hideous truth.

CHAPTER IV

COUNT SAMOVAL

Miss Armytage's own notions of what might be fit and proper for her virginal ears were by no means coincident with Lady O'Moy's. Thus, although you have seen her pass into the private quarters of the adjutant's establishment, and although, in fact, she did withdraw to her own room, she found it impossible to abide there a prey to doubt and misgivings as to what Dick Butler might have done—doubt and misgivings, be it understood, entertained purely on Una's account and not at all on Dick's.

By the corridor spanning the archway on the southern side of the quadrangle, and serving as a connecting bridge between the adjutant's private and official quarters, Miss Armytage took her way to Sir Terence's work-room, knowing that she would find Captain Tremayne there, and assuming that he would be alone.

"May I come in?" she asked him from the doorway.

He sprang to his feet. "Why, certainly, Miss Armytage." For so imperturbable a young man he seemed oddly breathless in his eagerness to welcome her. "Are you looking for O'Moy? He left me nearly half-an-hour ago to go to breakfast, and I was just about to follow."

"I scarcely dare detain you, then."

"On the contrary. I mean... not at all. But... were you wanting me?"

She closed the door, and came forward into the room, moving with that supple grace peculiarly her own.

"I want you to tell me something, Captain Tremayne, and I want you to be frank with me."

"I hope I could never be anything else."

"I want you to treat me as you would treat a man, a friend of your own sex."

Tremayne sighed. He had recovered from the surprise of her coming and was again his imperturbable self.

"I assure you that is the last way in which I desire to treat you. But if you insist—"

"I do." She had frowned slightly at the earlier part of his speech, with its subtle, half-jesting gallantry, and she spoke sharply now.

"I bow to your will," said Captain Tremayne.

"What has Dick Butler been doing?"

40

He looked into her face with sharply questioning eyes.

"What was it that happened at Tavora?"

He continued to look at her. "What have you heard?" he asked at last.

"Only that he has done something at Tavora for which the consequences, I gather, may be grave. I am anxious for Una's sake to know what it is."

"Does Una know?"

"She is being told now. Count Samoval let slip just what I have outlined. And she has insisted upon being told everything."

"Then why did you not remain to hear?"

"Because they sent me away on the plea that—oh, on the silly plea of my youth and innocence, which were not to be offended."

"But which you expect me to offend?"

"No. Because I can trust you to tell me without offending."

"Sylvia!" It was a curious exclamation of satisfaction and of gratitude for the implied confidence. We must admit that it betrayed a selfish forgetfulness of Dick Butler and his troubles, but it is by no means clear that it was upon such grounds that it offended her.

She stiffened perceptibly. "Really, Captain Tremayne!"

"I beg your pardon," said he. "But you seemed to imply—" He checked, at a loss.

Her colour rose. "Well, sir? What do you suggest that I implied or seemed to imply?" But as suddenly her manner changed. "I think we are too concerned with trifles where the matter on which I have sought you is a serious one."

"It is of the utmost seriousness," he admitted gravely.

"Won't you tell me what it is?"

He told her quite simply the whole story, not forgetting to give prominence to the circumstances extenuating it in Butler's favour. She listened with a deepening frown, rather pale, her head bowed.

"And when he is taken," she asked, "what—what will happen to him?"

"Let us hope that he will not be taken."

"But if he is—if he is?" she insisted almost impatiently.

Captain Tremayne turned aside and looked out of the window. "I should welcome the news that he is dead," he said softly. "For if he is taken he will find no mercy at the hands of his own people."

"You mean that he will be shot?" Horror charged her voice, dilated her eyes.

"Inevitably."

A shudder ran through her, and she covered her face with her

41

hands. When she withdrew then Tremayne beheld the lovely countenance transformed. It was white and drawn.

"But surely Terence can save him!" she cried piteously.

He shook his head, his lips tight pressed. "'There is no man less able to do so."

"What do you mean? Why do you say that?"

He looked at her, hesitating for a moment, then answered her: "'O'Moy has pledged his word to the Portuguese Government that Dick Butler shall be shot when taken."

"Terence did that?"

"He was compelled to it. Honour and duty demanded no less of him. I alone, who was present and witnessed the undertaking, know what it cost him and what he suffered. But he was forced to sink all private considerations. It was a sacrifice rendered necessary, inevitable for the success of this campaign." And he proceeded to explain to her all the circumstances that were interwoven with Lieutenant Butler's ill-timed offence. "Thus you see that from Terence you can hope for nothing. His honour will not admit of his wavering in this matter."

"Honour?" She uttered the word almost with contempt. "And what of Una?"

"I was thinking of Una when I said I should welcome the news of Dick's death somewhere in the hills. It is the best that can be hoped for."

"I thought you were Dick's friend, Captain Tremayne."

"Why, so I have been; so I am. Perhaps that is another reason why I should hope that he is dead."

"Is it no reason why you should do what you can to save him?"

He looked at her steadily for an instant, calm under the reproach of her eyes.

"Believe me, Miss Armytage, if I saw a way to save him, to do anything to help him, I should seize it, both for the sake of my friendship for himself and because of my affection for Una. Since you yourself are interested in him, that is an added reason for me. But it is one thing to admit willingness to help and another thing actually to afford help. What is there that I can do? I assure you that I have thought of the matter. Indeed for days I have thought of little else. But I can see no light. I await events. Perhaps a chance may come."

Her expression had softened. "I see." She put out a hand generously to ask forgiveness. "I was presumptuous, and I had no right to speak as I did."

He took the hand. "I should never question your right to speak to me in any way that seemed good to you," he assured her.

"I had better go to Una. She will be needing me, poor child. I am grateful to you, Captain Tremayne, for your confidence and for telling me." And thus she left him very thoughtful, as concerned for Una as she was herself.

Now Una O'Moy was the natural product of such treatment. There had ever been something so appealing in her lovely helplessness and fragility that all her life others had been concerned to shelter her from every wind that blew. Because it was so she was what she was; and because she was what she was it would continue to be so.

But Lady O'Moy at the moment did not stand in such urgent need of Miss Armytage as Miss Armytage imagined. She had heard the appalling story of her brother's escapade, but she had been unable to perceive in what it was so terrible as it was declared. He had made a mistake. He had invaded the convent under a misapprehension, for which it was ridiculous to blame him. It was a mistake which any man might have made in a foreign country. Lives had been lost, it is true; but that was owing to the stupidity of other people—of the nuns who had run for shelter when no danger threatened save in their own silly imaginations, and of the peasants who had come blundering to their assistance where no assistance was required; the latter were the people responsible for the bloodshed, since they had attacked the dragoons. Could it be expected of the dragoons that they should tamely suffer themselves to be massacred?

Thus Lady O'Moy upon the affair of Tavora. The whole thing appeared to her to be rather silly, and she refused seriously to consider that it could have any grave consequences for Dick. His continued absence made her anxious. But if he should come to be taken, surely his punishment would be merely a formal matter; at the worst he might be sent home, which would be a very good thing, for after all the climate of the Peninsula had never quite suited him.

In this fashion she nimbly pursued a train of vitiated logic, passing from inconsequence to inconsequence. And O'Moy, thankful that she should take such a view as this—mercifully hopeful that the last had been heard of his peccant and vexatious brother-in-law—content, more than content, to leave her comforted such illusions.

And then, while she was still discussing the matter in terms of comparative calm, came an orderly to summon him away, so that he left her in the company of Samoval.

The Count had been deeply shocked by the discovery that Dick Butler was Lady O'Moy's brother, and a little confused that he himself in his ignorance should have been the means of bringing to her knowledge a painful matter that touched her so closely and that hitherto had been so carefully concealed from her by her husband. He was thankful that she should take so optimistic a view, and quick to perceive O'Moy's charitable desire to leave her optimism undispelled. But he was no less quick to perceive the opportunities which the circumstances afforded him to further a certain deep intrigue upon which he was engaged.

Therefore he did not take his leave just yet. He sauntered with Lady O'Moy on the terrace above the wooded slopes that screened the village of Alcantara, and there discovered her mind to be even more frivolous and unstable than his perspicuity had hitherto suspected. Under stress Lady O'Moy could convey the sense that she felt deeply. She could be almost theatrical in her displays of emotion. But these were as transient as they were intense. Nothing that was not immediately present to her senses was ever capable of a deep impression upon her spirit, and she had the facility characteristic of the self-loving and self-indulgent of putting aside any matter that was unpleasant. Thus, easily self-persuaded, as we have seen, that this escapade of Richard's was not to be regarded too seriously, and that its consequences were not likely to be grave, she chattered with gay inconsequence of other things—of the dinner-party last week at the house of the Marquis of Minas, that prominent member of the council of Regency, of the forthcoming ball to be given by the Count of Redondo, of the latest news from home, the latest fashion and the latest scandal, the amours of the Duke of York and the shortcomings of Mr. Perceval.

Samoval, however, did not intend that the matter of her brother should be so entirely forgotten, so lightly treated. Deliberately at last he revived it.

Considering her as she leant upon the granite balustrade, her pink sunshade aslant over her shoulder, her flimsy lace shawl festooned from the crook of either arm and floating behind her, a wisp of cloudy vapour, Samoval permitted himself a sigh.

She flashed him a sidelong glance, arch and rallying.

"You are melancholy, sir—a poor compliment," she told him.

But do not misunderstand her. Hers was an almost childish coquetry, inevitable fruit of her intense femininity, craving ever the worship of the sterner sex and the incense of its flattery. And Samoval, after all, young, noble, handsome, with a half-sinister reputation, was something of a figure of romance, as a good many women had discovered to their cost.

He fingered his snowy stock, and bent upon her eyes of glowing adoration. "Dear Lady O'Moy," his tenor voice was soft and soothing as a caress, "I sigh to think that one so adorable, so entirely

44

made for life's sunshine and gladness, should have cause for a moment's uneasiness, perhaps for secret grief, at the thought of the peril of her brother."

Her glance clouded under this reminder. Then she pouted and made a little gesture of impatience. "Dick is not in peril," she answered. "He is foolish to remain so long in hiding, and of course he will have to face unpleasantness when he is found. But to say that he is in peril is... just nonsense. Terence said nothing of peril. He agreed with me that Dick will probably be sent home. Surely you don't think—"

"No, no." He looked down, studying his hessians for a moment, then his dark eyes returned to meet her own. "I shall see to it that he is in no danger. You may depend upon me, who ask but the happy chance to serve you. Should there be any trouble, let me know at once, and I will see to it that all is well. Your brother must not suffer, since he is your brother. He is very blessed and enviable in that."

She stared at him, her brows knitting. "But I don't understand."

"Is it not plain? Whatever happens, you must not suffer, Lady O'Moy. No man of feeling, and I least of any, could endure it. And since if your brother were to suffer that must bring suffering to you, you may count upon me to shield him."

"You are very good, Count. But shield him from what?"

"From whatever may threaten. The Portuguese Government may demand in self-protection, to appease the clamour of the people stupidly outraged by this affair, that an example shall be made of the offender."

"Oh, but how could they? With what reason?" She displayed a vague alarm, and a less vague impatience of such hypotheses.

He shrugged. "The people are like that—a fierce, vengeful god to whom appeasing sacrifices must be offered from time to time. If the people demand a scapegoat, governments usually provide one. But be comforted." In his eagerness of reassurance he caught her delicate mittened hand in his own, and her anxiety rendering her heedless, she allowed it to lie there gently imprisoned. "Be comforted. I shall be here to guard him. There is much that I can do and you may depend upon me to do it—for your sake, dear lady. The Government will listen to me. I would not have you imagine me capable of boasting. I have influence with the Government, that is all; and I give you my word that so far as the Portuguese Government is concerned your brother shall take no harm."

She looked at him for a long moment with moist eyes, moved and flattered by his earnestness and intensity of homage. "I take

45

this very kindly in you, sir. I have no thanks that are worthy," she said, her voice trembling a little. "I have no means of repaying you. You have made me very happy, Count."

He bent low over the frail hand he was holding.

"Your assurance that I have made you happy repays me very fully, since your happiness is my tenderest concern. Believe me, dear lady, you may ever count Jeronymo de Samoval your most devoted and obedient slave."

He bore the hand to his lips and held it to them for a long moment, whilst with heightened colour and eyes that sparkled, more, be it confessed, from excitement than from gratitude, she stood passively considering his bowed dark head.

As he came erect again a movement under the archway caught his eye, and turning he found himself confronting Sir Terence and Miss Armytage, who were approaching. If it vexed him to have been caught by a husband notoriously jealous in an attitude not altogether uncompromising, Samoval betrayed no sign of it.

With smooth self-possession he hailed O'Moy:

"General, you come in time to enable me to take my leave of you. I was on the point of going."

"So I perceived," said O'Moy tartly. He had almost said: "So I had hoped."

His frosty manner would have imposed constraint upon any man less master of himself than Samoval. But the Count ignored it, and ignoring it delayed a moment to exchange amiabilities politely with Miss Armytage, before taking at last an unhurried and unperturbed departure.

But no sooner was he gone than O'Moy expressed himself full frankly to his wife.

"I think Samoval is becoming too attentive and too assiduous."

"He is a dear," said Lady O'Moy.

"That is what I mean," replied Sir Terence grimly.

"He has undertaken that if there should be any trouble with the Portuguese Government about Dick's silly affair he will put it right."

"Oh!" said O'Moy, "that was it?" And out of his tender consideration for her said no more.

But Sylvia Armytage, knowing what she knew from Captain Tremayne, was not content to leave the matter there. She reverted to it presently as she was going indoors alone with her cousin.

"Una," she said gently, "I should not place too much faith in Count Samoval and his promises."

46

"What do you mean?" Lady O'Moy was never very tolerant of advice, especially from an inexperienced young girl.

"I do not altogether trust him. Nor does Terence."

"Pooh! Terence mistrusts every man who looks at me. My dear, never marry a jealous man," she added with her inevitable inconsequence.

"He is the last man—the Count, I mean—to whom, in your place, I should go for assistance if there is trouble about Dick." She was thinking of what Tremayne had told her of the attitude of the Portuguese Government, and her clear-sighted mind perceived an obvious peril in permitting Count Samoval to become aware of Dick's whereabouts should they ever be discovered.

"What nonsense, Sylvia! You conceive the oddest and most foolish notions sometimes. But of course you have no experience of the world." And beyond that she refused to discuss the matter, nor did the wise Sylvia insist.

CHAPTER V

THE FUGITIVE

Although Dick Butler might continue missing in the flesh, in the spirit he and his miserable affair seem to have been ever present and ubiquitous, and a most fruitful source of trouble.

It would be at about this time that there befell in Lisbon the deplorable event that nipped in the bud the career of that most promising young officer, Major Berkeley of the famous Die-Hards, the 29th Foot.

Coming into Lisbon on leave from his regiment, which was stationed at Abrantes, and formed part of the division under Sir Rowland Hill, the major happened into a company that contained at least one member who was hostile to Lord Wellington's conduct of the campaign, or rather to the measures which it entailed. As in the case of the Principal Souza, prejudice drove him to take up any weapon that came to his hand by means of which he could strike a blow at a system he deplored.

Since we are concerned only indirectly with the affair, it may be stated very briefly. The young gentleman in question was a Portuguese officer and a nephew of the Patriarch of Lisbon, and the particular criticism to which Major Berkeley took such just exception concerned the very troublesome Dick Butler. Our patrician ventured to comment with sneers and innuendoes upon the fact that the lieutenant of dragoons continued missing, and he went so far as to indulge in a sarcastic prophecy that he never would be found.

Major Berkeley, stung by the slur thus slyly cast upon British honour, invited the young gentleman to make himself more explicit.

"I had thought that I was explicit enough," says young impudence, leering at the stalwart red-coat. "But if you want it more clearly still, then I mean that the undertaking to punish this ravisher of nunneries is one that you English have never intended to carry out. To save your faces you will take good care that Lieutenant Butler is never found. Indeed I doubt if he was ever really missing."

Major Berkeley was quite uncompromising and downright. I am afraid he had none of the graces that can exalt one of these affairs.

"Ye're just a very foolish liar, sir, and you deserve a good caning," was all he said, but the way in which he took his cane from under his arm was so suggestive of more to follow there and then that several of the company laid preventive hands upon him instantly.

The Patriarch's nephew, very white and very fierce to hear himself addressed in terms which—out of respect for his august and powerful uncle—had never been used to him before, demanded instant satisfaction. He got it next morning in the shape of half-an-ounce of lead through his foolish brain, and a terrible uproar ensued. To appease it a scapegoat was necessary. As Samoval so truly said, the mob is a ferocious god to whom sacrifices must be made. In this instance the sacrifice, of course, was Major Berkeley. He was broken and sent home to cut his pigtail (the adornment still clung to by the 29th) and retire into private life, whereby the British army was deprived of an officer of singularly brilliant promise. Thus, you see, the score against poor Richard Butler—that foolish victim of wine and circumstance—went on increasing.

But in my haste to usher Major Berkeley out of a narrative which he touches merely at a tangent, I am guilty of violating the chronological order of the events. The ship in which Major Berkeley went home to England and the rural life was the frigate Telemachus, and the Telemachus had but dropped anchor in the Tagus at the date with which I am immediately concerned. She came with certain stores and a heavy load of mails for the troops, and it would be a full fortnight before she would sail again for home. Her officers would be ashore during the time, the welcome guests of the officers of the garrison, bearing their share in the gaieties with which the latter strove to kill the time of waiting for events, and Marcus Glennie, the captain of the frigate, an old friend of Tremayne's, was by virtue of that friendship an almost daily visitor at the adjutant's quarters.

But there again I am anticipating. The Telemachus came to her moorings in the Tagus, at which for the present we may leave her, on the morning of the day that was to close with Count Redondo's semi-official ball. Lady O'Moy had risen late, taking from one end of the day what she must relinquish to the other, that thus fully rested she might look her best that night. The greater part of the afternoon was devoted to preparation. It was amazing even to herself what an amount of detail there was to be considered, and from Sylvia she received but very indifferent assistance. There were times when she regretfully suspected in Sylvia a lack of proper womanliness, a taint almost of masculinity. There was to Lady O'Moy's mind something very wrong about a woman who preferred a canter to a waltz. It was unnatural; it was suspicious; she was not quite sure that it wasn't vaguely immoral.

At last there had been dinner—to which she came a full half-hour late, but of so ravishing and angelic an appearance that the sight of her was sufficient to mollify Sir Terence's impatience and stifle the withering sarcasms he had been laboriously preparing. After dinner—which was taken at six o'clock—there was still an hour to spare before the carriage would come to take them into Lisbon.

Sir Terence pleaded stress of work, occasioned by the arrival of the Telemachus that morning, and withdrew with Tremayne to the official quarters, to spend that hour in disposing of some of the many matters awaiting his attention. Sylvia, who to Lady O'Moy's exasperation seemed now for the first time to give a thought to what she should wear that night, went off in haste to gown herself, and so Lady O'Moy was left to her own resources—which I assure you were few indeed.

The evening being calm and warm, she sauntered out into the open. She was more or less annoyed with everybody—with Sir Terence and Tremayne for their assiduity to duty, and with Sylvia for postponing all thought of dressing until this eleventh hour, when she might have been better employed in beguiling her ladyship's loneliness. In this petulant mood, Lady O'Moy crossed the quadrangle, loitered a moment by the table and chairs placed under the trellis, and considered sitting there to await the others. Finally, however, attracted by the glory of the sunset behind the hills towards Abrantes, she sauntered out on to the terrace, to the intense thankfulness of a poor wretch who had waited there for the past ten hours in the almost despairing hope that precisely such a thing might happen.

She was leaning upon the balustrade when a rustle in the pines below drew her attention. The rustle worked swiftly upwards and round to the bushes on her right, and her eyes, faintly startled, followed its career, what time she stood tense and vaguely frightened.

Then the bushes parted and a limping figure that leaned heavily upon a stick disclosed itself; a shaggy, red-bearded man in the garb of a peasant; and marvel of marvels!—this figure spoke her name sharply, warningly almost, before she had time to think of screaming.

"Una! Una! Don't move!"

The voice was certainly the voice of Mr. Butler. But how came that voice into the body of this peasant? Terrified, with drumming pulses, yet obedient to the injunction, she remained without speech or movement, whilst crouching so as to keep below the level of the balustrade the man crept forward until he was immediately before and below her.

She stared into that haggard face, and through the half-mask of stubbly beard gradually made out the features of her brother.

"Richard!" The name broke from her in a scream.

"'Sh!" He waved his hands in wild alarm to repress her. "For God's sake, be quiet! It's a ruined man I am if they find me here. You'll have heard what's happened to me?"

She nodded, and uttered a half-strangled "Yes."

"Is there anywhere you can hide me? Can you get me into the house without being seen? I am almost starving, and my leg is on fire. I was wounded three days ago to make matters worse than they were already. I have been lying in the woods there watching for the chance to find you alone since sunrise this morning, and it's devil a bite or sup I've had since this time yesterday."

"Poor, poor Richard!" She leaned down towards him in an attitude of compassionate, ministering grace. "But why? Why did you not come up to the house and ask for me? No one would have recognised you."

"Terence would if he had seen me."

"But Terence wouldn't have mattered. Terence will help you."

"Terence!" He almost laughed from excess of bitterness, labouring under an egotistical sense of wrong. "He's the last man I should wish to meet, as I have good reason to know. If it hadn't been for that I should have come to you a month ago—immediately after this trouble of mine. As it is, I kept away until despair left me no other choice. Una, on no account a word of my presence to Terence."

"But... he's my husband!"

"Sure, and he's also adjutant-general, and if I know him at all he's the very man to place official duty and honour and all the rest of it above family considerations."

"Oh, Richard, how little you know Terence! How wrong you are to misjudge him like this!"

"Right or wrong, I'd prefer not to take the risk. It might end in my being shot one fine morning before long."

"Richard!"

"For God's sake, less of your Richard! It's all the world will be hearing you. Can you hide me, do you think, for a day or two? If you can't, I'll be after shifting for myself as best I can. I've been playing the part of an English overseer from Bearsley's wine farm, and it has brought me all the way from the Douro in safety. But the strain of it and the eternal fear of discovery are beginning to break me. And now there's this infernal wound. I was assaulted by a footpad near Abrantes, as if I was worth robbing. Anyhow I gave the fellow more than I took. Unless I have rest I think I shall go mad and give myself up to the provost-marshal to be shot and done with."

51

"Why do you talk of being shot? You have done nothing to deserve that. Why should you fear it?"

Now Mr. Butler was aware—having gathered the information lately on his travels—of the undertaking given by the British to the Council of Regency with regard to himself. But irresponsible egotist though he might be, yet in common with others he was actuated by the desire which his sister's fragile loveliness inspired in every one to spare her unnecessary pain or anxiety.

"It's not myself will take any risks," he said again. "We are at war, and when men are at war killing becomes a sort of habit, and one life more or less is neither here nor there." And upon that he renewed his plea that she should hide him if she could and that on no account should she tell a single soul—and Sir Terence least of any—of his presence.

Having driven him to the verge of frenzy by the waste of precious moments in vain argument, she gave him at last the promise he required. "Go back to the bushes there," she bade him, "and wait until I come for you. I will make sure that the coast is clear."

Contiguous to her dressing-room, which overlooked the quadrangle, there was a small alcove which had been converted into a storeroom for the array of trunks and dress boxes that Lady O'Moy had brought from England. A door opening directly from her dressing room communicated with this alcove, and of that door Bridget, her maid, was in possession of the key.

As she hurried now indoors she happened to meet Bridget on the stairs. The maid announced herself on her way to supper in the servants' quarters, and apologised for her presumption in assuming that her ladyship would no further require her services that evening. But since it fell in so admirably with her ladyship's own wishes, she insisted with quite unusual solicitude, with vehemence almost, that Bridget should proceed upon her way.

"Just give me the key of the alcove," she said. "There are one or two things I want to get."

"Can't I get them, your ladyship?"

"Thank you, Bridget. I prefer to get them, myself."

There was no more to be said. Bridget produced a bunch of keys, which she surrendered to her mistress, having picked out for her the one required.

Lady O'Moy went up, to come down again the moment that Bridget had disappeared. The quadrangle was deserted, the household disposed of, and it wanted yet half-an-hour to the time for which the carriage was ordered. No moment could have been more propitious. But in any case no concealment was attempted—

since, if detected it must have provoked suspicions hardly likely to be aroused in any other way.

When Lady O'Moy returned indoors in the gathering dusk she was followed at a respectful distance by the limping fugitive, who might, had he been seen, have been supposed some messenger, or perhaps some person employed about the house or gardens coming to her ladyship for instructions. No one saw them, however, and they gained the dressing-room and thence the alcove in complete safety.

There, whilst Richard, allowing his exhaustion at last to conquer him, sank heavily down upon one of his sister's many trunks, recking nothing of the havoc wrought in its priceless contents, her ladyship all a-tremble collapsed limply upon another.

But there was no rest for her. Richard's wound required attention, and he was faint for want of meat and drink. So having procured him the wherewithal to wash and dress his hurt—a nasty knife-slash which had penetrated to the bone of his thigh, the very sight of which turned her ladyship sick and faint—she went to forage for him in a haste increased by the fact that time was growing short.

On the dining-room sideboard, from the remains of dinner, she found and furtively abstracted what she needed—best part of a roast chicken, a small loaf and a half-flask of Collares. Mullins, the butler, would no doubt be exercised presently when he discovered the abstraction. Let him blame one of the footmen, Sir Terence's orderly, or the cat. It mattered nothing to Lady O'Moy.

Having devoured the food and consumed the wine, Richard's exhaustion assumed the form of a lethargic torpor. To sleep was now his overmastering desire. She fetched him rugs and pillows, and he made himself a couch upon the floor. She had demurred, of course, when he himself had suggested this. She could not conceive of any one sleeping anywhere but in a bed. But Dick made short work of that illusion.

"Haven't I been in hiding for the last six weeks?" he asked her. "And haven't I been thankful to sleep in a ditch? And wasn't I campaigning before that? I tell you I couldn't sleep in a bed. It's a habit I've lost entirely."

Convinced, she gave way.

"We'll talk to-morrow, Una," he promised her, as he stretched himself luxuriously upon that hard couch. "But meanwhile, on your life, not a word to any one. You understand?"

"Of course I understand, my poor Dick."

She stooped to kiss him. But he was fast asleep already.

She went out and locked the door, and when, on the point of setting out for Count Redondo's, she returned the bunch of keys to Bridget the key of the alcove was missing.

"I shall require it again in the morning, Bridget," she explained lightly. And then added kindly, as it seemed: "Don't wait for me, child. Get to bed. I shall be late in coming home, and I shall not want you."

CHAPTER VI

MISS ARMYTAGE'S PEARLS

Lady O'Moy and Miss Armytage drove alone together into Lisbon. The adjutant, still occupied, would follow as soon as he possibly could, whilst Captain Tremayne would go on directly from the lodgings which he shared in Alcantara with Major Carruthers—also of the adjutant's staff—whither he had ridden to dress some twenty minutes earlier.

"Are you ill, Una?" had been Sylvia's concerned greeting of her cousin when she came within the range of the carriage lamps. "You are pale as a ghost." To this her ladyship had replied mechanically that a slight headache troubled her.

But now that they sat side by side in the well upholstered carriage Miss Armytage became aware that her companion was trembling.

"Una, dear, whatever is the matter?"

Had it not been for the dominant fear that the shedding of tears would render her countenance unsightly, Lady O'Moy would have yielded to her feelings and wept. Heroically in the cause of her own flawless beauty she conquered the almost overmastering inclination.

"I—I have been so troubled about Richard," she faltered. "It is preying upon my mind."

"Poor dear!" In sheer motherliness Miss Armytage put an arm about her cousin and drew her close. "We must hope for the best."

Now if you have understood anything of the character of Lady O'Moy you will have understood that the burden of a secret was the last burden that such a nature was capable of carrying. It was because Dick was fully aware of this that he had so emphatically and repeatedly impressed upon her the necessity for saying not a word to any one of his presence. She realised in her vague way—or rather she believed it since he had assured her—that there would be grave danger to him if he were discovered. But discovery was one thing, and the sharing of a confidence as to his presence another. That confidence must certainly be shared.

Lady O'Moy was in an emotional maelstrom that swept her towards a cataract. The cataract might inspire her with dread, standing as it did for death and disaster, but the maelstrom was not to be resisted. She was helpless in it, unequal to breasting such strong waters, she who in all her futile, charming life had been borne snugly in safe crafts that were steered by others.

Remained but to choose her confidant. Nature suggested Terence. But it was against Terence in particular that she had been warned. Circumstance now offered Sylvia Armytage. But pride, or vanity if you prefer it, denied her here. Sylvia was an inexperienced young girl, as she herself had so often found occasion to remind her cousin. Moreover, she fostered the fond illusion that Sylvia looked to her for precept, that upon Sylvia's life she exercised a precious guiding influence. How, then, should the supporting lean upon the supported? Yet since she must, there and then, lean upon something or succumb instantly and completely, she chose a middle course, a sort of temporary assistance.

"I have been imagining things," she said. "It may be a premonition, I don't know. Do you believe in premonitions, Sylvia?"

"Sometimes," Sylvia humoured her.

"I have been imagining that if Dick is hiding, a fugitive, he might naturally come to me for help. I am fanciful, perhaps," she added hastily, lest she should have said too much. "But there it is. All day the notion has clung to me, and I have been asking myself desperately what I should do in such a case."

"Time enough to consider it when it happens, Una. After all—"

"I know," her ladyship interrupted on that ever-ready note of petulance of hers. "I know, of course. But I think I should be easier in my mind if I could find an answer to my doubt. If I knew what to do, to whom to appeal for assistance, for I am afraid that I should be very helpless myself. There is Terence, of course. But I am a little afraid of Terence. He has got Dick out of so many scrapes, and he is so impatient of poor Dick. I am afraid he doesn't understand him, and so I should be a little frightened of appealing to Terence again."

"No," said Sylvia gravely, "I shouldn't go to Terence. Indeed he is the last man to whom I should go."

"You say that too!" exclaimed her ladyship.

"Why?" quoth Sylvia sharply. "Who else has said it?"

There was a brief pause in which Lady O'Moy shuddered. She had been so near to betraying herself. How very quick and shrewd Sylvia was! She made, however, a good recovery.

"Myself, of course. It is what I have thought myself. There is Count Samoval. He promised that if ever any such thing happened he would help me. And he assured me I could count upon him. I think it may have been his offer that made me fanciful."

"I should go to Sir Terence before I went to Count Samoval. By which I mean that I should not go to Count Samoval at all under any circumstances. I do not trust him."

"You said so once before, dear," said Lady O'Moy.

"And you assured me that I spoke out of the fullness of my ignorance and inexperience."

"Ah, forgive me."

"There is nothing to forgive. No doubt you were right. But remember that instinct is most alive in the ignorant and inexperienced, and that instinct is often a surer guide than reason. Yet if you want reason, I can supply that too. Count Samoval is the intimate friend of the Marquis of Minas, who remains a member of the Government, and who next to the Principal Souza was, and no doubt is, the most bitter opponent of the British policy in Portugal. Yet Count Samoval, one of the largest landowners in the north, and the nobleman who has perhaps suffered most severely from that policy, represents himself as its most vigorous supporter."

Lady O'Moy listened in growing amazement. Also she was a little shocked. It seemed to her almost indecent that a young girl should know so much about politics—so much of which she herself, a married woman, and the wife of the adjutant-general, was completely in ignorance.

"Save us, child!" she ejaculated. "You are so extraordinarily informed."

"I have talked to Captain Tremayne," said Sylvia. "He has explained all this."

"Extraordinary conversation for a young man to hold with a young girl," pronounced her ladyship. "Terence never talked of such things to me."

"Terence was too busy making love to you," said Sylvia, and there was the least suspicion of regret in her almost boyish voice.

"That may account for it," her ladyship confessed, and fell for a moment into consideration of that delicious and rather amusing past, when O'Moy's ferocious hesitancy and flaming jealousy had delighted her with the full perception of her beauty's power. With a rush, however, the present forced itself back upon her notice. "But I still don't see why Count Samoval should have offered me assistance if he did not intend to grant it when the time came."

Sylvia explained that it was from the Portuguese Government that the demand for justice upon the violator of the nunnery at Tavora emanated, and that Samoval's offer might be calculated to obtain him information of Butler's whereabouts when they became known, so that he might surrender him to the Government.

"My dear!" Lady O'Moy was shocked almost beyond expression. "How you must dislike the man to suggest that he could be such a—such a Judas."

"I do not suggest that he could be. I warn you never to run the

57

risk of testing him. He may be as honest in this matter as he pretends. But if ever Dick were to come to you for help, you must take no risk."

The phrase was a happier one than Sylvia could suppose. It was almost the very phrase that Dick himself had used; and its reiteration by another bore conviction to her ladyship.

"To whom then should I go?" she demanded plaintively. And Sylvia, speaking with knowledge, remembering the promise that Tremayne had given her, answered readily: "There is but one man whose assistance you could safely seek. Indeed I wonder you should not have thought of him in the first instance, since he is your own, as well as Dick's lifelong friend."

"Ned Tremayne?" Her ladyship fell into thought. "Do you know, I am a little afraid of Ned. He is so very sober and cold. You do mean Ned—don't you?"

"Whom else should I mean?"

"But what could he do?"

"My dear, how should I know? But at least I know—for I think I can be sure of this—that he will not lack the will to help you; and to have the will, in a man like Captain Tremayne, is to find a way."

The confident, almost respectful, tone in which she spoke arrested her ladyship's attention. It promptly sent her off at a tangent:

"You like Ned, don't you, dear?"

"I think everybody likes him." Sylvia's voice was now studiously cold.

"Yes; but I don't mean quite in that way." And then before the subject could be further pursued the carriage rolled to a standstill in a flood of light from gaping portals, scattering a mob of curious sight-seers intersprinkled with chairmen, footmen, linkmen and all the valetaille that hovers about the functions of the great world.

The carriage door was flung open and the steps let down. A brace of footmen, plump as capons, in gorgeous liveries, bowed powdered heads and proffered scarlet arms to assist the ladies to alight.

Above in the crowded, spacious, colonnaded vestibule at the foot of the great staircase they were met-by Captain Tremayne, who had just arrived with Major Carruthers, both resplendent in full dress, and Captain Marcus Glennie of the Telemachus in blue and gold. Together they ascended the great staircase, lined with chatting groups, and ablaze with uniforms, military, naval and diplomatic, British and Portuguese, to be welcomed above by the Count and Countess of Redondo.

Lady O'Moy's entrance of the ballroom produced the effect to

58

which custom had by now inured her. Soon she found herself the centre of assiduous attentions. Cavalrymen in blue, riflemen in green, scarlet officers of the line regiments, winged light-infantrymen, rakishly pelissed, gold-braided hussars and all the smaller fry of court and camp fluttered insistently about her. It was no novelty to her who had been the recipient of such homage since her first ball five years ago at Dublin Castle, and yet the wine of it had gone ever to her head a little. But to-night she was rather pale and listless, her rose-petal loveliness emphasised thereby perhaps. An unusual air of indifference hung about her as she stood there amid this throng of martial jostlers who craved the honour of a dance and at whom she smiled a thought mechanically over the top of her slowly moving fan.

The first quadrille impended, and the senior service had carried off the prize from under the noses of the landsmen. As she was swept away by Captain Glennie, she came face to face with Tremayne, who was passing with Sylvia on his arm. She stopped and tapped his arm with her fan.

"You haven't asked to dance, Ned," she reproached him.

"With reluctance I abstained."

"But I don't intend that you shall. I have something to say to you." He met her glance, and found it oddly serious—most oddly serious for her. Responding to its entreaty, he murmured a promise in courteous terms of delight at so much honour.

But either he forgot the promise or did not conceive its redemption to be an urgent matter, for the quadrille being done he sauntered through one of the crowded ante-rooms with Miss Armytage and brought her to the cool of a deserted balcony above the garden. Beyond this was the river, agleam with the lights of the British fleet that rode at anchor on its placid bosom.

"Una will be waiting for you," Miss Armytage reminded him. She was leaning on the sill of the balcony. Standing erect beside her, he considered the graceful profile sharply outlined against a background of gloom by the light from the windows behind them. A heavy curl of her dark hair lay upon a neck as flawlessly white as the rope of pearls that swung from it, with which her fingers were now idly toying. It were difficult to say which most engaged his thoughts: the profile; the lovely line of neck; or the rope of pearls. These latter were of price, such things as it might seldom—and then only by sacrifice—lie within the means of Captain Tremayne to offer to the woman whom he took to wife.

He so lost himself upon that train of thought that she was forced to repeat her reminder.

"Una will be waiting for you, Captain Tremayne."

"Scarcely as eagerly," he answered, "as others will be waiting for you."

She laughed amusedly, a frank, boyish laugh. "I thank you for not saying as eagerly as I am waiting for others."

"Miss Armytage, I have ever cultivated truth."

"But we are dealing with surmise."

"Oh, no surmise at all. I speak of what I know."

"And so do I." And yet again she repeated: "Una will be waiting for you."

He sighed, and stiffened slightly. "Of course if you insist," said he, and made ready to reconduct her.

She swung round as if to go, but checked, and looked him frankly in the eyes.

"Why will you for ever be misunderstanding me?" she challenged him.

"Perhaps it is the inevitable result of my overanxiety to understand."

"Then begin by taking me more literally, and do not read into my words more meaning than I intend to give them. When I say Una is waiting for you, I state a simple fact, not a command that you shall go to her. Indeed I want first to talk to you."

"If I might take you literally now—"

"Should I have suffered you to bring me here if I did not?"

"I beg your pardon," he said, contrite, and something shaken out of his imperturbability. "Sylvia," he ventured very boldly, and there checked, so terrified as to be a shame to his brave scarlet, gold-laced uniform.

"Yes?" she said. She was leaning upon the balcony again, and in such a way now that he could no longer see her profile. But her fingers were busy at the pearls once more, and this he saw, and seeing, recovered himself.

"You have something to say to me?" he questioned in his smooth, level voice.

Had he not looked away as he spoke he might have observed that her fingers tightened their grip of the pearls almost convulsively, as if to break the rope. It was a gesture slight and trivial, yet arguing perhaps vexation. But Tremayne did not see it, and had he seen it, it is odds it would have conveyed no message to him.

There fell a long pause, which he did not venture to break. At last she spoke, her voice quiet and level as his own had been.

"It is about Una."

"I had hoped," he spoke very softly, "that it was about yourself."

60

She flashed round upon him almost angrily. "Why do you utter these set speeches to me?" she demanded. And then before he could recover from his astonishment to make any answer she had resumed a normal manner, and was talking quickly.

She told him of Una's premonitions about Dick. Told him, in short, what it was that Una desired to talk to him about.

"You bade her come to me?" he said.

"Of course. After your promise to me."

He was silent and very thoughtful for a moment. "I wonder that Una needed to be told that she had in me a friend," he said slowly.

"I wonder to whom she would have gone on her own impulse?"

"To Count Samoval," Miss Armytage informed him.

"Samoval!" he rapped the name out sharply. He was clearly angry. "That man! I can't understand why O'Moy should suffer him about the house so much."

"Terence, like everybody else, will suffer anything that Una wishes."

"Then Terence is more of a fool than I ever suspected."

There was a brief pause. "If you were to fail Una in this," said Miss Armytage presently, "I mean that unless you yourself give her the assurance that you are ready to do what you can for Dick, should the occasion arise, I am afraid that in her present foolish mood she may still avail herself of Count Samoval. That would be to give Samoval a hold upon her; and I tremble to think what the consequences might be. That man is a snake—a horror."

The frankness with which she spoke was to Tremayne full evidence of her anxiety. He was prompt to allay it.

"She shall have that assurance this very evening," he promised.

"I at least have not pledged my word to anything or to any one. Even so," he added slowly, "the chances of my services being ever required grow more slender every day. Una may be full of premonitions about Dick. But between premonition and event there is something of a gap."

Again a pause, and then: "I am glad," said Miss Armytage, "to think that Una has a friend, a trustworthy friend, upon whom she can depend. She is so incapable of depending upon herself. All her life there has been some one at hand to guide her and screen her from unpleasantness until she has remained just a sweet, dear child to be taken by the hand in every dark lane of life."

"But she has you, Miss Armytage."

"Me?" Miss Armytage spoke deprecatingly. "I don't think I am

61

a very able or experienced guide. Besides, even such as I am, she may not have me very long now. I had letters from home this morning. Father is not very well, and mother writes that he misses me. I am thinking of returning soon."

"But—but you have only just come!"

She brightened and laughed at the dismay in his voice. "Indeed, I have been here six weeks." She looked out over the shimmering moonlit waters of the Tagus and the shadowy, ghostly ships of the British fleet that rode at anchor there, and her eyes were wistful. Her fingers, with that little gesture peculiar to her in moments of constraint, were again entwining themselves in her rope of pearls. "Yes," she said almost musingly, "I think I must be going soon."

He was dismayed. He realised that the moment for action had come. His heart was sounding the charge within him. And then that cursed rope of pearls, emblem of the wealth and luxury in which she had been nurtured, stood like an impassable abattis across his path.

"You—you will be glad to go, of course?" he suggested.

"Hardly that. It has been very pleasant here." She sighed.

"We shall miss you very much," he said gloomily. "The house at Monsanto will not be the same when you are gone. Una will be lost and desolate without you."

"It occurs to me sometimes," she said slowly, "that the people about Una think too much of Una and too little of themselves."

It was a cryptic speech. In another it might have signified a spitefulness unthinkable in Sylvia Armytage; therefore it puzzled him very deeply. He stood silent, wondering what precisely she might mean, and thus in silence they continued for a spell. Then slowly she turned and the blaze of light from the windows fell about her irradiantly. She was rather pale, and her eyes were of a suspiciously excessive brightness. And again she made use of the phrase:

"Una will be waiting for you."

Yet, as before, he stood silent and immovable, considering her, questioning himself, searching her face and his own soul. All he saw was that rope of shimmering pearls.

"And after all, as yourself suggested, it is possible that others may be waiting for me," she added presently.

Instantly he was crestfallen and contrite. "I sincerely beg your pardon, Miss Armytage," and with a pang of which his imperturbable exterior gave no hint he proffered her his arm.

She took it, barely touching it with her finger-tips, and they re-entered the ante-room.

"When do you think that you will be leaving?" he asked her gently.

There was a note of harshness in the voice that answered him.

"I don't know yet. But very soon. The sooner the better, I think."

And then the sleek and courtly Samoval, detaching from, seeming to materialise out of, the glittering throng they had entered, was bowing low before her, claiming her attention. Knowing her feelings, Tremayne would not have relinquished her, but to his infinite amazement she herself slipped her fingers from his scarlet sleeve, to place them upon the black one that Samoval was gracefully proffering, and greeted Samoval with a gay raillery as oddly in contrast with her grave demeanour towards the captain as with her recent avowal of detestation for the Count.

Stricken and half angry, Tremayne stood looking after them as they receded towards the ballroom. To increase his chagrin came a laugh from Miss Armytage, sharp and rather strident, floating towards him, and Miss Armytage's laugh was wont to be low and restrained. Samoval, no doubt, had resources to amuse a woman— even a woman who instinctively, disliked him—resources of which Captain Tremayne himself knew nothing.

And then some one tapped him on the shoulder. A very tall, hawk-faced man in a scarlet coat and tightly strapped blue trousers stood beside him. It was Colquhoun Grant, the ablest intelligence officer in Wellington's service.

"Why, Colonel!" cried Tremayne, holding out his hand. "I didn't know you were in Lisbon."

"I arrived only this afternoon." The keen eyes flashed after the disappearing figures of Sylvia and her cavalier. "Tell me, what is the name of the irresistible gallant who has so lightly ravished you of your quite delicious companion?"

"Count Samoval," said Tremayne shortly.

Grant's face remained inscrutable. "Really!" he said softly. "So that is Jeronymo de Samoval, eh? How very interesting. A great supporter of the British policy; therefore an altruist, since himself he is a sufferer by it; and I hear that he has become a great friend of O'Moy's."

"He is at Monsanto a good deal certainly," Tremayne admitted.

"Most interesting." Grant was slowly nodding, and a faint smile curled his thin, sensitive lips. "But I'm keeping you, Tremayne, and no doubt you would be dancing. I shall perhaps see you to-morrow. I shall be coming up to Monsanto."

And with a wave of the hand he passed on and was gone.

CHAPTER VII

THE ALLY

Tremayne elbowed his way through the gorgeous crowd, exchanging greetings here and there as he went, and so reached the ballroom during a pause in the dancing. He looked round for Lady O'Moy, but he could see her nowhere, and would never have found her had not Carruthers pointed out a knot of officers and assured him that the lady was in the heart of it and in imminent peril of being suffocated.

Thither the captain bent his steps, looking neither to right nor left in his singleness of purpose. Thus it happened that he saw neither O'Moy, who had just arrived, nor the massive, decorated bulk of Marshal Beresford, with whom the adjutant stood in conversation on the skirts of the throng that so assiduously worshipped at her ladyship's shrine.

Captain Tremayne went through the group with all a sapper's skill at piercing obstacles, and so came face to face with the lady of his quest. Seeing her so radiant now, with sparkling eyes and ready laugh, it was difficult to conceive her haunted by any such anxieties as Miss Armytage had mentioned. Yet the moment she perceived him, as if his presence acted as a reminder to lift her out of the delicious present, something of her gaiety underwent eclipse.

Child of impulse that she was, she gave no thought to her action and the construction it might possibly bear in the minds of men chagrined and slighted.

"Why, Ned," she cried, "you have kept me waiting." And with a complete and charming ignoring of the claims of all who had been before him, and who were warring there for precedence of one another, she took his arm in token that she yielded herself to him before even the honour was so much as solicited.

With nods and smiles to right and left—a queen dismissing her court—she passed on the captain's arm through the little crowd that gave way before her dismayed and intrigued, and so away.

O'Moy, who had been awaiting a favourable moment to present the marshal by the marshal's own request, attempted to thrust forward now with Beresford at his side. But the bowing line of officers whose backs were towards him effectively barred his progress, and before they had broken up that formation her ladyship and her cavalier were out of sight, lost in the moving crowd.

64

The marshal laughed good-humouredly. "The infallible reward of patience," said he. And O'Moy laughed with him. But the next moment he was scowling at what he overheard.

"On my soul, that was impudence!" an Irish infantryman had protested.

"Have you ever heard," quoth a heavy dragoon, who was also a heavy jester, "that in heaven the last shall be first? If you pay court to an angel you must submit to celestial customs."

"And bedad," rejoined the infantryman, "as there's no marryin' in heaven ye've got to make the best of it with other men's wives. Sure it's a great success that fellow should be in paradise. Did ye remark the way she melted to him beauty swooning at the sight of temptation! Bad luck to him! Who is he at all?"

They dispersed laughing and followed by O'Moy's scowling eyes. It annoyed him that his wife's thoughtless conduct should render her the butt of such jests as these, and perhaps a subject for lewd gossip. He would speak to her about it later. Meanwhile the marshal had linked arms with him.

"Since the privilege must be postponed," said he, "suppose that we seek supper. I have always found that a man can best heal in his stomach the wounds taken by his heart." His fleshy bulk afforded a certain prima-facie confirmation of the dictum.

With a roll more suggestive of the quarter-deck than the saddle, the great man bore off O'Moy in quest of material consolation. Yet as they went the adjutant's eyes raked the ballroom in quest of his wife. That quest, however, was unsuccessful, for his wife was already in the garden.

"I want to talk to you most urgently, Ned. Take me somewhere where we can be quite private," she had begged the captain. "Somewhere where there is no danger of being overheard."

Her agitation, now uncontrolled, suggested to Tremayne that the matter might be far more serious and urgent than Miss Armytage had represented it. He thought first of the balcony where he had lately been. But then the balcony opened immediately from the ante-room and was likely at any moment to be invaded. So, since the night was soft and warm, he preferred the garden. Her ladyship went to find a wrap, then arm in arm they passed out, and were lost in the shadows of an avenue of palm-trees.

"It is about Dick," she said breathlessly.

"I know—Miss Armytage told me."

"What did she tell you?"

"That you had a premonition that he might come to you for assistance."

"A premonition!" Her ladyship laughed nervously. "It is more than a premonition, Ned. He has come."

The captain stopped in his stride, and stood quite still.

"Come?" he echoed. "Dick?"

"Sh!" she warned him, and sank her voice from very instinct. "He came to me this evening, half an hour before we left home. I have put him in an alcove adjacent to my dressing-room for the present."

"You have left him there?" He was alarmed.

"Oh, there's no fear. No one ever goes there except Bridget. And I have locked the alcove. He's fast asleep. He was asleep before I left. The poor fellow was so worn and weary." Followed details of his appearance and a recital of his wanderings so far as he had made them known to her. "And he was so insistent that no one should know, not even Terence."

"Terence must not know," he said gravely.

"You think that too!"

"If Terence knows—well, you will regret it all the days of your life, Una."

He was so stern, so impressive, that she begged for explanation. He afforded it. "You would be doing Terence the utmost cruelty if you told him. You would be compelling him to choose between his honour and his concern for you. And since he is the very soul of honour, he must sacrifice you and himself, your happiness and his own, everything that makes life good for you both, to his duty."

She was aghast, for all that she was far from understanding. But he went on relentlessly to make his meaning clear, for the sake of O'Moy as much as for her own—for the sake of the future of these two people who were perhaps his dearest friends. He saw in what danger of shipwreck their happiness now stood, and he took the determination of clearly pointing out to her every shoal in the water through which she must steer her course.

"Since this has happened, Una, you must be told the whole truth; you must listen, and, above all, be reasonable. I am Dick's friend, as I am your own and Terence's. Your father was my best friend, perhaps, and my gratitude to him is unbounded, as I hope you know. You and Dick are almost as brother and sister to me. In spite of this—indeed, because of this, I have prayed for news that Dick was dead."

Her grasp interrupted him, and he felt the tightening clutch of her hands upon his arm in the gloom.

"I have prayed this for Dick's sake, and more than all for the sake of your happiness and Terence's. If Dick is taken the choice

66

before Terence is a tragic one. You will realise it when I tell you that duty forced him to pledge his word to the Portuguese Government that Dick should be shot when found."

"Oh!" It was a gasp of horror, of incredulity. She loosed his arm and drew away from him. "It is infamous! I can't believe it. I can't."

"It is true. I swear it to you. I was present, and I heard."

"And you allowed it?"

"What could I do? How could I interfere? Besides, the minister who demanded that undertaking knew nothing of the relationship between O'Moy and this missing officer."

"But—but he could have been told."

"That would have made no difference—unless it were to create fresh difficulties."

She stood there ghostly white against the gloom. A dry sob broke from her. "Terence did that! Terence did that!" she moaned. And then in a surge of anger: "I shall never speak to Terence again. I shall not live with him another day. It was infamous! Infamous!"

"It was not infamous. It was almost noble, almost heroic," he amazed her. "Listen, Una, and try to understand." He took her arm again and drew her gently on down that avenue of moonlight-fretted darkness.

"Oh, I understand," she cried bitterly. "I understand perfectly. He has always been hard on Dick! He has always made mountains out of molehills where Dick was concerned. He forgets that Dick is young a mere boy. He judges Dick from the standpoint of his own sober middle age. Why, he's an old man—a wicked old man!"

Thus her rage, hurling at O'Moy what in the insolence of her youth seemed the last insult.

"You are very unjust, Una. You are even a little stupid," he said, deeming the punishment necessary and salutary.

"Stupid! I stupid! I have never been called stupid before."

"But you have undoubtedly deserved to be," he assured her with perfect calm.

It took her aback by its directness, and for a moment left her without an answer. Then: "I think you had better leave me," she told him frostily. "You forget yourself."

"Perhaps I do," he admitted. "That is because I am more concerned to think of Dick and Terence and yourself. Sit down, Una."

They had reached a little circle by a piece of ornamental water, facing which a granite-hewn seat had been placed. She sank to it obediently, if sulkily.

"It may perhaps help you to understand what Terence has

done when I tell you that in his place, loving Dick as I do, I must have pledged myself precisely as he did or else despised myself for ever. And being pledged, I must keep my word or go in the same self-contempt." He elaborated his argument by explaining the full circumstances under which the pledge had been exacted. "But be in no doubt about it," he concluded. "If Terence knows of Dick's presence at Monsanto he has no choice. He must deliver him up to a firing party—or to a court-martial which will inevitably sentence him to death, no matter what the defence that Dick may urge. He is a man prejudged, foredoomed by the necessities of war. And Terence will do this although it will break his heart and ruin all his life. Understand me, then, that in enjoining you never to allow Terence to suspect that Dick is present, I am pleading not so much for you or for Dick, but for Terence himself—for it is upon Terence that the hardest and most tragic suffering must fall. Now do you understand?"

"I understand that men are very stupid," was her way of admitting it.

"And you see that you were wrong in judging Terence as you did?"

"I—I suppose so."

She didn't understand it all. But since Tremayne was so insistent she supposed there must be something in his point of view. She had been brought up in the belief that Ned Tremayne was common sense incarnate; and although she often doubted it—as you may doubt the dogmas of a religion in which you have been bred— yet she never openly rebelled against that inculcated faith. Above all she wanted to cry. She knew that it would be very good for her. She had often found a singular relief in tears when vexed by things beyond her understanding. But she had to think of that flock of gallants in the ballroom waiting to pay court to her and of her duty towards them of preserving her beauty unimpaired by the ravages of a vented sorrow.

Tremayne sat down beside her. "So now that we understand each other on that score, let us consider ways and means to dispose of Dick."

At once she was uplifted and became all eagerness.

"Yes, Yes. You will help me, Ned?"

"You can depend upon me to do all in human power."

He thought rapidly, and gave voice to some of his thoughts. "If I could I would take him to my lodgings at Alcantara. But Carruthers knows him and would see him there. So that is out of the question. Then again it is dangerous to move him about. At any moment he might be seen and recognised."

"Hardly recognised," she said. "His beard disguises him, and his dress—" She shuddered at the very thought of the figure he had cut, he, the jaunty, dandy Richard Butler.

"That is something, of course," he agreed. And then asked: "How long do you think that you could keep him hidden?"

"I don't know. You see, there's Bridget. She is the only danger, as she has charge of my dressing-room."

"It may be desperate, but—Can you trust her?"

"Oh, I am sure I can. She is devoted to me; she would do anything—"

"She must be bought as well. Devotion and gain when linked together will form an unbreakable bond. Don't let us be stingy, Una. Take her into your confidence boldly, and promise her a hundred guineas for her silence—payable on the day that Dick leaves the country."

"But how are we to get him out of the country?"

"I think I know a way. I can depend on Marcus Glennie. I may tell him the whole truth and the identity of our man, or I may not. I must think about that. But, whatever I decide, I am sure I can induce Glennie to take our fugitive home in the Telemachus and land him safely somewhere in Ireland, where he will have to lose himself for awhile. Perhaps for Glennie's sake it will be safer not to disclose Dick's identity. Then if there should be trouble later, Glennie, having known nothing of the real facts, will not be held responsible. I will talk to him to-night."

"Do you think he will consent?" she asked in strained anxiety—anxiety to have her anxieties dispelled.

"I am sure he will. I can almost pledge my word on it. Marcus would do anything to serve me. Oh, set your mind at rest. Consider the thing done. Keep Dick safely hidden for a week or so until the Telemachus is ready to sail—he mustn't go on board until the last moment, for several reasons—and I will see to the rest."

Under that confident promise her troubles fell from her, as lightly as they ever did.

"You are very good to me, Ned. Forgive me what I said just now. And I think I understand about Terence—poor dear old Terence."

"Of course you do." Moved to comfort her as he might have been moved to comfort a child, he flung his arm along the seat behind her, and patted her shoulder soothingly. "I knew you would understand. And not a word to Terence, not a word that could so much as awaken his suspicions. Remember that."

"Oh, I shall."

Fell a step upon the patch behind them crunching the gravel.

Captain Tremayne, his arm still along the back of the seat, and seeming to envelop her ladyship, looked over her shoulder. A tall figure was advancing briskly. He recognised it even in the gloom by its height and gait and swing for O'Moy's.

"Why, here is Terence," he said easily—so easily, with such frank and obvious honesty of welcome, that the anger in which O'Moy came wrapped fell from him on the instant, to be replaced by shame.

"I have been looking for you everywhere, my dear," he said to Una. "Marshal Beresford is anxious to pay you his respects before he leaves, and you have been so hedged about by gallants all the evening that it's devil a chance he's had of approaching you." There was a certain constraint in his voice, for a man may not recover instantly from such feelings as those which had fetched him hot-foot down that path at sight of those two figures sitting so close and intimate, the young man's arm so proprietorialy about the lady's shoulders—as it seemed.

Lady O'Moy sprang up at once, with a little silvery laugh that was singularly care-free; for had not Tremayne lifted the burden entirely from her shoulders?

"You should have married a dowd," she mocked him. "Then you'd have found her more easily accessible."

"Instead of finding her dallying in the moonlight with my secretary," he rallied back between good and ill humour. And he turned to Tremayne: "Damned indiscreet of you, Ned," he added more severely. "Suppose you had been seen by any of the scandalmongering old wives of the garrison? A nice thing for Una and a nice thing for me, begad, to be made the subject of fly-blown talk over the tea-cups."

Tremayne accepted the rebuke in the friendly spirit in which it appeared to be conveyed. "Sorry, O'Moy," he said. "You're quite right. We should have thought of it. Everybody isn't to know what our relations are." And again he was so manifestly honest and so completely at his ease that it was impossible to harbour any thought of evil, and O'Moy felt again the glow of shame of suspicions so utterly unworthy and dishonouring.

CHAPTER VIII

THE INTELLIGENCE OFFICER

In a small room of Count Redondo's palace, a room that had been set apart for cards, sat three men about a card-table. They were Count Samoval, the elderly Marquis of Minas, lean, bald and vulturine of aspect, with a deep-set eye that glared fiercely through a single eyeglass rimmed in tortoise-shell, and a gentleman still on the fair side of middle age, with a clear-cut face and iron-grey hair, who wore the dark green uniform of a major of Cacadores.

Considering his Portuguese uniform, it is odd that the low-toned, earnest conversation amongst them should have been conducted in French.

There were cards on the table; but there was no pretence of play. You might have conceived them a group of players who, wearied of their game, had relinquished it for conversation. They were the only tenants of the room, which was small, cedar-panelled and lighted by a girandole of sparkling crystal. Through the closed door came faintly from the distant ballroom the strains of the dance music.

With perhaps the single exception of the Principal Souza, the British policy had no more bitter opponent in Portugal than the Marquis of Minas. Once a member of the Council of Regency—before Souza had been elected to that body—he had quitted it in disgust at the British measures. His chief ground of umbrage had been the appointment of British officers to the command of the Portuguese regiments which formed the division under Marshal Beresford. In this he saw a deliberate insult and slight to his country and his countrymen. He was a man of burning and blinded patriotism, to whom Portugal was the most glorious nation in the world. He lived in his country's splendid past, refusing to recognise that the days of Henry the Navigator, of Vasco da Gama, of Manuel the Fortunate—days in which Portugal had been great indeed among the nations of the Old World were gone and done with. He respected Britons as great merchants and industrious traders; but, after all, merchants and traders are not the peers of fighters on land and sea, of navigators, conquerors and civilisers, such as his countrymen had been, such as he believed them still to be. That the descendants of Gamas, Cunhas, Magalhaes and Albuquerques—men whose names were indelibly written upon the very face of the world—should be passed over, whilst alien officers lead been brought in to train and command the Portuguese legions, was an affront to Portugal which Minas could never forgive.

It was thus that he had become a rebel, withdrawing from a government whose supineness he could not condone. For a while his rebellion had been passive, until the Principal Souza had heated him in the fire of his own rage and fashioned him into an intriguing instrument of the first power. He was listening intently now to the soft, rapid speech of the gentleman in the major's uniform.

"Of course, rumours had reached the Prince of this policy of devastation," he was saying, "but his Highness has been disposed to treat these rumours lightly, unable to see, as indeed are we all, what useful purpose such a policy could finally serve. He does not underrate the talents of milord Wellington as a commander. He does not imagine that he would pursue such operations out of pure wantonness; yet if such operations are indeed being pursued, what can they be but wanton? A moment, Count," he stayed Samoval, who was about to interrupt. His mind and manner were authoritative. "We know most positively from the Emperor's London agents that the war is unpopular in England; we know that public opinion is being prepared for a British retreat, for the driving of the British into the sea, as must inevitably happen once Monsieur le Prince decides to launch his bolt. Here in the Tagus the British fleet lies ready to embark the troops, and the British Cabinet itself" (he spoke more slowly and emphatically) "expects that embarkation to take place at latest in September, which is just about the time that the French offensive should be at its height and the French troops under the very walls of Lisbon. I admit that by this policy of devastation if, indeed, it be true—added to a stubborn contesting of every foot of ground, the French advance may be retarded. But the process will be costly to Britain in lives and money."

"And more costly still to Portugal," croaked the Marquis of Minas.

"And, as you, say, Monsieur le Marquis, more costly still to Portugal. Let me for a moment show you another side of the picture. The French administration, so sane, so cherishing, animated purely by ideas of progress, enforcing wise and beneficial laws, making ever for the prosperity and well-being of conquered nations, knows how to render itself popular wherever it is established. This Portugal knows already—or at least some part of it. There was the administration of Soult in Oporto, so entirely satisfactory to the people that it was no inconsiderable party was prepared, subject to the Emperor's consent, to offer him the crown and settle down peacefully under his rule. There was the administration of Junot in Lisbon. I ask you: when was Lisbon better governed?

"Contrast, for a moment, with these the present British administration—for it amounts to an administration. Consider the burning grievances that must be left behind by this policy of laying the country waste, of pauperising a million people of all degrees, driving them homeless from the lands on which they were born, after compelling them to lend a hand in the destruction of all that their labour has built up through long years. If any policy could better serve the purposes of France, I know it not. The people from here to Beira should be ready to receive the French with open arms, and to welcome their deliverance from this most costly and bitter British protection.

"Do you, Messieurs, detect a flaw in these arguments?"

Both shook their heads.

"Bien!" said the major of Portuguese Cacadores. "Then we reach one or two only possible conclusions: either these rumours of a policy of devastation which have reached the Prince of Esslingen are as utterly false as he believes them to be, or—"

"To my cost I know them to be true, as I have already told you," Samoval interrupted bitterly.

"Or," the major persisted, raising a hand to restrain the Count, "or there is something further that has not been yet discovered—a mystery the enucleation of which will shed light upon all the rest. Since you assure me, Monsieur le Comte, that milord Wellington's policy is beyond doubt, as reported to Monsieur, le Marechal, it but remains to address ourselves to the discovery of the mystery underlying it. What conclusions have you reached? You, Monsieur de Samoval, have had exceptional opportunities of observation, I understand."

"I am afraid my opportunities have been none so exceptional as you suppose," replied Samoval, with a dubious shake of his sleek, dark head. "At one time I founded great hopes in Lady O'Moy. But Lady O'Moy is a fool, and does not enjoy her husband's confidence in official matters. What she knows I know. Unfortunately it does not amount to very much. One conclusion, however, I have reached: Wellington is preparing in Portugal a snare for Massena's army."

"A snare? Hum!" The major pursed his full lips into a smile of scorn. "There cannot be a trap with two exits, my friend. Massena enters Portugal at Almeida and marches to Lisbon and the open sea. He may be inconvenienced or hampered in his march; but its goal is certain. Where, then, can lie the snare? Your theory presupposes an impassable barrier to arrest the French when they are deep in the country and an overwhelming force to cut off their retreat when that barrier is reached. The overwhelming force does not exist and cannot be manufactured; as for the barrier, no barrier that it lies

73

within human power to construct lies beyond French power to over-stride."

"I should not make too sure of that," Samoval warned him. "And you have overlooked something."

The major glanced at the Count sharply and without satisfaction. He accounted himself—trained as he had been under the very eye of the great Emperor—of some force in strategy and tactics, a player too well versed in the game to overlook the possible moves of an opponent.

"Ha!" he said, with the ghost of a sneer. "For instance, Monsieur le Comte?"

"The overwhelming force exists," said Samoval.

"Where is it then? Whence has it been created? If you refer to the united British and Portuguese troops, you will be good enough to bear in mind that they will be retreating before the Prince. They cannot at once be before and behind him."

The man's cool assurance and cooler contempt of Samoval's views stung the Count into some sharpness.

"Are you seeking information, sir, or are you bestowing it?" he inquired.

"Ah! Your pardon, Monsieur le Comte. I inquire of course. I put forward arguments to anticipate conditions that may possibly be erroneous."

Samoval waived the point. "There is another force besides the British and Portuguese troops that you have left out of your calculations."

"And that?" The major was still faintly incredulous.

"You should remember what Wellington obviously remembers: that a French army depends for its sustenance upon the country it is invading. That is why Wellington is stripping the French line of penetration as bare of sustenance as this card-table. If we assume the existence of the barrier—an impassable line of fortifications encountered within many marches of the frontier—we may also assume that starvation will be the overwhelming force that will cut off the French retreat."

The other's keen eyes flickered. For a moment his face lost its assurance, and it was Samoval's turn to smile. But the major made a sharp recovery. He slowly shook his iron-grey head.

"You have no right to assume an impassable barrier. That is an inadmissible hypothesis. There is no such thing as a line of fortifications impassable to the French."

"You will pardon me, Major, but it is yourself have no right to your own assumptions. Again you overlook something. I will grant that technically what you say is true. No fortifications can be built that cannot be destroyed—given adequate power, with which it is yet to prove that Massena not knowing what may await him, will be equipped.

"But let us for a moment take so much for granted, and now consider this: fortifications are unquestionably building in the region of Torres Vedras, and Wellington guards the secret so jealously that not even the British—either here or in England—are aware of their nature. That is why the Cabinet in London takes for granted an embarkation in September. Wellington has not even taken his Government into his confidence. That is the sort of man he is. Now these fortifications have been building since last October. Best part of eight months have already gone in their construction. It may be another two or three months before the French army reaches them. I do not say that the French cannot pass them, given time. But how long will it take the French to pull down what it will have taken ten or eleven months to construct? And if they are unable to draw sustenance from a desolate, wasted country, what time will they have at their disposal? It will be with them a matter of life or death. Having come so far they must reach Lisbon or perish; and if the fortifications can delay them by a single month, then, granted that all Lord Wellington's other dispositions have been duly carried out, perish they must. It remains, Monsieur le Major, for you to determine whether, with all their energy, with all their genius and all their valour, the French can—in an ill-nourished condition—destroy in a few weeks the considered labour of nearly a year."

The major was aghast. He had changed colour, and through his eyes, wide and staring, his stupefaction glared forth at them.

Minas uttered a dry cough under cover of his hand, and screwed up his eyeglass to regard the major more attentively. "You do not appear to have considered all that," he said.

"But, my dear Marquis," was the half-indignant answer, "why was I not told all this to begin with? You represented yourself as but indifferently informed, Monsieur de Samoval. Whereas—"

"So I am, my dear Major, as far as information goes. If I did not use these arguments before, it was because it seemed to me an impertinence to offer what, after all, are no more than the conclusions of my own constructive and deductive reasoning to one so well versed in strategy as yourself."

The major was silenced for a moment. "I congratulate you, Count," he said. "Monsieur le Marechal shall have your views without delay. Tell me," he begged. "You say these fortifications lie in the region of Torres Vedras. Can you be more precise?"

"I think so. But again I warn you that I can tell you only what I infer. I judge they will run from the sea, somewhere near the mouth of the Zizandre, in a semicircle to the Tagus, somewhere to the south of Santarem. I know that they do not reach as far north as San, because the roads there are open, whereas all roads to the south, where I am assuming that the fortifications lie, are closed and closely guarded."

"Why do you suggest a semicircle?"

"Because that is the formation of the hills, and presumably the line of heights would be followed."

"Yes," the major approved slowly. "And the distance, then, would be some thirty or forty miles?"

"Fully."

The major's face relaxed its gravity. He even smiled. "You will agree, Count, that in a line of that extent a uniform strength is out of the question. It must perforce present many weak, many vulnerable, places."

"Oh, undoubtedly."

"Plans of these lines must be in existence."

"Again undoubtedly. Sir Terence O'Moy will have plans in his possession showing their projected extent. Colonel Fletcher, who is in charge of the construction, is in constant communication with the adjutant, himself an engineer; and—as I partly imagine, partly infer from odd phrases that I have overheard—especially entrusted by Lord Wellington with the supervision of the works."

"Two things, then, are necessary," said the major promptly. "The first is, that the devastation of the country should be retarded, and as far as possible hindered altogether."

"That," said Minas, "you may safely leave to myself and Souza's other friends, the northern noblemen who have no intention of becoming the victims of British disinclination to pitched battles."

"The second—and this is more difficult—is that we should obtain by hook or by crook a plan of the fortifications." And he looked directly at Samoval.

The Count nodded slowly, but his face expressed doubt.

"I am quite alive to the necessity. I always have been. But—"

"To a man of your resource and intelligence—an intelligence of which you have just given such very signal proof—the matter should be possible." He paused a moment. Then: "If I understand you correctly, Monsieur de Samoval, your fortunes have suffered deeply, and you are almost ruined by this policy of Wellington's. You are offered the opportunity of making a magnificent recovery. The Emperor is the most generous paymaster in the world, and he is beyond measure impatient at the manner in which the campaign in the Peninsula is dragging on. He has spoken of it as an ulcer that is draining the Empire of its resources. For the man who could render

76

him the service of disclosing the weak spot in this armour, the Achilles heel of the British, there would be a reward beyond all your possible dreams. Obtain the plans, then, and—"

He checked abruptly. The door had opened, and in a Venetian mirror facing him upon the wall the major caught the reflection of a British uniform, the stiff gold collar surmounted by a bronzed hawk face with which he was acquainted.

"I beg your pardon, gentlemen," said the officer in Portuguese, "I was looking for—"

His voice became indistinct, so that they never knew who it was that he had been seeking when he intruded upon their privacy. The door had closed again and the reflection had vanished from the mirror. But there were beads of perspiration on the major's brow.

"It is fortunate," he muttered breathlessly, "that my back was towards him. I would as soon meet the devil face to face. I didn't dream he was in Lisbon."

"Who is he?" asked Minas.

"Colonel Grant, the British Intelligence officer. Phew! Name of a Name! What an escape!" The major mopped his brow with a silk handkerchief. "Beware of him, Monsieur de Samoval."

He rose. He was obviously shaken by the meeting.

"If one of you will kindly make quite sure that he is not about I think that I had better go. If we should meet everything might be ruined." Then with a change of manner he stayed Samoval, who was already on his way to the door. "We understand each other, then?" he questioned them. "I have my papers, and at dawn I leave Lisbon. I shall report your conclusions to the Prince, and in anticipation I may already offer you the expression of his profoundest gratitude. Meanwhile, you know what is to do. Opposition to the policy, and the plans of the fortifications—above all the plans."

He shook hands with them, and having waited until Samoval assured him that the corridor outside was clear, he took his departure, and was soon afterwards driving home, congratulating himself upon his most fortunate escape from the hawk eye of Colquhoun Grant.

But when in the dead of that night he was awakened to find a British sergeant with a halbert and six redcoats with fixed bayonets surrounding his bed it occurred to him belatedly that what one man can see in a mirror is also visible to another, and that Marshal Massena, Prince of Esslingen, waiting for information beyond Ciudad Rodrigo, would never enjoy the advantages of a report of Count Samoval's masterly constructive and deductive reasoning.

CHAPTER IX

THE GENERAL ORDER

Sir Terence sat alone in his spacious, severely furnished private room in the official quarters at Monsanto. On the broad carved writing-table before him there was a mass of documents relating to the clothing and accoutrement of the forces, to leaves of absence, to staff appointments; there were returns from the various divisions of the sick and wounded in hospital, from which a complete list was to be prepared for the Secretary of State for War at home; there were plans of the lines at Torres Vedras just received, indicating the progress of the works at various points; and there were documents and communications of all kinds concerned with the adjutant-general's multifarious and arduous duties, including an urgent letter from Colonel Fletcher suggesting that the Commander-in-Chief should take an early opportunity of inspecting in person the inner lines of fortification.

Sir Terence, however, sat back in his chair, his work neglected, his eyes dreamily gazing through the open window, but seeing nothing of the sun-drenched landscape beyond, a heavy frown darkening his bronzed and rugged face. His mind was very far from his official duties and the mass of reminders before him—this Augean stable of arrears. He was lost in thought of his wife and Tremayne.

Five days had elapsed since the ball at Count Redondo's, where Sir Terence had surprised the pair together in the garden and his suspicions had been fired by the compromising attitude in which he had discovered them. Tremayne's frank, easy bearing, so unassociable with guilt, had, as we know, gone far, to reassure him, and had even shamed him, so that he had trampled his suspicions underfoot. But other things had happened since to revive his bitter doubts. Daily, constantly, had he been coming upon Tremayne and Lady O'Moy alone together in intimate, confidential talk which was ever silenced on his approach. The two had taken to wandering by themselves in the gardens at all hours, a thing that had never been so before, and O'Moy detected, or imagined that he detected, a closer intimacy between them, a greater warmth towards the captain on the part of her ladyship.

Thus matters had reached a pass in which peace of mind was impossible to him. It was not merely what he saw, it was his knowledge of what was; it was his ever-present consciousness of his own age and his wife's youth; it was the memory of his ante-nuptial jealousy of Tremayne which had been awakened by the gossip of those days—a gossip that pronounced Tremayne Una Butler's poor suitor, too poor either to declare himself or to be accepted if he did. The old wound which that gossip had dealt him then was reopened now. He thought of Tremayne's manifest concern for Una; he remembered how in that very room some six weeks ago, when Butler's escapade had first been heard of, it was from avowed concern for Una that Tremayne had urged him to befriend and rescue his rascally brother-in-law. He remembered, too, with increasing bitterness that it was Una herself had induced him to appoint Tremayne to his staff.

There were moments when the conviction of Tremayne's honesty, the thought of Tremayne's unswerving friendship for himself, would surge up to combat and abate the fires of his devastating jealousy.

But evidence would kindle those fires anew until they flamed up to scorch his soul with shame and anger. He had been a fool in that he had married a woman of half his years; a fool in that he had suffered her former lover to be thrown into close association with her.

Thus he assured himself. But he would abide by his folly, and so must she. And he would see to it that whatever fruits that folly yielded, dishonour should not be one of them. Through all his darkening rage there beat the light of reason. To avert, he bethought him, was better than to avenge. Nor were such stains to be wiped out by vengeance. A cuckold remains a cuckold though he take the life of the man who has reduced him to that ignominy.

Tremayne must go before the evil transcended reparation. Let him return to his regiment and do his work of sapping and mining elsewhere than in O'Moy's household.

Eased by that resolve he rose, a tall, martial figure, youth and energy in every line of it for all his six and forty years. Awhile he paced the room in thought. Then, suddenly, with hands clenched behind his back, he checked by the window, checked on a horrible question that had flashed upon his tortured mind. What if already the evil should be irreparable? What proof had he that it was not so?

The door opened, and Tremayne himself came in quickly.

"Here's the very devil to pay, sir," he announced, with that odd mixture of familiarity towards his friend and deference to his chief.

O'Moy looked at him in silence with smouldering, questioning eyes, thinking of anything but the trouble which the captain's air and manner heralded.

"Captain Stanhope has just arrived from headquarters with messages for you. A terrible thing has happened, sir. The dispatches from home by the Thunderbolt which we forwarded from here three weeks ago reached Lord Wellington only the day before yesterday."

Sir Terence became instantly alert.

"Garfield, who carried them, came into collision at Penalva with an officer of Anson's Brigade. There was a meeting, and Garfield was shot through the lung. He lay between life and death for a fortnight, with the result that the dispatches were delayed until he recovered sufficiently to remember them and to have them forwarded by other hands. But you had better see Stanhope himself."

The aide-de-camp came in. He was splashed from head to foot in witness of the fury with which he had ridden, his hair was caked with dust and his face haggard. But he carried himself with soldierly uprightness, and his speech was brisk. He repeated what Tremayne had already stated, with some few additional details.

"This wretched fellow sent Lord Wellington a letter dictated from his bed, in which he swore that the duel was forced upon him, and that his honour allowed him no alternative. I don't think any feature of the case has so deeply angered Lord Wellington as this stupid plea. He mentioned that when Sir John Moore was at Herrerias, in the course of his retreat upon Corunna, he sent forward instructions for the leading division to halt at Lugo, where he designed to deliver battle if the enemy would accept it. That dispatch was carried to Sir David Baird by one of Sir John's aides, but Sir David forwarded it by the hand of a trooper who got drunk and lost it. That, says Lord Wellington, is the only parallel, so far as he is aware, of the present case, with this difference, that whilst a common trooper might so far fail to appreciate the importance of his mission, no such lack of appreciation can excuse Captain Garfield."

"I am glad of that," said Sir Terence, who had been bristling. "For a moment I imagined that it was to be implied I had been as indiscreet in my choice of a messenger as Sir David Baird."

"No, no, Sir Terence. I merely repeated Lord Wellington's words that you may realise how deeply angered he is. If Garfield recovers from his wound he will be tried by court-martial. He is under open arrest meanwhile, as is his opponent in the duel—a Major Sykes of the 23rd Dragoons. That they will both be broke is beyond doubt. But that is not all. This affair, which might have had such grave consequences, coming so soon upon the heels of Major Berkeley's business, has driven Lord Wellington to a step regarding which this letter will instruct you."

Sir Terence broke the seal. The letter, penned by a secretary, but bearing Wellington's own signature, ran as follows:

"The bearer, Captain Stanhope, will inform you of the particulars of this disgraceful business of Captain Garfield's. The affair following so soon upon that of Major Berkeley has determined me to make it clearly understood to the officers in his Majesty's service that they have been sent to the Peninsula to fight the French and not each other or members of the civilian population. While this campaign continues, and as long as I am in charge of it, I am determined not to suffer upon any plea whatever the abominable practice of duelling among those under my command. I desire you to publish this immediately in general orders, enjoining upon officers of all ranks without exception the necessity to postpone the settlement of private quarrels at least until the close of this campaign. And to add force to this injunction you will make it known that any infringement of this order will be considered as a capital offence; that any officer hereafter either sending or accepting a challenge will, if found guilty by a general court-martial, be immediately shot."

Sir Terence nodded slowly.

"Very well," he said. "The measure is most wise, although I doubt if it will be popular. But, then, unpopularity is the fate of wise measures. I am glad the matter has not ended more seriously. The dispatches in question, so far as I can recollect, were not of great urgency."

"There is something more," said Captain Stanhope. "The dispatches bore signs of having been tampered with."

"Tampered with?" It was a question from Tremayne, charged with incredulity. "But who would have tampered with them?"

"There were signs, that is all. Garfield was taken to the house of the parish priest, where he lay lost until he recovered sufficiently to realise his position for himself. No doubt you will have a schedule of the contents of the dispatch, Sir Terence?"

"Certainly. It is in your possession, I think, Tremayne."

Tremayne turned to his desk, and a brief search in one of its well-ordered drawers brought to light an oblong strip of paper folded and endorsed. He unfolded and spread it on Sir Terence's table, whilst Captain Stanhope, producing a note with which he came equipped, stooped to check off the items. Suddenly he stopped, frowned, and finally placed his finger under one of the lines of Tremayne's schedule, carefully studying his own note for a moment.

"Ha!" he said quietly at last. "What's this?" And he read: "'Note from Lord Liverpool of reinforcements to be embarked for

Lisbon in June or July.'" He looked at the adjutant and the adjutant's secretary. "That would appear to be the most important document of all—indeed the only document of any vital importance. And it was not included in the dispatch as it reached Lord Wellington."

The three looked gravely at one another in silence.

"Have you a copy of the note, sir?" inquired the aide-de-camp.

"Not a copy—but a summary of its contents, the figures it contained, are pencilled there on the margin," Tremayne answered.

"Allow me, sir," said Stanhope, and taking up a quill from the adjutant's table he rapidly copied the figures. "Lord Wellington must have this memorandum as soon as possible. The rest, Sir Terence, is of course a matter for yourself. You will know what to do. Meanwhile I shall report to his lordship what has occurred. I had best set out at once."

"If you will rest for an hour, and give my wife the pleasure of your company at luncheon, I shall have a letter ready for Lord Wellington," replied Sir Terence. "Perhaps you'll see to it, Tremayne," he added, without waiting for Captain Stanhope's answer to an invitation which amounted to a command.

Thus Stanhope was led away, and Sir Terence, all other matters forgotten for the moment, sat down to write his letter.

Later in the day, after Captain Stanhope had taken his departure, the duty fell to Tremayne of framing the general order and seeing to the dispatch of a copy to each division.

"I wonder," he said to Sir Terence, "who will be the first to break it?"

"Why, the fool who's most anxious to be broke himself," answered Sir Terence.

There appeared to be reservations about it in Tremayne's mind.

"It's a devilish stringent regulation," he criticised.

"But very salutary and very necessary."

"Oh, quite." Tremayne's agreement was unhesitating. "But I shouldn't care to feel the restraint of it, and I thank heaven I have no enemy thirsting for my blood."

Sir Terence's brow darkened. His face was turned away from his secretary. "How can a man be confident of that?" he wondered.

"Oh, a clean conscience, I suppose," laughed Tremayne, and he gave his attention to his papers.

Frankness, honesty and light-heartedness rang so clear in the words that they sowed in Sir Terence's mind fresh doubts of the galling suspicion he had been harbouring.

"Do you boast a clean conscience, eh, Ned?" he asked, not

without a lurking shame at this deliberate sly searching of the other's mind. Yet he strained his ears for the answer.

"Almost clean," said Tremayne. "Temptation doesn't stain when it's resisted, does it?"

Sir Terence trembled. But he controlled himself.

"Nay, now, that's a question for the casuists. They right answer you that it depends upon the temptation." And he asked point-blank: "What's tempting you?"

Tremayne was in a mood for confidences, and Sir Terence was his friend. But he hesitated. His answer to the question was an irrelevance.

"It's just hell to be poor, O'Moy," he said.

The adjutant turned to stare at him. Tremayne was sitting with his head resting on one hand, the fingers thrusting through the crisp fair hair, and there was gloom in his clear-cut face, a dullness in the usually keen grey eyes.

"Is there anything on your mind?" quoth Sir Terence.

"Temptation," was the answer. "It's an unpleasant thing to struggle against."

"But you spoke of poverty?"

"To be sure. If I weren't poor I could put my fortunes to the test, and make an end of the matter one way or the other."

There was a pause. "Sure I hope I am the last man to force a confidence, Ned," said O'Moy. "But you certainly seem as if it would do you good to confide."

Tremayne shook himself mentally. "I think we had better deal with the matter of this dispatch that was tampered with at Penalva."

"So we will, to be sure. But it can wait a minute." Sir Terence pushed back his chair, and rose. He crossed slowly to his secretary's side. "What's on your mind, Ned?" he asked with abrupt solicitude, and Ned could not suspect that it was the matter on Sir Terence's own mind that was urging him—but urging him hopefully.

Captain Tremayne looked up with a rueful smile. "I thought you boasted that you never forced a confidence." And then he looked away. "Sylvia Armytage tells me that she is thinking of returning to England."

For a moment the words seemed to Sir Terence a fresh irrelevance; another attempt to change the subject. Then quite suddenly a light broke upon his mind, shedding a relief so great and joyous that he sought to check it almost in fear.

"It is more than she has told me," he answered steadily. "But then, no doubt, you enjoy her confidence."

Tremayne flashed him a wry glance and looked away again.

"Alas!" he said, and fetched a sigh.

83

"And is Sylvia the temptation, Ned?"

Tremayne was silent for a while, little dreaming how Sir Terence hung upon his answer, how impatiently he awaited it.

"Of course," he said at last. "Isn't it obvious to any one?" And he grew rhapsodical: "How can a man be daily in her company without succumbing to her loveliness, to her matchless grace of body and of mind, without perceiving that she is incomparable, peerless, as much above other women as an angel perhaps might be above herself?"

Before his glum solemnity, and before something else that Tremayne could not suspect, Sir Terence exploded into laughter. Of the immense and joyous relief in it his secretary caught no hint; all he heard was its sheer amusement, and this galled and shamed him. For no man cares to be laughed at for such feelings as Tremayne had been led into betraying.

"You think it something to laugh at?" he said tartly.

"Laugh, is it?" spluttered Sir Terence. "God grant I don't burst a blood-vessel."

Tremayne reddened. "When you've indulged your humour, sir," he said stiffly, "perhaps you'll consider the matter of this dispatch."

But Sir Terence laughed more uproariously than ever. He came to stand beside Tremayne, and slapped him heartily on the shoulder.

"Ye'll kill me, Ned!" he protested. "For God's sake, not so glum. It's that makes ye ridiculous."

"I am sorry you find me ridiculous."

"Nay, then, it's glad ye ought to be. By my soul, if Sylvia tempts you, man, why the devil don't ye just succumb and have done with it? She's handsome enough and well set up with her air of an Amazon, and she rides uncommon straight, begad! Indeed it's a broth of a girl she is in the hunting-field, the ballroom, or at the breakfast-table, although riper acquaintance may discover her not to be quite all that you imagine her at present. Let your temptation lead you then, entirely, and good luck to you, my boy."

"Didn't I tell you, O'Moy," answered the captain, mollified a little by the sympathy and good feeling peeping through the adjutant's boisterousness, "that poverty is just hell. It's my poverty that's in the way."

"And is that all? Then it's thankful you should be that Sylvia Armytage has got enough for two."

"That's just it."

"Just what?"

"The obstacle. I could marry a poor woman. But Sylvia—"

84

"Have you spoken to her?"

Tremayne was indignant. "How do you suppose I could?"

"It'll not have occurred to you that the lady may have feelings which having aroused you ought to be considering?"

A wry smile and a shake of the head was Tremayne's only answer; and then Carruthers came in fresh from Lisbon, where he had been upon business connected with the commissariat, and to Tremayne's relief the subject was perforce abandoned.

Yet he marvelled several times that day that the hilarity he should have awakened in Sir Terence continued to cling to the adjutant, and that despite the many vexatious matters claiming attention he should preserve an irrepressible and almost boyish gaiety.

Meanwhile, however, the coming of Carruthers had brought the adjutant a moment's seriousness, and he reverted to the business of Captain Garfield. When he had mentioned the missing note, Carruthers very properly became grave. He was a short, stiffly built man with a round, good-humoured, rather florid face.

"The matter must be probed at once, sir," he ventured. "We know that we move in a tangle of intrigues and espionage. But such a thing as this has never happened before. Have you anything to go upon?"

"Captain Stanhope gave us nothing," said the adjutant.

"It would be best perhaps to get Grant to look into it," said Tremayne.

"If he is still in Lisbon," said Sir Terence.

"I passed him in the street an hour ago," replied Carruthers.

"Then by all means let a note be sent to him asking him if he will step up to Monsanto as soon as he conveniently can. You might see to it, Tremayne."

CHAPTER X

THE STIFLED QUARREL

It was noon of the next day before Colonel Grant came to the house at Monsanto from whose balcony floated the British flag, and before whose portals stood a sentry in the tall bearskin of the grenadiers.

He found the adjutant alone in his room, and apologised for the delay in responding to his invitation, pleading the urgency of other matters that he had in hand.

"A wise enactment this of Lord Wellington's," was his next comment. "I mean this prohibition of duelling. It may be resented by some of our young bloods as an unwarrantable interference with their privileges, but it will do a deal of good, and no one can deny that there is ample cause for the measure."

"It is on the subject of the cause that I'm wanting to consult you," said Sir Terence, offering his visitor a chair. "Have you been informed of the details? No? Let me give you them." And he related how the dispatch bore signs of having been tampered with, and how the only document of any real importance came to be missing from it.

Colonel Grant, sitting with his sabre across his knees, listened gravely and thoughtfully. In the end he shrugged his shoulders, the keen hawk face unmoved.

"The harm is done, and cannot very well be repaired. The information obtained, no doubt on behalf of Massena, will by now be on its way to him. Let us be thankful that the matter is not more grave, and thankful, too, that you were able to supply a copy of Lord Liverpool's figures. What do you want me to do?"

"Take steps to discover the spy whose existence is disclosed by this event."

Colquhoun Grant smiled. "That is precisely the matter which has brought me to Lisbon."

"How?" Sir Terence was amazed. "You knew?"

"Oh, not that this had happened. But that the spy—or rather a network of espionage—existed. We move here in a web of intrigue wrought by ill-will, self-interest, vindictiveness and every form of malice. Whilst the great bulk of the Portuguese people and their leaders are loyally co-operating with us, there is a strong party opposing us which would prefer even to see the French prevail. Of course you are aware of this. The heart and brain of all this is—as I

86

gather the Principal Souza. Wellington has compelled his retirement from the Government. But if by doing so he has restricted the man's power for evil, he has certainly increased his will for evil and his activities.

"You tell me that Garfield was cared for by the parish priest at Penalva. There you are. Half the priesthood of the country are on Souza's side, since the Patriarch of Lisbon himself is little more than a tool of Souza's. What happens? This priest discovers that the British officer whom he has so charitably put to bed in his house is the bearer of dispatches. A loyal man would instantly have communicated with Marshal Beresford at Thomar. This fellow, instead, advises the intriguers in Lisbon. The captain's dispatches are examined and the only document of real value is abstracted. Of course it would be difficult to establish a case against the priest, and it is always vexatious and troublesome to have dealings with that class, as it generally means trouble with the peasantry. But the case is as clear as crystal."

"But the intriguers here? Can you not deal with them?"

"I have them under observation," replied the colonel. "I already knew the leaders, Souza's lieutenants in Lisbon, and I can put my hand upon them at any moment. If I have not already done so it is because I find it more profitable to leave them at large; it is possible, indeed, that I may never proceed to extremes against them. Conceive that they have enabled me to seize La Fleche, the most dangerous, insidious and skilful of all Napoleon's agents. I found him at Redondo's ball last week in the uniform of a Portuguese major, and through him I was able to track down Souza's chief instrument—I discovered them closeted with him in one of the card-rooms."

"And you didn't arrest them?"

"Arrest them! I apologised for my intrusion, and withdrew. La Fleche took his leave of them. He was to have left Lisbon at dawn equipped with a passport countersigned by yourself, my dear adjutant."

"What's that?"

"A passport for Major Vieira of the Portuguese Cacadores. Do you remember it?"

"Major Vieira!" Sir Terence frowned thoughtfully. Suddenly he recollected. "But that was countersigned by me at the request of Count Samoval, who represented himself a personal friend of the major's."

"So indeed he is. But the major in question was La Fleche nevertheless."

"And Samoval knew this?"

Sir Terence was incredulous.

Colonel Grant did not immediately answer the question. He preferred to continue his narrative. "That night I had the false major arrested very quietly. I have caused him to disappear for the present. His Lisbon friends believe him to be on his way to Massena with the information they no doubt supplied him. Massena awaits his return at Salamanca, and will continue to wait. Thus when he fails to be seen or heard of there will be a good deal of mystification on all sides, which is the proper state of mind in which to place your opponents. Lord Liverpool's figures, let me add, were not among the interesting notes found upon him—possibly because at that date they had not yet been obtained."

"And you say that Samoval was aware of the man's real identity?" insisted Sir Terence, still incredulous. "Aware of it?" Colonel Grant laughed shortly. "Samoval is Souza's principal agent—the most dangerous man in Lisbon and the most subtle. His sympathies are French through and through."

Sir Terence stared at him in frank amazement, in utter unbelief. "Oh, impossible!" he ejaculated at last.

"I saw Samoval for the first time," said Colonel Grant by way of answer, "in Oporto at the time of Soult's occupation. He did not call himself Samoval just then, any more than I called myself Colquhoun Grant. He was very active there in the French interest; I should indeed be more precise and say in Bonaparte's interest, for he was the man instrumental in disclosing to Soult the Bourbon conspiracy which was undermining the marshal's army. You do not know, perhaps, that French sympathy runs in Samoval's family. You may not be aware that the Portuguese Marquis of Alorna, who holds a command in the Emperor's army, and is at present with Massena at Salamanca, is Samoval's cousin."

"But," faltered Sir Terence, "Count Samoval has been a regular visitor here for the past three months."

"So I understand," said Grant coolly. "If I had known of it before I should have warned you. But, as you are aware, I have been in Spain on other business. You realise the danger of having such a man about the place. Scraps of information—"

"Oh, as to that," Sir Terence interrupted, "I can assure you that none have fallen from my official table."

"Never be too sure, Sir Terence. Matters here must ever be under discussion. There are your secretaries and the ladies—and Samoval has a great way with the women. What they know you may wager that he knows."

"They know nothing."

"That is a great deal to say. Little odds and ends now; a hint at one time; a word dropped at another; these things picked up naturally by feminine curiosity and retailed thoughtlessly under Samoval's charming suasion and display of Britannic sympathies. And Samoval has the devil's own talent for bringing together the pieces of a puzzle. Take the lines now: you may have parted with no details. But mention of them will surely have been made in this household. However," he broke off abruptly, "that is all past and done with. I am as sure as you are that any real indiscretions in this household are unimaginable, and so we may be confident that no harm has yet been done. But you will gather from what I have now told you that Samoval's visits here are not a mere social waste of time. That he comes, acquires familiarity and makes himself the friend of the family with a very definite aim in view."

"He does not come again," said Sir Terence, rising.

"That is more than I should have ventured to suggest. But it is a very wise resolve. It will need tact to carry it out, for Samoval is a man to be handled carefully."

"I'll handle him carefully, devil a fear," said Sir Terence. "You can depend upon my tact."

Colonel Grant rose. "In this matter of Penalva, I will consider further. But I do not think there is anything to be done now. The main thing is to stop up the outlets through which information reaches the French, and that is my chief concern. How is the stripping of the country proceeding now?"

"It was more active immediately after Souza left the Government. But the last reports announce a slackening again."

"They are at work in that, too, you see. Souza will not slumber while there's vengeance and self-interest to keep him awake." And he held out his hand to take his leave.

"You'll stay to luncheon?" said Sir Terence. "It is about to be served."

"You are very kind, Sir Terence."

They descended, to find luncheon served already in the open under the trellis vine, and the party consisted of Lady O'Moy, Miss Armytage, Captain Tremayne, Major Carruthers, and Count Samoval, of whose presence this was the adjutant's first intimation.

As a matter of fact the Count had been at Monsanto for the past hour, the first half of which he had spent most agreeably on the terrace with the ladies. He had spoken so eulogistically of the genius of Lord Wellington and the valour of the British soldier, and, particularly-of the Irish soldier, that even Sylvia's instinctive distrust and dislike of him had been lulled a little for the moment.

"And they must prevail," he had exclaimed in a glow of enthusiasm, his dark eyes flashing. "It is inconceivable that they should ever yield to the French, although the odds of numbers may lie so heavily against them."

"Are the odds of numbers so heavy?" said Lady O'Moy in surprise, opening wide those almost childish eyes of hers.

"Alas! anything from three to five to one. Ah, but why should we despond on that account?" And his voice vibrated with renewed confidence. "The country is a difficult one, easy to defend, and Lord Wellington's genius will have made the best of it. There are, for example, the fortifications at Torres Vedras."

"Ah yes! I have heard of them. Tell me about them, Count."

"Tell you about them, dear lady? Shall I carry perfumes to the rose? What can I tell you that you do not know so much better than myself?"

"Indeed, I know nothing. Sir Terence is ridiculously secretive," she assured him, with a little frown of petulance. She realised that her husband did not treat her as an intelligent being to be consulted upon these matters. She was his wife, and he had no right to keep secrets from her. In fact she said so.

"Indeed no," Samoval agreed. "And I find it hard to credit that it should be so."

"Then you forget," said Sylvia, "that these secrets are not Sir Terence's own. They are the secrets of his office."

"Perhaps so," said the unabashed Samoval. "But if I were Sir Terence I should desire above all to allay my wife's natural anxiety. For I am sure you must be anxious, dear Lady O'Moy.'"

"Naturally," she agreed, whose anxieties never transcended the fit of her gowns or the suitability of a coiffure. "But Terence is like that."

"Incredible!" the Count protested, and raised his dark eyes to heaven as if invoking its punishment upon so unnatural a husband. "Do you tell me that you have never so much as seen the plans of these fortifications?"

"The plans, Count!" She almost laughed.

"Ah!" he said. "I dare swear then that you do not even know of their existence." He was jocular now.

"I am sure that she does not," said Sylvia, who instinctively felt that the conversation was following an undesirable course.

"Then you are wrong," she was assured. "I saw them once, a week ago, in Sir Terence's room."

"Why, how would you know them if you saw them?" quoth Sylvia, seeking to cover what might be an indiscretion.

"Because they bore the name: 'Lines of Torres Vedras.' I remember."

"And this unsympathetic Sir Terence did not explain them to you?" laughed Samoval.

"Indeed, he did not."

"In fact, I could swear that he locked them away from you at once?" the Count continued on a jocular note.

"Not at once. But he certainly locked them away soon after, and whilst I was still there."

"In your place, then," said Samoval, ever on the same note of banter, "I should have been tempted to steal the key."

"Not so easily done," she assured him. "It never leaves his person. He wears it on a gold chain round his neck."

"What, always?"

"Always, I assure you."

"Too bad," protested Samoval. "Too bad, indeed. What, then, should you have done, Miss Armytage?"

It was difficult to imagine that he was drawing information from them, so bantering and frivolous was his manner; more difficult still to conceive that he had obtained any. Yet you will observe that he had been placed in possession of two facts: that the plans of the lines of Torres Vedras were kept locked up in Sir Terence's own room—in the strong-box, no doubt—and that Sir Terence always carried the key on a gold chain worn round his neck.

Miss Armytage laughed. "Whatever I might do, I should not be guilty of prying into matters that my husband kept hidden."

"Then you admit a husband's right to keep matters hidden from his wife?"

"Why not?"

"Madam," Samoval bowed to her, "your future husband is to be envied on yet another count."

And thus the conversation drifted, Samoval conceiving that he had obtained all the information of which Lady O'Moy was possessed, and satisfied that he had obtained all that for the moment he required. How to proceed now was a more difficult matter, to be very seriously considered—how to obtain from Sir Terence the key in question, and reach the plans so essential to Marshal Massena.

He was at table with them, as you know, when Sir Terence and Colonel Grant arrived. He and the colonel were presented to each other, and bowed with a gravity quite cordial on the part of Samoval, who was by far the more subtle dissembler of the two. Each knew the other perfectly for what he was; yet each was in complete ignorance of the extent of the other's knowledge of himself; and certainly neither betrayed anything by his manner.

At table the conversation was led naturally enough by

Tremayne to Wellington's general order against duelling. This was inevitable when you consider that it was a topic of conversation that morning at every table to which British officers sat down. Tremayne spoke of the measure in terms of warm commendation, thereby provoking a sharp disagreement from Samoval. The deep and almost instinctive hostility between these two men, which had often been revealed in momentary flashes, was such that it must invariably lead them to take opposing sides in any matter admitting of contention.

"In my opinion it is a most arbitrary and degrading enactment," said Samoval. "I say so without hesitation, notwithstanding my profound admiration and respect for Lord Wellington and all his measures."

"Degrading?" echoed Grant, looking across at him. "In what can it be degrading, Count?"

"In that it reduces a gentleman to the level of the clod," was the prompt answer. "A gentleman must have his quarrels, however sweet his disposition, and a means must be afforded him of settling them."

"Ye can always thrash an impudent fellow," opined the adjutant.

"Thrash?" echoed Samoval. His sensitive lip curled in disdain. "To use your hands upon a man!" He shuddered in sheer disgust. "To one of my temperament it would be impossible, and men of my temperament are plentiful, I think."

"But if you were thrashed yourself?" Tremayne asked him, and the light in his grey eyes almost hinted at a dark desire to be himself the executioner.

Samoval's dark, handsome eyes considered the captain steadily. "To be thrashed myself?" he questioned. "My dear Captain, the idea of having hands laid upon me, soiling me, brutalising me, is so nauseating, so repugnant, that I assure you I should not hesitate to shoot the man who did it just as I should shoot any other wild beast that attacked me. Indeed the two instances are exactly parallel, and my country's courts would uphold in such a case the justice of my conduct."

"Then you may thank God," said O'Moy, "that you are not under British jurisdiction."

"I do," snapped Samoval, to make an instant recovery: "at least so far as the matter is concerned." And he elaborated: "I assure you, sirs, it will be an evil day for the nobility of any country when its Government enacts against the satisfaction that one gentleman has the right to demand from another who offends him."

"Isn't the conversation rather too bloodthirsty for a luncheon-table?" wondered Lady O'Moy. And tactlessly she added, thinking with flattery to mollify Samoval and cool his obvious heat: "You are yourself such a famous swordsman, Count."

And then Tremayne's dislike of the man betrayed him into his deplorable phrase.

"At the present time Portugal is in urgent need of her famous swordsmen to go against the French and not to increase the disorders at home."

A silence complete and ominous followed the rash words, and Samoval, white to the lips, pondered the imperturbable captain with a baleful eye.

"I think," he said at last, speaking slowly and softly, and picking his words with care, "I think that is innuendo. I should be relieved, Captain Tremayne, to hear you say that it is not."

Tremayne was prompt to give him the assurance. "No innuendo at all. A plain statement of fact."

"The innuendo I suggested lay in the application of the phrase. Do you make it personal to myself?"

"Of course not," said Sir Terence, cutting in and speaking sharply. "What an assumption!"

"I am asking Captain Tremayne," the Count insisted, with grim firmness, notwithstanding his deferential smile to Sir Terence.

"I spoke quite generally, sir," Tremayne assured him, partly under the suasion of Sir Terence's interposition, partly out of consideration for the ladies, who were looking scared. "Of course, if you choose to take it to yourself, sir, that is a matter for your own discretion. I think," he added, also with a smile, "that the ladies find the topic tiresome."

"Perhaps we may have the pleasure of continuing it when they are no longer present."

"Oh, as you please," was the indifferent answer. "Carruthers, may I trouble you to pass the salt? Lady O'Callaghan was complaining the other night of the abuse of salt in Portuguese cookery. It is an abuse I have never yet detected."

"I can't conceive Lady O'Callaghan complaining of too much salt in anything, begad," quoth O'Moy, with a laugh. "If you had heard the story she told me about—"

"Terence, my dear!" his wife checked him, her fine brows raised, her stare frigid.

"Faith, we go from bad to worse," said Carruthers. "Will you try to improve the tone of the conversation, Miss Armytage? It stands in urgent need of it."

With a general laugh, breaking the ice of the restraint that was in danger of settling about the table, a semblance of ease was

93

restored, and this was maintained until the end of the repast. At last the ladies rose, and, leaving the men at table, they sauntered off towards the terrace. But under the archway Sylvia checked her cousin.

"Una," she said gravely, "you had better call Captain Tremayne and take him away for the present."

Una's eyes opened wide. "Why?" she inquired.

Miss Armytage was almost impatient with her. "Didn't you see? Resentment is only slumbering between those men. It will break out again now that we have left them unless you can get Captain Tremayne away."

Una continued to look at her cousin, and then, her mind fastening ever upon the trivial to the exclusion of the important, her glance became arch. "For whom is your concern? For Count Samoval or Ned?" she inquired, and added with a laugh: "You needn't answer me. It is Ned you are afraid for."

"I am certainly not afraid for him," was the reply on a faint note of indignation. She had reddened slightly. "But I should not like to see Captain Tremayne or any other British officer embroiled in a duel. You forget Lord Wellington's order which they were discussing, and the consequences of infringing it."

Lady O'Moy became scared.

"You don't imagine—"

Sylvia spoke quickly: "I am certain that unless you take Captain Tremayne away, and at once, there will! be serious trouble."

And now behold Lady O'Moy thrown into a state of alarm that bordered upon terror. She had more reason than Sylvia could dream, more reason she conceived than Sylvia herself, to wish to keep Captain Tremayne out of trouble just at present. Instantly, agitatedly, she turned and called to him.

"Ned!" floated her silvery voice across the enclosed garden. And again: "Ned! I want you at once, please."

Captain Tremayne rose. Grant was talking briskly at the time, his intention being to cover Tremayne's retreat, which he himself desired. Count Samoval's smouldering eyes were upon the captain, and full of menace. But he could not be guilty of the rudeness of interrupting Grant or of detaining Captain Tremayne when a lady called him.

CHAPTER XI

THE CHALLENGE

Rebuke awaited Captain Tremayne at the hands of Lady O'Moy, and it came as soon as they were alone together sauntering in the thicket of pine and cork-oak on the slope of the hill below the terrace.

"How thoughtless of you, Ned, to provoke Count Samoval at such a time as this!"

"Did I provoke him? I thought it was the Count himself who was provoking." Tremayne spoke lightly.

"But suppose anything were to happen to you? You know the man's dreadful reputation."

Tremayne looked at her kindly. This apparent concern for himself touched him. "My dear Una, I hope I can take care of myself, even against so formidable a fellow; and after all a man must take his chances a soldier especially."

"But what of Dick?" she cried. "Do you forget that he is depending entirely upon you—that if you should fail him he will be lost?" And there was something akin to indignation in the protesting eyes she turned upon him.

For a moment Tremayne was so amazed that he was at a loss for an answer. Then he smiled. Indeed his inclination was to laugh outright. The frank admission that her concern which he had fondly imagined to be for himself was all for Dick betrayed a state of mind that was entirely typical of Una. Never had she been able to command more than one point of view of any question, and that point of view invariably of her own interest. All her life she had been accustomed to sacrifices great and small made by others on her own behalf, until she had come to look upon such sacrifices her absolute right.

"I am glad you reminded me," he said with an irony that never touched her. "You may depend upon me to be discreetness itself, at least until after Dick has been safely shipped."

"Thank you, Ned. You are very good to me." They sauntered a little way in silence. Then: "When does Captain Glennie sail?" she asked him. "Is it decided yet?"

"Yes. I have just heard from him that the Telemachus will put to sea on Sunday morning at two o'clock."

"At two o'clock in the morning! What an uncomfortable hour!"

"Tides, as King Canute discovered, are beyond mortal control. The Telemachus goes out with the ebb. And, after all, for our purposes surely no hour could be more suitable. If I come for Dick at midnight tomorrow that will just give us time to get him snugly aboard before she sails. I have made all arrangements with Glennie. He believes Dick to be what he has represented himself—one of Bearsley's overseers named Jenkinson, who is a friend of mine and who must be got out of the country quietly. Dick should thank his luck for a good deal. My chief anxiety was lest his presence here should be discovered by any one."

"Beyond Bridget not a soul knows that he is here not even Sylvia."

"You have been the soul of discreetness."

"Haven't I?" she purred, delighted to have him discover a virtue so unusual in her.

Thereafter they discussed details; or, rather, Tremayne discussed them. He would come up to Monsanto at twelve o'clock to-morrow night in a curricle in which he would drive Dick down to the river at a point where a boat would be waiting to take him out to the Telemachus. She must see that Dick was ready in time. The rest she could safely leave to him. He would come in through the official wing of the building. The guard would admit him without question, accustomed to seeing him come and go at all hours, nor would it be remarked that he was accompanied by a man in civilian dress when he departed. Dick was to be let down from her ladyship's balcony to the quadrangle by a rope ladder with which Tremayne would come equipped, having procured it for the purpose from the Telemachus.

She hung upon his arm, overwhelming him now with her gratitude, her parasol sheltering them both from the rays of the sun as they emerged from the thicket intro the meadowland in full view of the terrace where Count Samoval and Sir Terence were at that moment talking earnestly together.

You will remember that O'Moy had undertaken to provide that Count Samoval's visits to Monsanto should be discontinued. About this task he had gone with all the tact of which he had boasted himself master to Colquhoun Grant. You shall judge of the tact for yourself. No sooner had the colonel left for Lisbon, and Carruthers to return to his work, than, finding himself alone with the Count, Sir Terence considered the moment a choice one in which to broach the matter.

"I take it ye're fond of walking, Count," had been his singular opening move. They had left the table by now, and were sauntering together on the terrace.

"Walking?" said Samoval. "I detest it."

"And is that so? Well, well! Of course it's not so very far from your place at Bispo."

"Not more than half-a-league, I should say."

"Just so," said O'Moy. "Half-a-league there, and half-a-league back: a league. It's nothing at all, of course; yet for a gentleman who detests walking it's a devilish long tramp for nothing."

"For nothing?" Samoval checked and looked at his host in faint surprise. Then he smiled very affably. "But you must not say that, Sir Terence. I assure you that the pleasure of seeing yourself and Lady O'Moy cannot be spoken of as nothing."

"You are very good." Sir Terence was the very quintessence of courtliness, of concern for the other. "But if there were not that pleasure?"

"Then, of course, it would be different." Samoval was beginning to be slightly intrigued.

"That's it," said Sir Terence. "That's just what I'm meaning."

"Just what you're meaning? But, my dear General, you are assuming circumstances which fortunately do not exist."

"Not at present, perhaps. But they might."

Again Samoval stood still and looked at O'Moy. He found something in the bronzed, rugged face that was unusually sardonic. The blue eyes seemed to have become hard, and yet there were wrinkles about their corners suggestive of humour that might be mockery. The Count stiffened; but beyond that he preserved his outward calm whilst confessing that he did not understand Sir Terence's meaning.

"It's this way," said Sir Terence. "I've noticed that ye're not looking so very well lately, Count."

"Really? You think that?" The words were mechanical. The dark eyes continued to scrutinise that bronzed face suspiciously.

"I do, and it's sorry I am to see it. But I know what it is. It's this walking backwards and forwards between here and Bispo that's doing the mischief. Better give it up, Count. Better not come toiling up here any more. It's not good for your health. Why, man, ye're as white as a ghost this minute."

He was indeed, having perceived at last the insult intended. To be denied the house at such a time was to checkmate his designs, to set a term upon his crafty and subtle espionage, precisely in the season when he hoped to reap its harvest. But his chagrin sprang not at all from that. His cold anger was purely personal. He was a gentleman—of the fine flower, as he would have described himself—of the nobility of Portugal; and that a probably upstart Irish soldier—himself, from Samoval's point of view, a guest in that country—should deny him his house, and choose such terms of ill-

97

considered jocularity in which to do it, was an affront beyond all endurance.

For a moment passion blinded him, and it was only by an effort that he recovered and kept his self-control. But keep it he did. You may trust your practised duellist for that when he comes face to face with the necessity to demand satisfaction. And soon the mist of passion clearing from his keen wits, he sought swiftly for a means to fasten the quarrel upon Sir Terence in Sir Terence's own coin of galling mockery. Instantly he found it. Indeed it was not very far to seek. O'Moy's jealousy, which was almost a byword, as we know, had been apparent more than once to Samoval. Remembering it now, it discovered to him at once Sir Terence's most vulnerable spot, and cunningly Samoval proceeded to gall him there.

A smile spread gradually over his white face—a smile of immeasurable malice.

"I am having a very interesting and instructive morning in this atmosphere of Irish boorishness," said he. "First Captain Tremayne—"

"Now don't be after blaming old Ireland for Tremayne's shortcomings. Tremayne's just a clumsy mannered Englishman."

"I am glad to know there is a distinction. Indeed I might have perceived it for myself. In motives, of course, that distinction is great indeed, and I hope that I am not slow to discover it, and in your case to excuse it. I quite understand and even sympathise with your feelings, General."

"I am glad of that now," said Sir Terence, who had understood nothing of all this.

"Naturally," the Count pursued on a smooth, level note of amiability, "when a man, himself no longer young, commits the folly of taking a young and charming wife, he is to be forgiven when a natural anxiety drives him to lengths which in another might be resented." He bowed before the empurpling Sir Terence.

"Ye're a damned coxcomb, it seems," was the answering roar.

"Of course you would assume it. It was to be expected. I condone it with the rest. And because I condone it, because I sympathise with what in a man of your age and temperament must amount to an affliction, I hasten to assure you upon my honour that so far as I am concerned there are no grounds for your anxiety."

"And who the devil asks for your assurances? It's stark mad ye are to suppose that I ever needed them."

"Of course you must say that," Samoval insisted, with a confident and superior smile. He shook his head, his expression one of amused sorrow. "Sir Terence, you have knocked at the wrong door. You are youthful at least in your impulsiveness, but you are surely as blind as old Pantaloon in the comedy or you would see where your industry would be better employed in shielding your wife's honour and your own."

Goaded to fury, his blue eyes aflame now with passion, Sir Terence considered the sleek and subtle gentleman before him, and it was in that moment that the Count's subtlety soared to its finest heights. In a flash of inspiration he perceived the advantages to be drawn by himself from conducting this quarrel to extremes.

This is not mere idle speculation. Knowledge of the real motives actuating him rests upon the evidence of a letter which Samoval was to write that same evening to La Fleche—afterwards to be discovered—wherein he related what had passed, how deliberately he had steered the matter, and what he meant to do. His object was no longer the punishing of an affront. That would happen as a mere incident, a thing done, as it were, in passing. His real aim now was to obtain the keys of the adjutant's strong-box, which never left Sir Terence's person, and so become possessed of the plans of the lines of Torres Vedras. When you consider in the light of this the manner in which Samoval proceeded now you will admire with me at once the opportunism and the subtlety of the man.

"You'll be after telling me exactly what you mean," Sir Terence had said.

It was in that moment that Tremayne and Lady O'Moy came arm in arm into the open on the hill-side, half-a-mile away—very close and confidential. They came most opportunely to the Count's need, and he flung out a hand to indicate them to Sir Terence, a smile of pity on his lips.

"You need but to look to take the answer for yourself," said he.

Sir Terence looked, and laughed. He knew the secret of Ned Tremayne's heart and could laugh now with relish at that which hitherto had left him darkly suspicious.

"And who shall blame Lady O'Moy?" Count Samoval pursued. "A lady so charming and so courted must seek her consolation for the almost unnatural union Fate has imposed upon her. Captain Tremayne is of her own age, convenient to her hand, and for an Englishman not ill-looking."

He smiled at O'Moy with insolent compassion, and O'Moy, losing all his self-control, struck him slapped him resoundingly upon the cheek.

"Ye're a dirty liar, Samoval, a muck-rake," said he.

Samoval stepped back, breathing hard, one cheek red, the other white. Yet by a miracle he still preserved his self-control.

"I have proved my courage too often," he said, "to be under

99

the necessity of killing you for this blow. Since my honour is safe I will not take advantage of your overwrought condition."

"Ye'll take advantage of it whether ye like it or not," blazed Sir Terence at him. "I mean you to take advantage of it. D' ye think I'll suffer any man to cast a slur upon Lady O'Moy? I'll be sending my friends to wait on you to-day, Count; and—by God!—Tremayne himself shall be one of them."

Thus did the hot-headed fellow deliver himself into the hands of his enemy. Nor was he warned when he saw the sudden gleam in Samoval's dark eyes.

"Ha!" said the Count. It was a little exclamation of wicked satisfaction. "You are offering me a challenge, then?"

"If I may make so bold. And as I've a mind to shoot you dead—"

"Shoot, did you say?" Samoval interrupted gently.

"I said 'shoot'—and it shall be at ten paces, or across a handkerchief, or any damned distance you please."

The Count shook his head. He sneered. "I think not—not shoot." And he waved the notion aside with a hand white and slender as a woman's. "That is too English, or too Irish. The pistol, I mean—appropriately a fool's weapon." And he explained himself, explained at last his extraordinary forbearance under a blow. "If you think I have practised the small-sword every day of my life for ten years to suffer myself to be shot at like a rabbit in the end—ho, really!" He laughed aloud. "You have challenged me, I think, Sir Terence. Because I feared the predilection you have discovered, I was careful to wait until the challenge came from you. The choice of weapons lies, I think, with me. I shall instruct my friends to ask for swords."

"Sorry a difference will it make to me," said Sir Terence. "Anything from a horsewhip to a howitzer." And then recollection descending like a cold hand upon him chilled his hot rage, struck the fine Irish arrogance all out of him, and left him suddenly limp. "My God!" he said, and it was almost a groan. He detained Samoval, who had already turned to depart. "A moment, Count," he cried. "I— I had forgotten. There is the general order—Lord Wellington's enactment."

"Awkward, of course," said Samoval, who had never for a moment been oblivious of that enactment, and who had been carefully building upon it. "But you should have considered it before committing yourself so irrevocably."

Sir Terence steadied himself. He recovered his truculence. "Irrevocable or not, it will just have to be revocable. The meeting's impossible."

100

"I do not see the impossibility. I am not surprised you should shelter yourself behind an enactment; but you will remember this enactment does not apply to me, who am not a soldier."

"But it applies to me, who am not only a soldier, but the Adjutant-General here, the man chiefly responsible for seeing the order carried out. It would be a fine thing if I were the first to disregard it."

"I am afraid it is too late. You have disregarded it already, sir."

"How so?"

"The letter of the law is against sending or receiving a challenge, I think."

O'Moy was distracted. "Samoval," he said, drawing himself up, "I will admit that I have been a fool. I will apologise to you for the blow and for the word that accompanied it."

"The apology would imply that my statement was a true one and that you recognised it. If you mean that—"

"I mean nothing of the kind. Damme! I've a mind to horsewhip you, and leave it at that. D' ye think I want to face a firing party on your account?"

"I don't think there is the remotest likelihood of any such contingency," replied Samoval.

But O'Moy went headlong on. "And another thing. Where will I be finding a friend to meet your friends? Who will dare to act for me in view of that enactment?"

The Count considered. He was grave now. "Of course that is a difficulty," he admitted, as if he perceived it now for the first time. "Under the circumstances, Sir Terence, and entirely to accommodate you, I might consent to dispense with seconds."

"Dispense with seconds?" Sir Terence was horrified at the suggestion. "You know that that is irregular—that a charge of murder would lie against the survivor."

"Oh, quite so. But it is for your own convenience that I suggest it, though I appreciate your considerate concern on the score of what may happen to me afterwards should it come to be known that I was your opponent."

"Afterwards? After what?"

"After I have killed you."

"And is it like that?" cried O'Moy, his countenance inflaming again, his mind casting all prudence to the winds.

It followed, of course, that without further thought for anything but the satisfaction of his rage Sir Terence became as wax in the hands of Samoval's desires.

"Where do you suggest that we meet?" he asked.

"There is my place at Bispo. We should be private in the

gardens there. As for time, the sooner the better, though for secrecy's sake we had better meet at night. Shall we say at midnight?"

But Sir Terence would agree to none of this.

"To-night is out of the question for me. I have an engagement that will keep me until late. To-morrow night, if you will, I shall be at your service." And because he did not trust Samoval he added, as Samoval himself had almost reckoned: "But I should prefer not to come to Bispo. I might be seen going or returning."

"Since there are no such scruples on my side, I am ready to come to you here if you prefer it."

"It would suit me better."

"Then expect me promptly at midnight to-morrow, provided that you can arrange to admit me without my being seen. You will perceive my reasons."

"Those gates will be closed," said O'Moy, indicating the now gaping massive doors that closed the archway at night. "But if you knock I shall be waiting for you, and I will admit you by the wicket."

"Excellent," said Samoval suavely. "Then—until to-morrow night, General." He bowed with almost extravagant submission, and turning walked sharply away, energy and suppleness in every line of his slight figure, leaving Sir Terence to the unpleasant, almost desperate, thoughts that reflection must usher in as his anger faded.

CHAPTER XII

THE DUEL

It was a time of stress and even of temptation for Sir Terence. Honour and pride demanded that he should keep the appointment made with Samoval; common sense urged him at all costs to avoid it. His frame of mind, you see, was not at all enviable. At moments he would consider his position as adjutant-general, the enactment against duelling, the irregularity of the meeting arranged, and, consequently, the danger in which he stood on every score; at others he could think of nothing but the unpardonable affront that had been offered him and the venomously insulting manner in which it had been offered, and his rage welled up to blot out every consideration other than that of punishing Samoval.

For two days and a night he was a sort of shuttlecock tossed between these alternating moods, and he was still the same when he paced the quadrangle with bowed head and hands clasped behind him awaiting Samoval at a few minutes before twelve of the following night. The windows that looked down from the four sides of that enclosed garden were all in darkness. The members of the household had withdrawn over an hour ago and were asleep by now. The official quarters were closed. The rising moon had just mounted above the eastern wing and its white light fell upon the upper half of the facade of the residential site. The quadrangle itself remained plunged in gloom.

Sir Terence, pacing there, was considering the only definite conclusion he had reached. If there were no way even now of avoiding this duel, at least it must remain secret. Therefore it could not take place here in the enclosed garden of his own quarters, as he had so rashly consented. It should be fought upon neutral ground, where the presence of the body of the slain would not call for explanations by the survivor.

From distant Lisbon on the still air came softly the chimes of midnight, and immediately there was a sharp rap upon the little door set in one of the massive gates that closed the archway.

Sir Terence went to open the wicket, and Samoval stepped quickly over the sill. He was wrapped in a dark cloak, a broad-brimmed hat obscured his face. Sir Terence closed the door again. The two men bowed to each other in silence, and as Samoval's cloak fell open he produced a pair of duelling-swords swathed together in a skin of leather.

"You are very punctual, sir," said O'Moy.

"I hope I shall never be so discourteous as to keep an opponent waiting. It is a thing of which I have never yet been guilty," replied Samoval, with deadly smoothness in that reminder of his victorious past. He stepped forward and looked about the quadrangle. "I am afraid the moon will occasion us some delay," he said. "It were perhaps better to wait some five or ten minutes, by then the light in here should have improved."

"We can avoid the delay by stepping out into the open," said Sir Terence. "Indeed it is what I had to suggest in any case. There are inconveniences here which you may have overlooked."

But Samoval, who had purposes to serve of which this duel was but a preliminary, was of a very different mind.

"We are quite private here, your household being abed," he answered, "whilst outside one can never be sure even at this hour of avoiding witnesses and interruption. Then, again, the turf is smooth as a table on that patch of lawn, and the ground well known to both of us; that, I can assure you, is a very necessary condition in the dark and one not to be found haphazard in the open."

"But there is yet another consideration, sir. I prefer that we engage on neutral ground, so that the survivor shall not be called upon for explanations that might be demanded if we fought here."

Even in the gloom Sir Terence caught the flash of Samoval's white teeth as he smiled.

"You trouble yourself unnecessarily on my account," was the smoothly ironic answer. "No one has seen me come, and no one is likely to see me depart."

"You may be sure that no one shall, by God," snapped O'Moy, stung by the sly insolence of the other's assurance.

"Shall we get to work, then?" Samoval invited.

"If you're set on dying here, I suppose I must be after humouring you, and make the best of it. As soon as you please, then." O'Moy was very fierce.

They stepped to the patch of lawn in the middle of the quadrangle, and there Samoval threw off altogether his cloak and hat. He was closely dressed in black, which in that light rendered him almost invisible. Sir Terence, less practised and less calculating in these matters, wore an undress uniform, the red coat of which showed greyish. Samoval observed this rather with contempt than with satisfaction in the advantage it afforded him. Then he removed the swathing from the swords, and, crossing them, presented the hilts to Sir Terence. The adjutant took one and the Count retained the other, which he tested, thrashing the air with it so that it hummed like a whip. That done, however, he did not immediately fall on.

"In a few minutes the moon will be more obliging," he suggested. "If you would prefer to wait—"

But it occurred to Sir Terence that in the gloom the advantage might lie slightly with himself, since the other's superior sword-play would perhaps be partly neutralised. He cast a last look round at the dark windows.

"I find it light enough," he answered.

Samoval's reply was instantaneous. "On guard, then," he cried, and on the words, without giving Sir Terence so much as time to comply with the invitation, he whirled his point straight and deadly at the greyish outline of his opponent's body. But a ray of moonlight caught the blade and its livid flash gave Sir Terence warning of the thrust so treacherously delivered. He saved himself by leaping backwards—just saved himself with not an inch to spare—and threw up his blade to meet the thrust.

"Ye murderous villain," he snarled under his breath, as steel ground on steel, and he flung forward to the attack.

But from the gloom came a little laugh to answer him, and his angry lunge was foiled by an enveloping movement that ended in a ripost. With that they settled down to it, Sir Terence in a rage upon which that assassin stroke had been fresh fuel; the Count cool and unhurried, delaying until the moonlight should have crept a little farther, so as to enable him to make quite sure that his stroke when delivered should be final.

Meanwhile he pressed Sir Terence towards the side where the moonlight would strike first, until they were fighting close under the windows of the residential wing, Sir Terence with his back to them, Samoval facing them. It was Fate that placed them so, the Fate that watched over Sir Terence even now when he felt his strength failing him, his sword arm turning to lead under the strain of an unwonted exercise. He knew himself beaten, realised the dexterous ease, the masterly economy of vigour and the deadly sureness of his opponent's play. He knew that he was at the mercy of Samoval; he was even beginning to wonder why the Count should delay to make an end of a situation of which he was so completely master. And then, quite suddenly, even as he was returning thanks that he had taken the precaution of putting all his affairs in order, something happened.

A light showed; it flared up suddenly, to be as suddenly extinguished, and it had its source in the window of Lady O'Moy's dressing-room, which Samoval was facing.

That flash drawing off the Count's eyes for one instant, and leaving them blinded for another, had revealed him clearly at the same time to Sir Terence. Sir Terence's blade darted in, driven by all that was left of his spent strength, and Samoval, his eyes unseeing, in that moment had fumbled widely and failed to find the other's steel until he felt it sinking through his body, searing him from breast to back.

His arms sank to his sides quite nervelessly. He uttered a faint exclamation of astonishment, almost instantly interrupted by a cough. He swayed there a moment, the cough increasing until it choked him. Then, suddenly limp, he pitched forward upon his face, and lay clawing and twitching at Sir Terence's feet.

Sir Terence himself, scarcely realising what had taken place, for the whole thing had happened within the time of a couple of heart-beats, stood quite still, amazed and awed, in a half-crouching attitude, looking down at the body of the fallen man. And then from above, ringing upon the deathly stillness, he caught a sibilant whisper:

"What was that? 'Sh!"

He stepped back softly, and flattened himself instinctively against the wall; thence profoundly intrigued and vaguely alarmed on several scores he peered up at the windows of his wife's room whence the sound had come, whence the sudden light had come which—as he now realised—had given him the victory in that unequal contest. Looking up at the balcony in whose shadow he stood concealed, he saw two figures there—his wife's and another's—and at the same time he caught sight of something black that dangled from the narrow balcony, and peered more closely to discover a rope ladder.

He felt his skin roughening, bristling like a dog's; he was conscious of being cold from head to foot, as if the flow of his blood had been suddenly arrested; and a sense of sickness overcame him. And then to turn that horrible doubt of his into still more horrible certainty came a man's voice, subdued, yet not so subdued but that he recognised it for Ned Tremayne's.

"There's some one lying there. I can make out the figure."

"Don't go down! For pity's sake, come back. Come back and wait, Ned. If any one should come and find you we shall be ruined."

Thus hoarsely whispering, vibrating with terror, the voice of his wife reached O'Moy, to confirm him the unsuspecting blind cuckold that Samoval had dubbed him to his face, for which Samoval—warning the guilty pair with his last breath even as he had earlier so mockingly warned Sir Terence—had coughed up his soul on the turf of that enclosed garden.

Crouching there for a moment longer, a man bereft of

movement and of reason, stood O'Moy, conscious only of pain, in an agony of mind and heart that at one and the same time froze his blood and drew the sweat from his brow.

Then he was for stepping out into the open, and, giving flow to the rage and surging violence that followed, calling down the man who had dishonoured him and slaying him there under the eyes of that trull who had brought him to this shame. But he controlled the impulse, or else Satan controlled it for him. That way, whispered the Tempter, was too straight and simple. He must think. He must have time to readjust his mind to the horrible circumstances so suddenly revealed.

Very soft and silently, keeping well within the shadow of the wall, he sidled to the door which he had left ajar. Soundlessly he pushed it open, passed in and as soundlessly closed it again. For a moment he stood leaning heavily against its timbers, his breath coming in short panting sobs. Then he steadied himself and turning, made his way down the corridor to the little study which had been fitted up for him in the residential wing, and where sometimes he worked at night. He had been writing there that evening ever since dinner, and he had quitted the room only to go to his assignation with Samoval, leaving the lamp burning on his open desk.

He opened the door, but before passing in he paused a moment, straining his ears to listen for sounds overhead. His eyes, glancing up and down, were arrested by a thin blade of light under a door at the end of the corridor. It was the door of the butler's pantry, and the line of light announced that Mullins had not yet gone to bed. At once Sir Terence understood that, knowing him to be at work, the old servant had himself remained below in case his master should want anything before retiring.

Continuing to move without noise, Sir Terence entered his study, closed the door and crossed to his desk. Wearily he dropped into the chair that stood before it, his face drawn and ghastly, his smouldering eyes staring vacantly ahead. On the desk before him lay the letters that he had spent the past hours in writing—one to his wife; another to Tremayne; another to his brother in Ireland; and several others connected with his official duties, making provision for their uninterrupted continuance in the event of his not surviving the encounter.

Now it happened that amongst the latter there was one that was destined hereafter to play a considerable part; it was a note for the Commissary-General upon a matter that demanded immediate attention, and the only one of all those letters that need now survive. It was marked "Most Urgent," and had been left by him for delivery first thing in the morning. He pulled open a drawer and swept into it all the letters he had written save that one.

He locked that drawer; then unlocked another, and took thence a case of pistols. With shaking hands he lifted out one of the weapons to examine it, and all the while, of course, his thoughts were upon his wife and Tremayne. He was considering how well-founded had been his every twinge of jealousy; how wasted, how senseless the reactions of shame that had followed them; how insensate his trust in Tremayne's honesty, and, above all, with what crafty, treacherous subtlety Tremayne had drawn a red herring across the trail of his suspicions by pretending to an unutterable passion for Sylvia Armytage. It was perhaps that piece of duplicity, worthy, he thought, of the Iscariot himself, that galled Sir Terence now most sorely; that and the memory of his own silly credulity. He had been such a ready dupe. How those two together must have laughed at him! Oh, Tremayne had been very subtle! He had been the friend, the quasi-brother, parading his affection for the Butler family to excuse the familiarities with Lady O'Moy which he had permitted himself under Sir Terence's very eyes. O'Moy thought of them as he had seen them in the garden on the night of Redondo's ball, remembered the air of transparent honesty by which that damned hypocrite when discovered had deflected his just resentment.

Oh, there was no doubt that the treacherous blackguard had been subtle. But—by God!—subtlety should be repaid with subtlety! He would deal with Tremayne as cruelly as Tremayne had dealt with him; and his wanton wife, too, should be repaid in kind. He beheld the way clear, in a flash of wicked inspiration. He put back the pistol, slapped down the lid of the box and replaced it in its drawer.

He rose, took up the letter to the Commissary-general, stepped briskly to the door and pulled it open.

"Mullins!" he called sharply. "Are you there? Mullins?"

Came the sound of a scraping chair, and instantly that door at the end of the corridor was thrown open, and Mullins stood silhouetted against the light behind him. A moment he stood there, then came forward.

"You called, Sir Terence?"

"Yes." Sir Terence's voice was miraculously calm. His back was to the light and his face in shadow, so that its drawn, haggard look was not perceptible to the butler. "I am going to bed. But first I want you to step across to the sergeant of the guard with this letter for the Commissary-General. Tell him that it is of the utmost importance, and ask him to arrange to have it taken into Lisbon first thing in the morning."

Mullins bowed, venerable as an archdeacon in aspect and bearing, as he received the letter from his master: "Certainly, Sir Terence."

As he departed Sir Terence turned and slowly paced back to his desk, leaving the door open. His eyes had narrowed; there was a cruel, an almost evil smile on his lips. Of the generous, good-humoured nature imprinted upon his face every sign had vanished. His countenance was a mask of ferocity restrained by intelligence, cold and calculating.

Oh, he would pay the score that lay between himself and those two who had betrayed him. They should receive treachery for treachery, mockery for mockery, and for dishonour death. They had deemed him an old fool! What was the expression that Samoval had used—Pantaloon in the comedy? Well, well! He had been Pantaloon in the comedy so far. But now they should find him Pantaloon in the tragedy—nay, not Pantaloon at all, but Polichinelle, the sinister jester, the cynical clown, who laughs in murdering. And in anguished silence should they bear the punishment he would mete out to them, or else in no less anguished speech themselves proclaim their own dastardy to the world.

His wife he beheld now in a new light. It was out of vanity and greed that she had married him, because of the position in the world that he could give her. Having done so, at least she might have kept faith; she might have been honest, and abided by the bargain. If she had not done so, it was because honesty was beyond her shallow nature. He should have seen before what he now saw so clearly. He should have known her for a lovely, empty husk; a silly, fluttering butterfly; a toy; a thing of vanities, emotions, and nothing else.

Thus Sir Terence, cursing the day when he had mated with a fool. Thus Sir Terence whilst he stood there waiting for the outcry from Mullins that should proclaim the discovery of the body, and afford him a pretext for having the house searched for the slayer. Nor had he long to wait.

"Sir Terence! Sir Terence! For God's sake, Sir Terence!" he heard the voice of his old servant. Came the loud crash of the door thrust back until it struck the wall and quick steps along the passage.

Sir Terence stepped out to meet him.

"Why, what the devil—" he was beginning in his bluff, normal tones, when the servant, showing a white, scared face, cut him short.

"A terrible thing, Sir Terence! Oh, the saints protect us, a dreadful thing! This way, sir! There's a man killed—Count Samoval, I think it is!"

"What? Where?"

"Out yonder, in the quadrangle, sir."

"But—" Sir Terence checked. "Count Samoval, did ye say? Impossible!" and he went out quickly, followed by the butler.

In the quadrangle he checked. In the few minutes that were sped since he had left the place the moon had overtopped the roof of the opposite wing, so that full upon the enclosed garden fell now its white light, illumining and revealing.

There lay the black still form of Samoval supine, his white face staring up into the heavens, and beside him knelt Tremayne, whilst in the balcony above leaned her ladyship. The rope ladder, Sir Terence's swift glance observed, had disappeared.

He halted in his advance, standing at gaze a moment. He had hardly expected so much. He had conceived the plan of causing the house to be searched immediately upon Mullins's discovery of the body. But Tremayne's rashness in adventuring down in this fashion spared him even that necessity. True, it set up other difficulties. But he was not sure that the matter would not be infinitely more interesting thus.

He stepped forward, and came to a standstill beside the two— his dead enemy and his living one.

CHAPTER XIII

POLICHINELLE

"Why, Ned," he asked gravely, "what has happened?"

"It is Samoval," was Tremayne's quiet answer. "He is quite dead."

He stood up as he spoke, and Sir Terence observed with terrible inward mirth that his tone had the frank and honest ring, his bearing the imperturbable ease which more than once before had imposed upon him as the outward signs of an easy conscience. This secretary of his was a cool scoundrel.

"Samoval, is it?" said Sir Terence, and went down on one knee beside the body to make a perfunctory examination. Then he looked up at the captain.

"And how did this happen?"

"Happen?" echoed Tremayne, realising that the question was being addressed particularly to himself. "That is what I am wondering. I found him here in this condition."

"You found him here? Oh, you found him here in this condition! Curious!" Over his shoulder he spoke to the butler: "Mullins, you had better call the guard." He picked up the slender weapon that lay beside Samoval. "A duelling sword!" Then he looked searchingly about him until his eyes caught the gleam of the other blade near the wall, where himself he had dropped it. "Ah!" he said, and went to pick it up. "Very odd!" He looked up at the balcony, over the parapet of which his wife was leaning. "Did you see anything, my dear?" he asked, and neither Tremayne nor she detected the faint note of wicked mockery in the question.

There was a moment's pause before she answered him, faltering:

"N-no. I saw nothing." Sir Terence's straining ears caught no faintest sound of the voice that had prompted her urgently from behind the curtained windows.

"How long have you been there?" he asked her.

"A—a moment only," she replied, again after a pause. "I—I thought I heard a cry, and—and I came to see what had happened." Her voice shook with terror; but what she beheld would have been quite enough to account for that.

The guard filed in through the doors from the official quarters, a sergeant with a halbert in one hand and a lantern in the other, followed by four men, and lastly by Mullins. They halted and came to attention before Sir Terence. And almost at the same moment there was a sharp rattling knock on the wicket in the great closed gates through which Samoval had entered. Startled, but without showing any signs of it, Sir Terence bade Mullins go open, and in a general silence all waited to see who it was that came.

A tall man, bowing his shoulders to pass under the low lintel of that narrow door, stepped over the sill and into the courtyard. He wore a cocked hat, and as his great cavalry cloak fell open the yellow rays of the sergeant's lantern gleamed faintly on a British uniform. Presently, as he advanced into the quadrangle, he disclosed the aquiline features of Colquhoun Grant.

"Good-evening, General. Good-evening, Tremayne," he greeted one and the other. Then his eyes fell upon the body lying between them. "Samoval, eh? So I am not mistaken in seeking him here. I have had him under very close observation during the past day or two, and when one of my men brought me word tonight that he had left his place at Bispo on foot and alone, going along the upper Alcantara road, If had a notion that he might be coming to Monsanto and I followed. But I hardly expected to find this. How has it happened?"

"That is what I was just asking Tremayne," replied Sir Terence. "Mullins discovered him here quite by chance with the body."

"Oh!" said Grant, and turned to the captain. "Was it you then—"

"I?" interrupted Tremayne with sudden violence. He seemed now to become aware for the first time of the gravity of his position. "Certainly not, Colonel Grant. I heard a cry, and I came out to see what it was. I found Samoval here, already dead."

"I see," said Grant. "You were with Sir Terence, then, when this—"

"Nay," Sir Terence interrupted. "I have been alone since dinner, clearing up some arrears of work. I was in my study there when Mullins called me to tell me what he had discovered. It looks as if there had been a duel. Look at these swords." Then he turned to his secretary. "I think, Captain Tremayne," he said gravely, "that you had better report yourself under arrest to your colonel."

Tremayne stiffened suddenly. "Report myself under arrest?" he cried. "My God, Sir Terence, you don't believe that I—"

Sir Terence interrupted him. The voice in which he spoke was stern, almost sad; but his eyes gleamed with fiendish mockery the while. It was Polichinelle that spoke—Polichinelle that mocks what time he slays. "What were you doing here?" he asked, and it was like moving the checkmating piece.

112

Tremayne stood stricken and silent. He cast a desperate upward glance at the balcony overhead. The answer was so easy, but it would entail delivering Richard Butler to his death. Colonel Grant, following his upward glance, beheld Lady O'Moy for the first time. He bowed, swept off his cocked hat, and "Perhaps her ladyship," he suggested to Sir Terence, "may have seen something."

"I have already asked her," replied O'Moy.

And then she herself was feverishly assuring Colonel Grant that she had seen nothing at all, that she had heard a cry and had come out on to the balcony to see what was happening.

"And was Captain Tremayne here when you came out?" asked O'Moy, the deadly jester.

"Ye-es," she faltered. "I was only a moment or two before yourself."

"You see?" said Sir Terence heavily to Grant, and Grant, with pursed lips, nodded, his eyes moving from O'Moy to Tremayne.

"But, Sir Terence," cried Tremayne, "I give you my word—I swear to you—that I know absolutely nothing of how Samoval met his death."

"What were you doing here?" O'Moy asked again, and this time the sinister, menacing note of derision vibrated clearly in the question.

Tremayne for the first time in his honest, upright life found himself deliberately choosing between truth and falsehood. The truth would clear him—since with that truth he would produce witnesses to it, establishing his movements completely. But the truth would send a man to his death; and so for the sake of that man's life he was driven into falsehood.

"I was on my way to see you," he said.

"At midnight?" cried Sir Terence on a note of grim doubt. "To what purpose?"

"Really, Sir Terence, if my word is not sufficient, I refuse to submit to cross-examination."

Sir Terence turned to the sergeant of the guard, "How long is it since Captain Tremayne arrived?" he asked.

The sergeant stood to attention. "Captain Tremayne, sir, arrived rather more than half-an-hour ago. He came in a curricle, which is still waiting at the gates."

"Half-an-hour ago, eh?" said Sir Terence, and from Colquhoun Grant there was a sharp and audible intake of breath, expressive either of understanding, or surprise, or both. The adjutant looked at Tremayne again. "As my questions seem only to entangle you further," he said, "I think you had better do as I suggest without more protests: report yourself under arrest to Colonel Fletcher in the morning, sir."

Still Tremayne hesitated for a moment. Then drawing himself up, he saluted curtly. "Very well, sir," he replied.

"But, Terence—" cried her ladyship from above.

"Ah?" said Sir Terence, and he looked up. "You would say—?" he encouraged her, for she had broken off abruptly, checked again—although none below could guess it—by the one behind who prompted her.

"Couldn't you—couldn't you wait?" she was faltering, compelled to it by his question.

"Certainly. But for what?" quoth he, grimly sardonic.

"Wait until you have some explanation," she concluded lamely.

"That will be the business of the court-martial," he answered. "My duty is quite clear and simple; I think. You needn't wait, Captain Tremayne."

And so, without another word, Tremayne turned and departed. The soldiers, in compliance with the short command issued by Sir Terence, took up the body and bore it away to a room in the official quarters; and in their wake went Colonel Grant, after taking his leave of Sir Terence. Her ladyship vanished from the balcony and closed her windows, and finally Sir Terence, followed by Mullins, slowly, with bowed head and dragging steps, reentered the house. In the quadrangle, flooded now by the cold, white light of the moon, all was peace once more. Sir Terence turned into his study, sank into the chair by his desk and sat there awhile staring into vacancy, a diabolical smile upon his handsome, mobile mouth. Gradually the smile faded and horror overspread his face. Finally he flung himself forward and buried his head in his arms.

There were steps in the hall outside, a quick mutter of voices, and then the door of his study was flung open, and Miss Armytage came sharply to rouse him.

"Terence! What has happened to Captain Tremayne?"

He sat up stiffly, as she sped across the room to him. She was wrapped in a blue quilted bed-gown, her dark hair hung in two heavy plaits, and her bare feet had been hastily thrust into slippers.

Sir Terence looked at her with eyes that were dull and heavy and that yet seemed to search her white, startled face.

She set a hand on his shoulder, and looked down into his ravaged, haggard countenance. He seemed suddenly to have been stricken into an old man.

"Mullins has just told me that Captain Tremayne has been

114

ordered under arrest for—for killing Count Samoval. Is it true? Is it true?" she demanded wildly.

"It is true," he answered her, and there was a heavy, sneering curl on his upper lip.

"But—" She stopped, and put a hand to her throat; she looked as if she would stifle. She sank to her knees beside him, and caught his hand in both her own that were trembling. "Oh, you can't believe it! Captain Tremayne is not the man to do a murder."

"The evidence points to a duel," he answered dully.

"A duel!" She looked at him, and then, remembering what had passed that morning between Tremayne and Samoval, remembering, too, Lord Wellington's edict, "Oh, God!" she gasped. "Why did you let them take him?"

"They didn't take him. I ordered him under arrest. He will report himself to Colonel Fletcher in the morning."

"You ordered him? You! You, his friend!" Anger, scorn, reproach and sorrow all blending in her voice bore him a clear message.

He looked down at her most closely, and gradually compassion crept into his face. He set his hands on her shoulders, she suffering it passively, insensibly.

"You care for him, Sylvia?" he said, between inquiry and wonder. "Well, well! We are both fools together, child. The man is a dastard, a blackguard, a Judas, to be repaid with betrayal for betrayal. Forget him, girl. Believe me, he isn't worth a thought."

"Terence!" She looked in her turn into that distorted face. "Are you mad?" she asked him.

"Very nearly," he answered, with a laugh that was horrible to hear.

She drew back and away from him, bewildered and horrified. Slowly she rose to her feet. She controlled with difficulty the deep emotion swaying her. "Tell me," she said slowly, speaking with obvious effort, "what will they do to Captain Tremayne?"

"What will they do to him?" He looked at her. He was smiling. "They will shoot him, of course."

"And you wish it!" she denounced him in a whisper of horror.

"Above all things," he answered. "A more poetic justice never overtook a blackguard."

"Why do you call him that? What do you mean?"

"I will tell you—afterwards, after they have shot him; unless the truth comes out before."

"What truth do you mean? The truth of how Samoval came by his death?"

"Oh, no. That matter is quite clear, the evidence complete. I

115

mean—oh, I will tell you afterwards what I mean. It may help you to bear your trouble, thankfully."

She approached him again. "Won't you tell me now?" she begged him.

"No," he answered, rising, and speaking with finality. "Afterwards if necessary, afterwards. And now get back to bed, child, and forget the fellow. I swear to you that he isn't worth a thought. Later I shall hope to prove it to you."

"That you never will," she told him fiercely.

He laughed, and again his laugh was harsh and terrible in its bitter mockery. "Yet another trusting fool," he cried. "The world is full of them—it is made up of them, with just a sprinkling of knaves to batten on their folly. Go to bed, Sylvia, and pray for understanding of men. It is a possession beyond riches."

"I think you are more in need of it than I am," she told him, standing by the door.

"Of course you do. You trust, which is why you are a fool. Trust," he said, speaking the very language of Polichinelle, "is the livery of fools."

She went without answering him and toiled upstairs with dragging feet. She paused a moment in the corridor above, outside Una's door. She was in such need of communion with some one that for a moment she thought of going in. But she knew beforehand the greeting that would await her; the empty platitudes, the obvious small change of verbiage which her ladyship would dole out. The very thought of it restrained her, and so she passed on to her own room and a sleepless night in which to piece together the puzzle which the situation offered her, the amazing enigma of Sir Terence's seeming access of insanity.

And the only conclusion that she reached was that intertwined with the death of Samoval there was some other circumstance which had aroused in the adjutant an unreasoning hatred of his friend, converting him into Tremayne's bitterest enemy, intent—as he had confessed—upon seeing him shot for that night's work. And because she knew them both for men of honour above all, the enigma was immeasurably deepened.

Had she but obeyed the transient impulse to seek Lady O'Moy she might have discovered all the truth at once. For she would have come upon her ladyship in a frame of mind almost as distraught as her own; and she might—had she penetrated to the dressing-room where her ladyship was—have come upon Richard Butler at the same time.

Now, in view of what had happened, her ladyship, ever impulsive, was all for going there and then to her husband to confess the whole truth, without pausing to reflect upon the consequences to others than Ned Tremayne. As you know, it was beyond her to see a thing from two points of view at one and the same time. It was also beyond her brother—the failing, as I think I have told you, was a family one—and her brother saw this matter only from the point of view of his own safety.

"A single word to Terence," he had told her, putting his back to the door of the dressing-room to bar her intended egress, "and you realise that it will be a court-martial and a firing party for me."

That warning effectively checked her. Yet certain stirrings of conscience made her think of the man who had imperilled himself for her sake and her brother's.

"But, Dick, what is to become of Ned?" she had asked him.

"Oh, Ned will be all right. What is the evidence against him after all? Men are not shot for things they haven't done. Justice will out, you know. Leave Ned to shift for himself for the present. Anyhow his danger isn't grave, nor is it immediate, and mine is."

Helplessly distraught, she sank to an ottoman. The night had been a very trying one for her ladyship. She gave way to tears.

"It is all your fault, Dick," she reproached him.

"Naturally you would blame me," he said with resignation—the complete martyr.

"If only you had been ready at the time, as he told you to be, there would have been no delays, and you would have got away before any of this happened."

"Was it my fault that I should have reopened my wound—bad luck to it!—in attempting to get down that damned ladder?" he asked her. "Is it my fault that I am neither an ape nor an acrobat? Tremayne should have come up at once to assist me, instead of waiting until he had to come up to help me bandage my leg again. Then time would not have been lost, and very likely my life with it." He came to a gloomy conclusion.

"Your life? What do you mean, Dick?"

"Just that. What are my chances of getting away now?" he asked her. "Was there ever such infernal luck as mine? The Telemachus will sail without me, and the only man who could and would have helped me to get out of this damned country is under arrest. It's clear I shall have to shift for myself again, and I can't even do that for a day or two with my leg in this state. I shall have to go back into that stuffy store-cupboard of yours till God knows when." He lost all self-control at the prospect and broke into imprecations of his luck.

She attempted to soothe him. But he wasn't easy to soothe.

"And then," he grumbled on, "you have so little sense that you want to run straight off to Terence and explain to him what Tremayne was doing here. You might at least have the grace to wait until I am off the premises, and give me the mercy of a start before you set the dogs on my trail."

"Oh, Dick, Dick, you are so cruel!" she protested. "How can you say such things to me, whose only thought is for you, to save you."

"Then don't talk any more about telling Terence," he replied.

"I won't, Dick. I won't." She drew him down beside her on the ottoman and her fingers smoothed his rather tumbled red hair, just as her words attempted to smooth the ruffles in his spirit. "You know I didn't realise, or I should not have thought of it even. I was so concerned for Ned for the moment."

"Don't I tell you there's not the need?" he assured her. "Ned will be safe enough, devil a doubt. It's for you to keep to what you told them from the balcony; that you heard a cry, went out to see what was happening and saw Tremayne there bending over the body. Not a word more, and not a word less, or it will be all over with me."

CHAPTER XIV

THE CHAMPION

With the possible exception of her ladyship, I do not think that there was much sleep that night at Monsanto for any of the four chief actors in this tragicomedy. Each had his own preoccupations. Sylvia's we know. Mr. Butler found his leg troubling him again, and the pain of the reopened wound must have prevented him from sleeping even had his anxieties about his immediate future not sufficed to do so. As for Sir Terence, his was the most deplorable case of all. This man who had lived a life of simple and downright honesty in great things and in small, a man who had never stooped to the slightest prevarication, found himself suddenly launched upon the most horrible and infamous course of duplicity to encompass the ruin of another. The offence of that other against himself might be of the most foul and hideous, a piece of treachery that only treachery could adequately avenge; yet this consideration was not enough to appease the clamours of Sir Terence's self-respect.

In the end, however, the primary desire for vengeance and vengeance of the bitterest kind proved master of his mind. Captain Tremayne had been led by his villainy into a coil that should presently crush him, and Sir Terence promised himself an infinite balm for his outraged honour in the entertainment which the futile struggles of the victim should provide. With Captain Tremayne lay the cruel choice of submitting in tortured silence to his fate, or of turning craven and saving his miserable life by proclaiming himself a seducer and a betrayer. It should be interesting to observe how the captain would decide, and his punishment was certain whatever the decision that he took.

Sir Terence came to breakfast in the open, grey-faced and haggard, but miraculously composed for a man who had so little studied the art of concealing his emotions. Voice and glance were calm as he gave a good-morning to his wife and to Miss Armytage.

"What are you going to do about Ned?" was one of his wife's first questions.

It took him aback. He looked askance at her, marvelling at the steadiness with which she bore his glance, until it occurred to him that effrontery was an essential part of the equipment of all harlots.

"What am I going to do?" he echoed. "Why, nothing. The matter is out of my hands. I may be asked to give evidence; I may

119

even be called to sit upon the court-martial that will try him. My evidence can hardly assist him. My conclusions will naturally be based upon the evidence that is laid before the court."

Her teaspoon rattled in her saucer. "I don't understand you, Terence. Ned has always been your best friend."

"He has certainly shared everything that was mine."

"And you know," she went on, "that he did not kill Samoval."

"Indeed?" His glance quickened a little. "How should I know that?"

"Well... I know it, anyway."

He seemed moved by that statement. He leaned forward with an odd eagerness, behind which there was something terrible that went unperceived by her.

"Why did you not say so before? How do you know? What do you know?"

"I am sure that he did not."

"Yes, yes. But what makes you so sure? Do you possess some knowledge that you have not revealed?"

He saw the colour slowly shrinking from her cheeks under his burning gaze. So she was not quite shameless then, after all. There were limits to her effrontery.

"What knowledge should I possess?" she filtered.

"That is what I am asking."

She made a good recovery. "I possess the knowledge that you should possess yourself," she told him. "I know Ned for a man incapable of such a thing. I am ready to swear that he could not have done it."

"I see: evidence as to character." He sank back into his chair and thoughtfully stirred his chocolate. "It may weigh with the court. But I am not the court, and my mere opinions can do nothing for Ned Tremayne."

Her ladyship looked at him wildly. "The court?" she cried. "Do you mean that I shall have to give evidence?"

"Naturally," he answered. "You will have to say what you saw."

"But—but I saw nothing."

"Something, I think."

"Yes; but nothing that can matter."

"Still the court will wish to hear it and perhaps to examine you upon it."

"Oh no, no!" In her alarm she half rose, then sank again to her chair. "You must keep me out of this, Terence. I couldn't—I really couldn't."

He laughed with an affectation of indulgence, masking something else.

120

"Why," he said, "you would not deprive Tremayne of any of the advantages to be derived from your testimony? Are you not ready to bear witness as to his character? To swear that from your knowledge of the man you are sure he could not have done such a thing? That he is the very soul of honour, a man incapable of anything base or treacherous or sly?"

And then at last Sylvia, who had been watching them, and seeking to apply to what she heard the wild expressions that Sir Terence had used to herself last night, broke into the conversation.

"Why do you apply these words to Captain Tremayne?" she asked.

He turned sharply to meet the opposition he detected in her. "I don't apply them. On the contrary, I say that, as Una knows, they are not applicable."

"Then you make an unnecessary statement, a statement that has nothing to do with the case. Captain Tremayne has been arrested for killing Count Samoval in a duel. A duel may be a violation of the law as recently enacted by Lord Wellington, but it is not an offence against honour; and to say that a man cannot have fought a duel because a man is incapable of anything base or treacherous or sly is just to say a very foolish and meaningless thing."

"Oh, quite so," the adjutant, admitted. "But if Tremayne denies having fought, if he shelters himself behind a falsehood, and says that he has not killed Samoval, then I think the statement assumes some meaning."

"Does Captain Tremayne say that?" she asked him sharply.

"It is what I understood him to say last night when I ordered him under arrest."

"Then," said Sylvia, with full conviction, "Captain Tremayne did not do it."

"Perhaps he didn't," Sir Terence admitted. "The court will no doubt discover the truth. The truth, you know, must prevail," and he looked at his wife again, marking the fresh signs of agitation she betrayed.

Mullins coming to set fresh covers, the conversation was allowed to lapse. Nor was it ever resumed, for at that moment, with no other announcement save such as was afforded by his quick step and the click-click of his spurs, a short, slight man entered the quadrangle from the doorway of the official wing.

The adjutant, turning to look, caught his breath suddenly in an exclamation of astonishment.

"Lord Wellington!" he cried, and was immediately on his feet.

At the exclamation the new-comer checked and turned. He

121

wore a plain grey undress frock and white stock, buckskin breeches and lacquered boots, and he carried a riding-crop tucked under his left arm. His features were bold and sternly handsome; his fine eyes singularly piercing and keen in their glance; and the sweep of those eyes now took in not merely the adjutant, but the spread table and the ladies seated before it. He halted a moment, then advanced quickly, swept his cocked hat from a brown head that was but very slightly touched with grey, and bowed with a mixture of stiffness and courtliness to the ladies.

"Since I have intruded so unwittingly, I had best remain to make my apologies," he said. "I was on my way to your residential quarters, O'Moy, not imagining that I should break in upon your privacy in this fashion."

O'Moy with a great deference made haste to reassure him on the score of the intrusion, whilst the ladies themselves rose to greet him. He bore her ladyship's hand to his lips with perfunctory courtesy, then insisted upon her resuming her chair. Then he bowed—ever with that mixture of stiffness and deference—to Miss Armytage upon her being presented to him by the adjutant.

"Do not suffer me to disturb you," he begged them. "Sit down, O'Moy. I am not pressed, and I shall be monstrous glad of a few moments' rest. You are very pleasant here," and he looked about the luxuriant garden with approving eyes.

Sir Terence placed the hospitality of his table at his lordship's disposal. But the latter declined graciously.

"A glass of wine and water, if you will. No more. I breakfasted at Torres Vedras with Fletcher." Then to the look of astonishment on the faces of the ladies he smiled. "Oh yes," he assured them, "I was early astir, for time is very precious just at present, which is why I drop unannounced upon you from the skies, O'Moy." He took the glass that Mullins proffered on a salver, sipped from it, and set it down. "There is so much vexation, so much hindrance from these pestilential intriguers here in Lisbon, that I have thought it as well to come in person and speak plainly to the gentlemen of the Council of Regency." He was peeling off his stout riding-gloves as he spoke. "If this campaign is to go forward at all, it will go forward as I dispose. Then, too, I wanted to see Fletcher and the works. By gad, O'Moy, he has performed miracles, and I am very pleased with him—oh, and with you too. He told me how ably you have seconded him and counselled him where necessary. You must have worked night and day, O'Moy." He sighed. "I wish that I were as well served in every direction." And then he broke off abruptly. "But this is monstrous tedious for your ladyship, and for you, Miss Armytage. Forgive me."

Her ladyship protested the contrary, professing a deep interest in military matters, and inviting his lordship to continue. Lord Wellington, however, ignoring the invitation, turned the conversation upon life in Lisbon, inquiring hopefully whether they found the place afforded them adequate entertainment.

"Indeed yes," Lady O'Moy assured him. "We are very gay at times. There are private theatricals and dances, occasionally an official ball, and we are promised picnics and water-parties now that the summer is here."

"And in the autumn, ma'am, we may find you a little hunting," his lordship promised them. "Plenty of foxes; a rough country, though; but what's that to an Irishwoman?" He caught the quickening of Miss Armytage's eye. "The prospect interests you, I see."

Miss Armytage admitted it, and thus they made conversation for a while, what time the great soldier sipped his wine and water to wash the dust of his morning ride from his throat. When at last he set down an empty glass Sir Terence took this as the intimation of his readiness to deal with official matters, and, rising, he announced himself entirely at his lordship's service.

Lord Wellington claimed his attention for a full hour with the details of several matters that are not immediately concerned with this narrative. Having done, he rose at last from Sir Terence's desk, at which he had been sitting, and took up his riding-crop and cocked hat from the chair where he had placed them.

"And now," he said, "I think I will ride into Lisbon and endeavour to come to an understanding with Count Redondo and Don Miguel Forjas."

Sir Terence advanced to open the door. But Wellington checked him with a sudden sharp inquiry.

"You published my order against duelling, did you not?"

"Immediately upon receiving it, sir."

"Ha! It doesn't seem to have taken long for the order to be infringed, then." His manner was severe, his eyes stern. Sir Terence was conscious of a quickening of his pulses. Nevertheless his answer was calmly regretful:

"I am afraid not."

The great man nodded. "Disgraceful! I heard of it from Fletcher this morning. Captain What's-his-name had just reported himself under arrest, I understand, and Fletcher had received a note from you giving the grounds for this. The deplorable part of these things is that they always happen in the most troublesome manner conceivable. In Berkeley's case the victim was a nephew of the Patriarch's. Samoval, now, was a person of even greater consequence, a close friend of several members of the Council. His death will be deeply resented, and may set up fresh difficulties. It is monstrous vexatious." And abruptly he asked "What did they quarrel about?"

O'Moy trembled, and his glance avoided the other's gimlet eye. "The only quarrel that I am aware of between them," he said, "was concerned with this very enactment of your lordship's. Samoval proclaimed it infamous, and Tremayne resented the term. Hot words passed between them, but the altercation was allowed to go no further at the time by myself and others who were present."

His lordship had raised his brows. "By gad, sir," he ejaculated, "there almost appears to be some justification for the captain. He was one of your military secretaries, was he not?"

"He was."

"Ha! Pity! Pity!" His lordship was thoughtful for a moment. Then he dismissed the matter. "But then orders are orders, and soldiers must learn to obey implicitly. British soldiers of all degrees seem to find the lesson difficult. We must inculcate it more sternly, that is all."

O'Moy's honest soul was in torturing revolt against the falsehoods he had implied—and to this man of all men, to this man whom he reverenced above all others, who stood to him for the very fount of military honour and lofty principle! He was in such a mood that one more question on the subject from Wellington and the whole ghastly truth must have come pouring from his lips. But no other question came. Instead his lordship turned on the threshold and held out his hand.

"Not a step farther, O'Moy. I've left you a mass of work, and you are short of a secretary. So don't waste any of your time on courtesies. I shall hope still to find the ladies in the garden so that I may take my leave without inconveniencing them."

And he was gone, stepping briskly with clicking spurs, leaving O'Moy hunched now in his chair, his body the very expression of the dejection that filled his soul.

In the garden his lordship came upon Miss Armytage alone, still seated by the table under the trellis, from which the cloth had by now been removed. She rose at his approach and in spite of gesture to her to remain seated.

"I was seeking Lady O'Moy," said he, "to take my leave of her. I may not have the pleasure of coming to Monsanto again."

"She is on the terrace, I think," said Miss Armytage. "I will find her for your lordship."

"Let us find her together," he said amiably, and so turned and

124

went with her towards the archway. "You said your name is Armytage, I think?" he commented.

"Sir Terence said so."

His eyes twinkled. "You possess an exceptional virtue," said he. "To be truthful is common; to be accurate rare. Well, then, Sir Terence said so. Once I had a great friend of the name of Armytage. I have lost sight of him these many years. We were at school together in Brussels."

"At Monsieur Goubert's," she surprised him by saying. "That would be John Armytage, my uncle."

"God bless my soul, ma'am!" he ejaculated. "But I gathered you were Irish, and Jack Armytage came from Yorkshire."

"My mother is Irish, and we live in Ireland now. I was born there. But father, none the less, was John Armytage's brother."

He looked at her with increased interest, marking the straight, supple lines of her, and the handsome, high-bred face. His lordship, remember, never lacked an appreciative eye for a fine woman. "So you're Jack Armytage's niece. Give me news of him, my dear."

She did so. Jack Armytage was well and prospering, had made a rich marriage and retired from the Blues many years ago to live at Northampton. He listened with interest, and thus out of his boyhood friendship for her uncle, which of late years he had had no opportunity to express, sprang there and then a kindness for the niece. Her own personal charms may have contributed to it, for the great soldier was intensely responsive to the appeal of beauty.

They reached the terrace. Lady O'Moy was nowhere in sight. But Lord Wellington was too much engrossed in his discovery to be troubled.

"My dear," he said, "if I can serve you at any time, both for Jack's sake and your own, I hope that you will let me know of it."

She looked at him a moment, and he saw her colour come and go, arguing a sudden agitation.

"You tempt me, sir," she said, with a wistful smile.

"Then yield to the temptation, child," he urged her kindly, those keen, penetrating eyes of his perceiving trouble here.

"It isn't for myself," she responded. "Yet there is something I would ask you if I dare—something I had intended to ask you in any case if I could find the opportunity. To be frank, that is why I was waiting there in the garden just now. It was to waylay you. I hoped for a word with you."

"Well, well," he encouraged her. "It should be the easier now, since in a sense we find that we are old friends."

He was so kind, so gentle, despite that stern, strong face of his, that she melted at once to his persuasion.

125

"It is about Lieutenant Richard Butler," she began.

"Ah," said he lightly, "I feared as much when you said it was not for yourself you had a favour to ask."

But, looking at him, she instantly perceived how he had misunderstood her.

"Mr. Butler," she said, "is the officer who was guilty of the affair at Tavora."

He knit his brow in thought. "Butler-Tavora?" he muttered questioningly. Suddenly his memory found what it was seeking. "Oh yes, the violated nunnery." His thin lips tightened; the sternness of his ace increased. "Yes?" he inquired, but the tone was now forbidding.

Nevertheless she was not deterred. "Mr. Butler is Lady O'Moy's brother," she said.

He stared a moment, taken aback. "Good God! Ye don't say so, child! Her brother! O'Moy's brother-in-law! And O'Moy never said a word to me about it."

"What should he say? Sir Terence himself pledged his word to the Council of Regency that Mr. Butler would be shot when taken."

"Did he, egad!" He was still further surprised out of his sternness. "Something of a Roman this O'Moy in his conception of duty! Hum! The Council no doubt demanded this?"

"So I understand, my lord. Lady O'Moy, realising her brother's grave danger, is very deeply troubled."

"Naturally," he agreed. "But what can I do, Miss Armytage? What were the actual facts, do you happen to know?"

She recited them, putting the case bravely for the scapegrace Mr. Butler, dwelling particularly upon the error under which he was labouring, that he had imagined himself to be knocking at the gates of a monastery of Dominican friars, that he had broken into the convent because denied admittance, and because he suspected some treacherous reason for that denial.

He heard her out, watching her with those keen eyes of his the while.

"Hum! You make out so good a case for him that one might almost believe you instructed by the gentleman himself. Yet I gather that nothing has since been heard of him?"

"Nothing, sir, since he vanished from Tavora, nearly, two months ago. And I have only repeated to your lordship the tale that was told by the sergeant and the troopers who reported the matter to Sir Robert Craufurd on their return."

He was very thoughtful. Leaning on the balustrade, he looked out across the sunlit valley, turning his boldly chiselled profile to his companion. At last he spoke slowly, reflectively: "But if this were really so—a mere blunder—I see no sufficient grounds to threaten him with capital punishment. His subsequent desertion, if he has deserted—I mean if nothing has happened to him—is really the graver matter of the two."

"I gathered, sir, that he was to be sacrificed to the Council of Regency—a sort of scapegoat."

He swung round sharply, and the sudden blaze of his eyes almost terrified her. Instantly he was cold again and inscrutable. "Ah! You are oddly well informed throughout. But of course you would be," he added, with an appraising look into that intelligent face in which he now caught a faint likeness of Jack Armytage. "Well, well, my dear, I am very glad you have told me of this. If Mr. Butler is ever taken and in danger—there will be a court-martial, of course—send me word of it, and I will see what I can do, both for your sake and for the sake of strict justice."

"Oh, not for my sake," she protested, reddening slightly at the gentle imputation. "Mr. Butler is nothing to me—that is to say, he is just my cousin. It is for Una's sake that I am asking this."

"Why, then, for Lady O'Moy's sake, since you ask it," he replied readily. "But," he warned her, "say nothing of it until Mr. Butler is found." It is possible he believed that Butler never would be found. "And remember, I promise only to give the matter my attention. If it is as you represent it, I think you may be sure that the worst that will befall Mr. Butler will be dismissal from the service. He deserves that. But I hope I should be the last man to permit a British officer to be used as a scapegoat or a burnt-offering to the mob or to any Council of Regency. By the way, who told you this about a scapegoat?"

"Captain Tremayne."

"Captain Tremayne? Oh, the man who killed Samoval?"

"He didn't," she cried.

On that almost fierce denial his lordship looked at her, raising his eyebrows in astonishment.

"But I am told that he did, and he is under arrest for it this moment—for that, and for breaking my order against duelling."

"You were not told the truth, my lord. Captain Tremayne says that he didn't, and if he says so it is so."

"Oh, of course, Miss Armytage!" He was a man of unparalleled valour and boldness, yet so fierce was she in that moment that for the life of him he dared not have contradicted her.

"Captain Tremayne is the most honourable man I know," she continued, "and if he had killed Samoval he would never have denied it; he would have proclaimed it to all the world."

"There is no need for all this heat, my dear," he reassured her.

127

"The point is not one that can remain in doubt. The seconds of the duel will be forthcoming; and they will tell us who were the principals."

"There were no seconds," she informed him.

"No seconds!" he cried in horror. "D' ye mean they just fought a rough and tumble fight?"

"I mean they never fought at all. As for this tale of a duel, I ask your lordship: Had Captain Tremayne desired a secret meeting with Count Samoval, would he have chosen this of all places in which to hold it?"

"This?"

"This. The fight—whoever fought it—took place in the quadrangle there at midnight."

He was overcome with astonishment, and he showed it.

"Upon my soul," he said, "I do not appear to have been told any of the facts. Strange that O'Moy should never have mentioned that," he muttered, and then inquired suddenly: "Where was Tremayne arrested?"

"Here," she informed him.

"Here? He was here, then, at midnight? What was he doing here?"

"I don't know. But whatever he was doing, can your lordship believe that he would have come here to fight a secret duel?"

"It certainly puts a monstrous strain upon belief," said he. "But what can he have been doing here?"

"I don't know," she repeated. She wanted to add a warning of O'Moy. She was tempted to tell his lordship of the odd words that O'Moy had used to her last night concerning Tremayne. But she hesitated, and her courage failed her. Lord Wellington was so great a man, bearing the destinies of nations on his shoulders, and already he had wasted upon her so much of the time that belonged to the world and history, that she feared to trespass further; and whilst she hesitated came Colquhoun Grant clanking across the quadrangle looking for his lordship. He had come up, he announced, standing straight and stiff before them, to see O'Moy, but hearing of Lord Wellington's presence, had preferred to see his lordship in the first instance.

"And indeed you arrive very opportunely, Grant," his lordship confessed.

He turned to take his leave of Jack Armytage's niece.

"I'll not forget either Mr. Butler or Captain Tremayne," he promised her, and his stern face softened into a gentle, friendly smile. "They are very fortunate in their champion."

CHAPTER XV

THE WALLET

"A queer, mysterious business this death of Samoval," said Colonel Grant.

"So I was beginning to perceive," Wellington agreed, his brow dark.

They were alone together in the quadrangle under the trellis, through which the sun, already high, was dappling the table at which his lordship sat.

"It would be easier to read if it were not for the duelling swords. Those and the nature of Samoval's wound certainly point unanswerably to a duel. Otherwise there would be considerable evidence that Samoval was a spy caught in the act and dealt with out of hand as he deserved."

"How? Count Samoval a spy?"

"In the French interest," answered the colonel without emotion, "acting upon the instructions of the Souza faction, whose tool he had become." And Colonel Grant proceeded to relate precisely what he knew of Samoval.

Lord Wellington sat awhile in silence, cogitating. Then he rose, and his piercing eyes looked up at the colonel, who stood a good head taller than himself.

"Is this the evidence of which you spoke?"

"By no means," was the answer. "The evidence I have secured is much more palpable. I have it here." He produced a little wallet of red morocco bearing the initial "S" surmounted by a coronet. Opening it, he selected from it some papers, speaking the while. "I thought it as well before I left last night to make an examination of the body. This is what I found, and it contains, among other lesser documents, these to which I would draw your lordship's attention. First this." And he placed in Lord Wellington's hand a holograph note from the Prince of Esslingen introducing the bearer, M. de la Fleche, his confidential agent, who would consult with the Count, and thanking the Count for the valuable information already received from him.

His lordship sat down again to read the letter. "It is a full confirmation of what you have told me," he said calmly.

"Then this," said Colonel Grant, and he placed upon the table a note in French of the approximate number and disposition of the British troops in Portugal at the time. "The handwriting is

Samoval's own, as those who know it will have no difficulty in discerning. And now this, sir." He unfolded a small sketch map, bearing the title also in French: Probable position and extent of the fortifications north of Lisbon.

"The notes at the foot," he added, "are in cipher, and it is the ordinary cipher employed by the French, which in itself proves how deeply Samoval was involved. Here is a translation of it." And he placed before his chief a sheet of paper on which Lord Wellington read:

"This is based upon my own personal knowledge of the country, odd scraps of information received from time to time, and my personal verification of the roads closed to traffic in that region. It is intended merely as a guide to the actual locale of the fortifications, an exact plan of which I hope shortly to obtain."

His lordship considered it very attentively, but without betraying the least discomposure.

"For a man working upon such slight data as he himself confesses," was the quiet comment, "he is damnably accurate. It is as well, I think, that this did not reach Marshal Massena."

"My own assumption is that he put off sending it, intending to replace it by the actual plan—which he here confesses to the expectation of obtaining shortly."

"I think he died at the right moment. Anything else?"

"Indeed," said Colonel Grant, "I have kept the best for the last." And unfolding yet another document, he placed it in the hands of the Commander-in-Chief. It was Lord Liverpool's note of the troops to be embarked for Lisbon in June and July—the note abstracted from the dispatch carried by Captain Garfield.

His lordship's lips tightened as he considered it. "His death was timely indeed, damned timely; and the man who killed him deserves to be mentioned in dispatches. Nothing else, I suppose?"

"The rest is of little consequence, sir."

"Very well." He rose. "You will leave these with me, and the wallet as well, if you please. I am on my way to confer with the members of the Council of Regency, and I am glad to go armed with so stout a weapon as this. Whatever may be the ultimate finding of the court-martial, the present assumption must be that Samoval met the death of a spy caught in the act, as you suggested. That is the only conclusion the Portuguese Government can draw when I lay these papers before it. They will effectively silence all protests."

"Shall I tell O'Moy?" inquired the colonel.

"Oh, certainly," answered his lordship, instantly to change his mind. "Stay!" He considered, his chin in his hand, his eyes dreamy. "Better not, perhaps. Better not tell anybody. Let us keep this to

130

ourselves for the present. It has no direct bearing on the matter to be tried. By the way, when does the court-martial sit?"

"I have just heard that Marshal Beresford has ordered it to sit on Thursday here at Monsanto."

His lordship considered. "Perhaps I shall be present. I may be at Torres Vedras until then. It is a very odd affair. What is your own impression of it, Grant? Have you formed any?"

Grant smiled darkly. "I have been piecing things together. The result is rather curious, and still very mystifying, still leaving a deal to be explained, and somehow this wallet doesn't fit into the scheme at all."

"You shall tell me about it as we ride into Lisbon. I want you to come with me. Lady O'Moy must forgive me if I take French leave, since she is nowhere to be found."

The truth was, that her ladyship had purposely gone into hiding, after the fashion of suffering animals that are denied expression of their pain. She had gone off with her load of sorrow and anxiety into the thicket on the flank of Monsanto, and there Sylvia found her presently, dejectedly seated by a spring on a bank that was thick with flowering violets. Her ladyship was in tears, her mind swollen to bursting-point by the secret which it sought to contain but felt itself certainly unable to contain much longer.

"Why, Una dear," cried Miss Armytage, kneeling beside her and putting a motherly arm about that full-grown child, "what is this?"

Her ladyship wept copiously, the springs of her grief gushing forth in response to that sympathetic touch.

"Oh, my dear, I am so distressed. I shall go mad, I think. I am sure I have never deserved all this trouble. I have always been considerate of others. You know I wouldn't give pain to any one. And—and Dick has always been so thoughtless."

"Dick?" said Miss Armytage, and there was less sympathy in her voice. "It is Dick you are thinking about at present?"

"Of course. All this trouble has come through Dick. I mean," she recovered, "that all my troubles began with this affair of Dick's. And now there is Ned under arrest and to be court-martialled."

"But what has Captain Tremayne to do with Dick?"

"Nothing, of course," her ladyship agreed, with more than usual self-restraint. "But it's one trouble on another. Oh, it's more than I can bear."

"I know, my dear, I know," Miss Armytage said soothingly, and her own voice was not so steady.

"You don't know! How can you? It isn't your brother or your friend. It isn't as if you cared very much for either of them. If you

131

did, if you loved Dick or Ned, you might realise what I am suffering."

Miss Armytage's eyes looked straight ahead into the thick green foliage, and there was an odd smile, half wistful, half scornful, on her lips.

"Yet I have done what I could," she said presently. "I have spoken to Lord Wellington about them both."

Lady O'Moy checked her tears to look at her companion, and there was dread in her eyes.

"You have spoken to Lord Wellington?"

"Yes. The opportunity came, and I took it."

"And whatever did you tell him?" She was all a-tremble now, as she clutched Miss Armytage's hand.

Miss Armytage related what had passed; how she had explained the true facts of Dick's case to his lordship; how she had protested her faith that Tremayne was incapable of lying, and that if he said he had not killed Samoval it was certain that he had not done so; and, finally, how his lordship had promised to bear both cases in his mind.

"That doesn't seem very much," her ladyship complained.

"But he said that he would never allow a British officer to be made a scapegoat, and that if things proved to be as I stated them he would see that the worst that happened to Dick would be his dismissal from the army. He asked me to let him know immediately if Dick were found."

More than ever was her ladyship on the very edge of confiding. A chance word might have broken down the last barrier of her will. But that word was not spoken, and so she was given the opportunity of first consulting her brother.

He laughed when he heard the story.

"A trap to take me, that's all," he pronounced it. "My dear girl, that stiff-necked martinet knows nothing of forgiveness for a military offence. Discipline is the god at whose shrine he worships." And he afforded her anecdotes to illustrate and confirm his assertion of Lord Wellington's ruthlessness. "I tell you," he concluded, "it's nothing but a trap to catch me. And if you had been fool enough to yield, and to have blabbed of my presence to Sylvia, you would have had it proved to you."

She was terrified and of course convinced, for she was easy of conviction, believing always the last person to whom she spoke. She sat down on one of the boxes that furnished that cheerless refuge of Mr. Butler's.

"Then what's to become of Ned?" she cried. "Oh, I had hoped that we had found a way out at last."

132

He raised himself on his elbow on the camp-bed they had fitted up for him.

"Be easy now," he bade her impatiently. "They can't do anything to Ned until they find him guilty; and how are they going to find him guilty when he's innocent?"

"Yes; but the appearances!"

"Fiddlesticks!" he answered her—and the expression chosen was a mere concession to her sex, and not at all what Mr. Butler intended. "Appearances can't establish guilt. Do be sensible, and remember that they will have to prove that he killed Samoval. And you can't prove a thing to be what it isn't. You can't!"

"Are you sure?"

"Certain sure," he replied with emphasis.

"Do you know that I shall have to give evidence before the court?" she announced resentfully.

It was an announcement that gave him pause. Thoughtfully he stroked his abominable tuft of red beard. Then he dismissed the matter with a shrug and a smile.

"Well, and what of it?" he cried. "They are not likely to bully you or cross-examine you. Just tell them what you saw from the balcony. Indeed you can't very well say anything else, or they will see that you are lying, and then heaven alone knows what may happen to you, as well as to me."

She got up in a pet. "You're callous, Dick—callous!" she told him. "Oh, I wish you had never come to me for shelter."

He looked at her and sneered. "That's a matter you can soon mend," he told her. "Call up Terence and the others and have me shot. I promise I shall make no resistance. You see, I'm not able to resist even if I would."

"Oh, how can you think it?" She was indignant.

"Well, what is a poor devil to think? You blow hot and cold all in a breath. I'm sick and ill and feverish," he continued with self-pity, "and now even you find me a trouble. I wish to God they'd shoot me and make an end. I'm sure it would be best for everybody."

And now she was on her knees beside him, soothing him; protesting that he had misunderstood her; that she had meant—oh, she didn't know what she had meant, she was so distressed on his account.

"And there's never the need to be," he assured her. "Surely you can be guided by me if you want to help me. As soon as ever my leg gets well again I'll be after fending for myself, and trouble you no further. But if you want to shelter me until then, do it thoroughly,

133

and don't give way to fear at every shadow without substance that falls across your path."

She promised it, and on that promise left him; and, believing him, she bore herself more cheerfully for the remainder of the day. But that evening after they had dined her fears and anxieties drove her at last to seek her natural and legal protector.

Sir Terence had sauntered off towards the house, gloomy and silent as he had been throughout the meal. She ran after him now, and came tripping lightly at his side up the steps. She put her arm through his.

"Terence dear, you are not going back to work again?" she pleaded.

He stopped, and from his fine height looked down upon her with a curious smile. Slowly he disengaged his arm from the clasp of her own. "I am afraid I must," he answered coldly. "I have a great deal to do, and I am short of a secretary. When this inquiry is over I shall have more time to myself, perhaps." There was something so repellent in his voice, in his manner of uttering those last words, that she stood rebuffed and watched him vanish into the building.

Then she stamped her foot and her pretty mouth trembled.

"Oaf!" she said aloud.

CHAPTER XVI

THE EVIDENCE

The board of officers convened by Marshal Beresford to form the court that was to try Captain Tremayne, was presided over by General Sir Harry Stapleton, who was in command of the British troops quartered in Lisbon. It included, amongst others, the adjutant-general, Sir Terence O'Moy; Colonel Fletcher of the Engineers, who had come in haste from Torres Vedras, having first desired to be included in the board chiefly on account of his friendship for Tremayne; and Major Carruthers. The judge-advocate's task of conducting the case against the prisoner was deputed to the quartermaster of Tremayne's own regiment, Major Swan.

The court sat in a long, cheerless hall, once the refectory of the Franciscans, who had been the first tenants of Monsanto. It was stone-flagged, the windows set at a height of some ten feet from the ground, the bare, whitewashed walls hung with very wooden portraits of long-departed kings and princes of Portugal who had been benefactors of the order.

The court occupied the abbot's table, which was set on a shallow dais at the end of the room—a table of stone with a covering of oak, over which a green cloth had been spread; the officers—twelve in number, besides the president—sat with their backs to the wall, immediately under the inevitable picture of the Last Supper.

The court being sworn, Captain Tremayne was brought in by the provost-marshal's guard and given a stool placed immediately before and a few paces from the table. Perfectly calm and imperturbable, he saluted the court, and sat down, his guards remaining some paces behind him.

He had declined all offers of a friend to represent him, on the grounds that the court could not possibly afford him a case to answer.

The president, a florid, rather pompous man, who spoke with a faint lisp, cleared his throat and read the charge against the prisoner from the sheet with which he had been supplied—the charge of having violated the recent enactment against duelling made by the Commander-in-Chief of his Majesty's forces in the Peninsula, in so far as he had fought: a duel with Count Jeronymo de Samoval, and of murder in so far as that duel, conducted in an irregular manner, and without any witnesses, had resulted in the death of the said Count Jeronymo de Samoval.

"How say you, then, Captain Tremayne?" the judge-advocate challenged him. "Are you guilty of these charges or not guilty?"

"Not guilty."

The president sat back and observed the prisoner with an eye that was officially benign. Tremayne's glance considered the court and met the concerned and grave regard of his colonel, of his friend Carruthers and of two other friends of his own regiment, the cold indifference of three officers of the Fourteenth—then stationed in Lisbon with whom he was unacquainted, and the utter inscrutability of O'Moy's rather lowering glance, which profoundly intrigued him, and, lastly, the official hostility of Major Swan, who was on his feet setting forth the case against him. Of the remaining members of the court he took no heed.

From the opening address it did not seem to Captain Tremayne as if this case—which had been hurriedly prepared by Major Swan, chiefly that same morning would amount to very much. Briefly the major announced his intention of establishing to the satisfaction of the court how, on the night of the 28th of May, the prisoner, in flagrant violation of an enactment in a general order of the 26th of that same month, had engaged in a duel with Count Jeronymo de Samoval, a peer of the realm of Portugal.

Followed a short statement of the case from the point of view of the prosecution, an anticipation of the evidence to be called, upon which the major thought—rather sanguinely, opined Captain Tremayne—to convict the accused. He concluded with an assurance that the evidence of the prisoner's guilt was as nearly direct as evidence could be in a case of murder.

The first witness called was the butler, Mullins. He was introduced by the sergeant-major stationed by the double doors at the end of the hall from the ante-room where the witnesses commanded to be present were in waiting.

Mullins, rather less venerable than usual, as a consequence of agitation and affliction on behalf of Captain Tremayne, to whom he was attached, stated nervously the facts within his knowledge. He was occupied with the silver in his pantry, having remained up in case Sir Terence, who was working late in his study, should require anything before going to bed. Sir Terence called him, and—

"At what time did Sir Terence call you?" asked the major.

"It was ten minutes past twelve, sir, by the clock in my pantry."

"You are sure that the clock was right?"

"Quite sure, sir; I had put it right that same evening."

136

"Very well, then. Sir Terence called you at ten minutes past twelve. Pray continue."

"He gave me a letter addressed to the Commissary-general. 'Take that,' says he, 'to the sergeant of the guard at once, and tell him to be sure that it is forwarded to the Commissary-General first thing in the morning.' I went out at once, and on the lawn in the quadrangle I saw a man lying on his back on the grass and another man kneeling beside him. I ran across to them. It was a bright, moonlight night—bright as day it was, and you could see quite clear. The gentleman that was kneeling looks up, at me, and I sees it was Captain Tremayne, sir. 'What's this, Captain dear?' says I. 'It's Count Samoval, and he's kilt,' says he, 'for God's sake, go and fetch somebody.' So I ran back to tell Sir Terence, and Sir Terence he came out with me, and mighty startled he was at what he found there. 'What's happened?' says he, and the captain answers him just as he had answered me: 'It's Count Samoval, and he's kilt.' 'But how did it happen?' says Sir Terence. 'Sure and that's just what I want to know,' says the captain; 'I found him here.' And then Sir Terence turns to me, and 'Mullins,' says he, 'just fetch the guard,' and of course, I went at once."

"Was there any one else present?" asked the prosecutor.

"Not in the quadrangle, sir. But Lady O'Moy was on the balcony of her room all the time."

"Well, then, you fetched the guard. What happened when you returned?"

"Colonel Grant arrived, sir, and I understood him to say that he had been following Count Samoval..."

"Which way did Colonel Grant come?" put in the president.

"By the gate from the terrace."

"Was it open?"

"No, sir. Sir Terence himself went to open the wicket when Colonel Grant knocked."

Sir Harry nodded and Major Swan resumed the examination.

"What happened next?"

"Sir Terence ordered the captain under arrest."

"Did Captain Tremayne submit at once?"

"Well, not quite at once, sir. He naturally made some bother. 'Good God!' he says, 'ye'll never be after thinking I kilt him? I tell you I just found him here like this.' 'What were ye doing here, then?' says Sir Terence. 'I was coming to see you,' says the captain. 'What about?' says Sir Terence, and with that the captain got angry, said he refused to be cross-questioned and went off to report himself under arrest as he was bid."

That closed the butler's evidence, and the judge-advocate looked across at the prisoner.

"Have you any questions for the witness?" he inquired.

"None," replied Captain Tremayne. "He has given his evidence very faithfully and accurately."

Major Swan invited the court to question the witness in any manner it considered desirable. The only one to avail himself of the invitation was Carruthers, who, out of his friendship and concern for Tremayne—and a conviction of Tremayne's innocence begotten chiefly by that friendship desired to bring out anything that might tell in his favour.

"What was Captain Tremayne's bearing when he spoke to you and to Sir Terence?"

"Quite as usual, sir."

"He was quite calm, not at all perturbed?"

"Devil a bit; not until Sir Terence ordered him under arrest, and then he was a little hot."

"Thank you, Mullins."

Dismissed by the court, Mullins would have departed, but that upon being told by the sergeant-major that he was at liberty to remain if he chose he found a seat on one of the benches ranged against the wall.

The next witness was Sir Terence, who gave his evidence quietly from his place at the board immediately on the president's right. He was pale, but otherwise composed, and the first part of his evidence was no more than a confirmation of what Mullins had said, an exact and strictly truthful statement of the circumstances as he had witnessed them from the moment when Mullins had summoned him.

"You were present, I believe, Sir Terence," said Major Swan, "at an altercation that arose on the previous day between Captain Tremayne and the deceased?"

"Yes. It happened at lunch here at Monsanto."

"What was the nature of it?"

"Count Samoval permitted himself to criticise adversely Lord Wellington's enactment against duelling, and Captain Tremayne defended it. They became a little heated, and the fact was mentioned that Samoval himself was a famous swordsman. Captain Tremayne made the remark that famous swordsmen were required by Count Samoval's country to, save it from invasion. The remark was offensive to the deceased, and although the subject was abandoned out of regard for the ladies present, it was abandoned on a threat from Count Samoval to continue it later."

"Was it so continued?"

138

"Of that I have no knowledge."

Invited to cross-examine the witness, Captain Tremayne again declined, admitting freely that all that Sir Terence had said was strictly true. Then Carruthers, who appeared to be intent to act as the prisoner's friend, took up the examination of his chief.

"It is of course admitted that Captain Tremayne enjoyed free access to Monsanto practically at all hours in his capacity as your military secretary, Sir Terence?"

"Admitted," said Sir Terence.

"And it is therefore possible that he might have come upon the body of the deceased just as Mullins came upon it?"

"It is possible, certainly. The evidence to come will no doubt determine whether it is a tenable opinion."

"Admitting this, then, the attitude in which Captain Tremayne was discovered would be a perfectly natural one? It would be natural that he should investigate the identity and hurt of the man he found there?"

"Certainly."

"But it would hardly be natural that he should linger by the body of a man he had himself slain, thereby incurring the risk of being discovered?"

"That is a question for the court rather than for me."

"Thank you, Sir Terence." And, as no one else desired to question him, Sir Terence resumed his seat, and Lady O'Moy was called.

She came in very white and trembling, accompanied by Miss Armytage, whose admittance was suffered by the court, since she would not be called upon to give evidence. One of the officers of the Fourteenth seated on the extreme right of the table made gallant haste to set a chair for her ladyship, which she accepted gratefully.

The oath administered, she was invited gently by Major Swan to tell the court what she knew of the case before them.

"But—but I know nothing," she faltered in evident distress, and Sir Terence, his elbow leaning on the table, covered his mouth with his hand that its movements might not betray him. His eyes glowered upon her with a ferocity that was hardly dissembled.

"If you will take the trouble to tell the court what you saw from your balcony," the major insisted, "the court will be grateful."

Perceiving her agitation, and attributing it to nervousness, moved also by that delicate loveliness of hers, and by deference to the adjutant-generates lady, Sir Harry Stapleton intervened.

"Is Lady O'Moy's evidence really necessary?" he asked. "Does it contribute any fresh fact regarding the discovery of the body?"

"No, sir," Major Swan admitted. "It is merely a corroboration of what we have already heard from Mullins and Sir Terence."

"Then why unnecessarily distress this lady?"

"Oh, for my own part, sir—" the prosecutor was submitting, when Sir Terence cut in:

"I think that in the prisoner's interest perhaps Lady O'Moy will not mind being distressed a little." It was at her he looked, and for her and Tremayne alone that he intended the cutting lash of sarcasm concealed from the rest of the court by his smooth accent. "Mullins has said, I think, that her ladyship was on the balcony when he came into the quadrangle. Her evidence therefore, takes us further back in point of time than does Mullins's." Again the sarcastic double meaning was only for those two. "Considering that the prisoner is being tried for his life, I do not think we should miss anything that may, however slightly, affect our judgment."

"Sir Terence is right, I think, sir," the judge-advocate supported.

"Very well, then," said the president. "Proceed, if you please."

"Will you be good enough to tell the court, Lady O'Moy, how you came to be upon the balcony?"

Her pallor had deepened, and her eyes looked more than ordinarily large and child-like as they turned this way and that to survey the members of the court. Nervously she dabbed her lips with a handkerchief before answering mechanically as she had been schooled:

"I heard a cry, and I ran out—"

"You were in bed at the time, of course?" quoth her husband, interrupting.

"What on earth has that to do with it, Sir Terence?" the president rebuked him, out of his earnest desire to cut this examination as short as possible.

"The question, sir, does not seem to me to be without point," replied O'Moy. He was judicially smooth and self-contained. "It is intended to enable us to form an opinion as to the lapse of time between her ladyship's hearing the cry and reaching the balcony."

Grudgingly the president admitted the point, and the question was repeated.

"Ye-es," came Lady O'Moy's tremulous, faltering answer, "I was in bed."

"But not asleep—or were you asleep?" rapped O'Moy again, and in answer to the president's impatient glance again explained himself: "We should know whether perhaps the cry might not have been repeated several times before her ladyship heard it. That is of value."

"It would be more regular," ventured the judge-advocate, "if Sir Terence would reserve his examination of the witness until she has given her evidence."

"Very well," grumbled Sir Terence, and he sat back, foiled for the moment in his deliberate intent to torture her into admissions that must betray her if made.

"I was not asleep," she told the court, thus answering her husband's last question. "I heard the cry, and ran to the balcony at once. That—that is all."

"But what did you see from the balcony?" asked Major Swan.

"It was night, and of course—it—it was dark," she answered.

"Surely not dark, Lady O'Moy? There was a moon, I think—a full moon?"

"Yes; but—but—there was a good deal of shadow in the garden, and—and I couldn't see anything at first."

"But you did eventually?"

"Oh, eventually! Yes, eventually." Her fingers were twisting and untwisting the handkerchief they held, and her distressed loveliness was very piteous to see. Yet it seems to have occurred to none of them that this distress and the minor contradictions into which it led her were the result of her intent to conceal the truth, of her terror lest it should nevertheless be wrung from her. Only O'Moy, watching her and reading in her every word and glance and gesture the signs of her falsehood, knew the hideous thing she strove to hide, even, it seemed, at the cost of her lover's life. To his lacerated soul her torture was a balm. Gloating, he watched her, then, and watched her lover, marvelling at the blackguard's complete self-mastery and impassivity even now.

Major Swan was urging her gently.

"Eventually, then, what was it that you saw?"

"I saw a man lying on the ground, and another kneeling over him, and then—almost at once—Mullins came out, and—"

"I don't think we need take this any further, Major Swan," the president again interposed. "We have heard what happened after Mullins came out."

"Unless the prisoner wishes—" began the judge-advocate.

"By no means," said Tremayne composedly. Although outwardly impassive, he had been watching her intently, and it was his eyes that had perturbed her more than anything in that court. It was she who must determine for him how to proceed; how far to defend himself. He had hoped that by now Dick Butler might have been got away, so that it would have been safe to tell the whole truth, although he began to doubt how far that could avail him, how far, indeed, it would be believed in the absence of Dick Butler. Her

141

evidence told him that such hopes as he may have entertained had been idle, and that he must depend for his life simply upon the court's inability to bring the guilt home to him. In this he had some confidence, for, knowing himself innocent, it seemed to him incredible that he could be proven guilty. Failing that, nothing short of the discovery of the real slayer of Samoval could save him—and that was a matter wrapped in the profoundest mystery. The only man who could conceivably have fought Samoval in such a place was Sir Terence himself. But then it was utterly inconceivable that in that case Sir Terence, who was the very soul of honour, should not only keep silent and allow another man to suffer, but actually sit there in judgment upon that other; and, besides, there was no quarrel, nor ever had been, between Sir Terence and Samoval.

"There is," Major Swan was saying, "just one other matter upon which I should like to question Lady O'Moy." And thereupon he proceeded to do so: "Your ladyship will remember that on the day before the event in which Count Samoval met his death he was one of a small luncheon party at your house here in Monsanto."

"Yes," she replied, wondering fearfully what might be coming now.

"Would your ladyship be good enough to tell the court who were the other members of that party?"

"It—it was hardly a party, sir," she answered, with her unconquerable insistence upon trifles. "We were just Sir Terence and myself, Miss Armytage, Count Samoval, Colonel Grant, Major Carruthers and Captain Tremayne."

"Can your ladyship recall any words that passed between the deceased and Captain Tremayne on that occasion—words of disagreement, I mean?"

She knew that there had been something, but in her benumbed state of mind she was incapable of remembering what it was. All that remained in her memory was Sylvia's warning after she and her cousin had left the table, Sylvia's insistence that she should call Captain Tremayne away to avoid trouble between himself and the Count. But, search as she would, the actual subject of disagreement eluded her. Moreover, it occurred to her suddenly, and sowed fresh terror in her soul, that, whatever it was, it would tell against Captain Tremayne.

"I—I am afraid I don't remember," she faltered at last.

"Try to think, Lady O'Moy."

"I—I have tried. But I—I can't." Her voice had fallen almost to a whisper.

"Need we insist?" put in the president compassionately.

"There are sufficient witnesses as to what passed on that occasion without further harassing her ladyship."

"Quite so, sir," the major agreed in his dry voice. "It only remains for the prisoner to question the witness if he so wishes."

Tremayne shook his head. "It is quite unnecessary, sir," he assured the president, and never saw the swift, grim smile that flashed across Sir Terence's stern face.

Of the court Sir Terence was the only member who could have desired to prolong the painful examination of her ladyship. But he perceived from the president's attitude that he could not do so without betraying the vindictiveness actuating him; and so he remained silent for the present. He would have gone so far as to suggest that her ladyship should be invited to remain in court against the possibility of further evidence being presently required from her but that he perceived there was no necessity to do so. Her deadly anxiety concerning the prisoner must in itself be sufficient to determine her to remain, as indeed it proved. Accompanied and half supported by Miss Armytage, who was almost as pale as herself, but otherwise very steady in her bearing, Lady O'Moy made her way, with faltering steps to the benches ranged against the side wall, and sat there to hear the remainder of the proceedings.

After the uninteresting and perfunctory evidence of the sergeant of the guard who had been present when the prisoner was ordered under arrest, the next witness called was Colonel Grant. His testimony was strictly in accordance with the facts which we know him to have witnessed, but when he was in the middle of his statement an interruption occurred.

At the extreme right of the dais on which the table stood there was a small oaken door set in the wall and giving access to a small ante-room that was known, rightly or wrongly, as the abbot's chamber. That anteroom communicated directly with what was now the guardroom, which accounts for the new-comer being ushered in that way by the corporal at the time.

At the opening of that door the members of the court looked round in sharp annoyance, suspecting here some impertinent intrusion. The next moment, however, this was changed to respectful surprise. There was a scraping of chairs and they were all on their feet in token of respect for the slight man in the grey undress frock who entered. It was Lord Wellington.

Saluting the members of the court with two fingers to his cocked hat, he immediately desired them to sit, peremptorily waving his hand, and requesting the president not to allow his entrance to interrupt or interfere with the course of the inquiry.

"A chair here for me, if you please, sergeant," he called and, when it was fetched, took his seat at the end of the table, with his back to the door through which he had come and immediately facing the prosecutor. He retained his hat, but placed his riding-crop on the table before him; and the only thing he would accept was an officer's notes of the proceedings as far as they had gone, which that officer himself was prompt to offer. With a repeated injunction to the court to proceed, Lord Wellington became instantly absorbed in the study of these notes.

Colonel Grant, standing very straight and stiff in the originally red coat which exposure to many weathers had faded to an autumnal brown, continued and concluded his statement of what he had seen and heard on the night of the 28th of May in the garden at Monsanto.

The judge-advocate now invited him to turn his memory back to the luncheon-party at Sir Terence's on the 27th, and to tell the court of the altercation that had passed on that occasion between Captain Tremayne and Count Samoval.

"The conversation at table," he replied, "turned, as was perhaps quite natural, upon the recently published general order prohibiting duelling and making it a capital offence for officers in his Majesty's service in the Peninsula. Count Samoval stigmatised the order as a degrading and arbitrary one, and spoke in defence of single combat as the only honourable method of settling differences between gentlemen. Captain Tremayne dissented rather sharply, and appeared to resent the term 'degrading' applied by the Count to the enactment. Words followed, and then some one—Lady O'Moy, I think, and as I imagine with intent to soothe the feelings of Count Samoval, which appeared to be ruffled—appealed to his vanity by mentioning the fact that he was himself a famous swordsman. To this Captain Tremayne's observation was a rather unfortunate one, although I must confess that I was fully in sympathy with it at the time. He said, as nearly as I remember, that at the moment Portugal was in urgent need of famous swords to defend her from invasion and not to increase the disorders at home."

Lord Wellington looked up from the notes and thoughtfully stroked his high-bridged nose. His stern, handsome face was coldly impassive, his fine eyes resting upon the prisoner, but his attention all to what Colonel Grant was saying.

"It was a remark of which Samoval betrayed the bitterest resentment. He demanded of Captain Tremayne that he should be more precise, and Tremayne replied that, whilst he had spoken generally, Samoval was welcome to the cap if he found it fitted him. To that he added a suggestion that, as the conversation appeared to be tiresome to the ladies, it would be better to change its topic.

Count Samoval consented, but with the promise, rather threateningly delivered, that it should be continued at another time. That, sir, is all, I think."

"Have you any questions for the witness, Captain Tremayne?" inquired the judge-advocate.

As before, Captain Tremayne's answer was in the negative, coupled with the now usual admission that Colonel Grant's statement accorded perfectly with his own recollection of the facts.

The court, however, desired enlightenment on several subjects. Came first of all Carruthers's inquiries as to the bearing of the prisoner when ordered under arrest, eliciting from Colonel Grant a variant of the usual reply.

"It was not inconsistent with innocence," he said.

It was an answer which appeared to startle the court, and perhaps Carruthers would have acted best in Tremayne's interest had he left the question there. But having obtained so much he eagerly sought for more.

"Would you say that it was inconsistent with guilt?" he cried.

Colonel Grant smiled slowly, and slowly shook his head. "I fear I could not go so far, as that," he answered, thereby plunging poor Carruthers into despair.

And now Colonel Fletcher voiced a question agitating the minds of several members of the count.

"Colonel Grant," he said, "you have told us that on the night in question you had Count Samoval under observation, and that upon word being brought to you of his movements by one of your agents you yourself followed him to Monsanto. Would you be good enough to tell the court why you were watching the deceased's movements at the time?"

Colonel Grant glanced at Lord Wellington. He smiled a little reflectively and shook his head.

"I am afraid that the public interest will not allow me to answer your question. Since, however, Lord Wellington himself is present, I would suggest that you ask his lordship whether I am to give you the information you require."

"Certainly not," said his lordship crisply, without awaiting further question. "Indeed, one of my reasons for being present is to ensure that nothing on that score shall transpire."

There followed a moment's silence. Then the president ventured a question. "May we ask, sir, at least whether Colonel Grant's observation of Count Samoval resulted from any knowledge of, or expectation of, this duel that was impending?"

"Certainly you may ask that," Lord Wellington, consented.

"It did not, sir," said Colonel Grant in answer to the question.

145

"What grounds had you, Colonel Grant, for assuming that Count Samoval was going to Monsanto?" the president asked.

"Chiefly the direction taken."

"And nothing else?"

"I think we are upon forbidden ground again," said Colonel Grant, and again he looked at Lord Wellington for direction.

"I do not see the point of the question," said Lord Wellington, replying to that glance. "Colonel Grant has quite plainly informed the court that his observation of Count Samoval had no slightest connection with this duel, nor was inspired by any knowledge or suspicion on his part that any such duel was to be fought. With that I think the court should be content. It has been necessary for Colonel Grant to explain to the court his own presence at Monsanto at midnight on the 28th. It would have been better, perhaps, had he simply stated that it was fortuitous, although I can understand that the court might have hesitated to accept such a statement. That, however, is really all that concerns the matter. Colonel Grant happened to be there. That is all that the court need remember. Let me add the assurance that it would not in the least assist the court to know more, so far as the case under consideration is concerned."

In view of that the president notified that he had nothing further to ask the witness, and Colonel Grant saluted and withdrew to a seat near Lady O'Moy.

There followed the evidence of Major Carruthers with regard to the dispute between Count Samoval and Captain Tremayne, which substantially bore out what Sir Terence and Colonel Grant had already said, notwithstanding that it manifested a strong bias in favour of the prisoner.

"The conversation which Samoval threatened to resume does not appear to have been resumed," he added in conclusion.

"How can you say that?" Major Swan asked him.

"I may state my opinion, sir," flashed Carruthers, his chubby face reddening.

"Indeed, sir, you may not," the president assured him. "You are upon oath to give evidence of facts directly within your own personal knowledge."

"It is directly within my own personal knowledge that Captain Tremayne was called away from the table by Lady O'Moy, and that he did not have another opportunity of speaking with Count Samoval that day. I saw the Count leave shortly after, and at the time Captain Tremayne was still with her ladyship—as her ladyship can testify if necessary. He spent the remainder of the afternoon with me at work, and we went home together in the evening. We share the same lodging in Alcantara."

146

"There was still all of the next day," said Sir Harry. "Do you say that the prisoner was never out of your sight on that day too?"

"I do not; but I can't believe—"

"I am afraid you are going to state opinions again," Major Swan interposed.

"Yet it is evidence of a kind," insisted Carruthers, with the tenacity of a bull-dog. He looked as if he would make it a personal matter between himself and Major Swan if he were not allowed to proceed. "I can't believe that Captain Tremayne would have embroiled himself further with Count Samoval. Captain Tremayne has too high a regard for discipline and for orders, and he is the least excitable man I have ever known. Nor do I believe that he would have consented to meet Samoval without my knowledge."

"Not perhaps unless Captain Tremayne desired to keep the matter secret, in view of the general order, which is precisely what it is contended that he did."

"Falsely contended, then," snapped Major Carruthers, to be instantly rebuked by the president.

He sat down in a huff, and the judge-advocate called Private Bates, who had been on sentry duty on the night of the 28th, to corroborate the evidence of the sergeant of the guard as to the hour at which the prisoner had driven up to Monsanto in his curricle.

Private Bates having been heard, Major Swan announced that he did not propose to call any further witnesses, and resumed his seat. Thereupon, to the president's invitation, Captain Tremayne replied that he had no witnesses to call at all.

"In that case, Major Swan," said Sir Harry, "the court will be glad to hear you further."

And Major Swan came to his feet again to address the court for the prosecution.

CHAPTER XVII

BITTER WATER

Major Swan may or may not have been a gifted soldier. History is silent on the point. But the surviving records of the court-martial with which we are concerned go to show that he was certainly not a gifted speaker. His vocabulary was limited, his rhetoric clumsy, and Major Carruthers denounces his delivery as halting, his very voice dull and monotonous; also his manner, reflecting his mind on this occasion, appears to have been perfectly unimpassioned. He had been saddled with a duty and he must perform it. He would do so conscientiously to the best of his ability, for he seems to have been a conscientious man; but he could not be expected to put his heart into the matter, since he was not inflamed by any zeal born of conviction, nor had he any of the incentives of a civil advocate to sway his audience by all possible means.

Nevertheless the facts themselves, properly marshalled, made up a dangerous case against the prisoner. Major Swan began by dwelling upon the evidence of motive: there had been a quarrel, or the beginnings of a quarrel, between the deceased and the accused; the deceased had shown himself affronted, and had been heard quite unequivocally to say that the matter could not be left at the stage at which it was interrupted at Sir Terence's luncheon-table. Major Swan dwelt for a moment upon the grounds of the quarrel. They were by no means discreditable to the accused, but it was singularly unfortunate, ironical almost, that he should have involved himself in a duel as a result of his out-spoken defence of a wise measure which made duelling in the British army a capital offence. With that, however, he did not think that the court was immediately concerned. By the duel itself the accused had offended against the recent enactment, and, moreover, the irregular manner in which the encounter had been conducted, without seconds or witnesses, rendered the accused answerable to a charge of murder, if it could be proved that he actually did engage and kill the deceased. Major Swan thought this could be proved.

The irregularity of the meeting must be assigned to the enactment against which it offended. A matter which, under other circumstances, considering the good character borne by Captain Tremayne, would have been quite incomprehensible, was, he thought, under existing circumstances, perfectly clear. Because Captain Tremayne could not have found any friend to act for him, he was forced to forgo witnesses to the encounter, and because of the consequences to himself of the encounter's becoming known, he was forced to contrive that it should be held in secret. They knew, from the evidence of Colonel Grant and Major Carruthers, that the meeting was desired by Count Samoval, and they were therefore entitled to assume that, recognising the conditions arising out of the recent enactment, the deceased had consented that the meeting should take place in this irregular fashion, since otherwise it could not have been held at all, and he would have been compelled to forgo the satisfaction he desired.

He passed to the consideration of the locality chosen, and there he confessed that he was confronted with a mystery. Yet the mystery would have been no less in the case of any other opponent than Captain Tremayne, since it was clear beyond all doubt that a duel had been fought and Count Samoval killed, and no less clear that it was a premeditated combat, and that the deceased had gone to Monsanto expressly to engage in it, since the duelling swords found had been identified as his property and must have been carried by him to the encounter.

The mystery, he repeated, would have been no less in the case of any other opponent than Captain Tremayne; indeed, in the case of some other opponent it might even have been deeper. It must be remembered, after all, that the place was one to which the accused had free access at all hours.

And it was clearly proven that he availed himself of that access on the night in question. Evidence had been placed before the court showing that he had come to Monsanto in a curricle at twenty minutes to twelve at the latest, and there was abundant evidence to show that he was found kneeling beside the body of the dead man at ten minutes past twelve—the body being quite warm at the time and the breath hardly out of it, proving that he had fallen but an instant before the arrival of Mullins and the other witnesses who had testified.

Unless Captain Tremayne could account to the satisfaction of the court for the manner in which he had spent that half-hour, Major Swan did not perceive, when all the facts of motive and circumstance were considered, what conclusion the court could reach other than that Captain Tremayne was guilty of the death of Count Jeronymo de Samoval in a single combat fought under clandestine and irregular conditions, transforming the deed into technical murder.

Upon that conclusion the major sat down to mop a brow that was perspiring freely. From Lady O'Moy in the background came faintly, the sound of a half-suppressed moan. Terrified, she clutched the hand of Miss Armytage,—and found that hand to lie like a thing of ice in her own, yet she suspected nothing of the deep agitation under her companion's outward appearance of calm.

Captain Tremayne rose slowly to address the court in reply to the prosecution. As he faced his, judges now he met the smouldering eyes of Sir Terence considering him with such malevolence that he was shocked and bewildered. Was he prejudged already, and by his best friend? If so, what must be the attitude of the others? But the kindly, florid countenance of the president was friendly and encouraging; there was eager anxiety for him in the gaze of his friend Caruthers. He glanced at Lord Wellington sitting at the table's end sternly inscrutable, a mere spectator, yet one whose habit of command gave him an air that was authoritative and judicial.

At length he began to speak. He had considered his defence, and he had based it mainly upon a falsehood—since the strict truth must have proved ruinous to Richard Butler.

"My answer, gentlemen," he said, "will be a very brief one as brief, indeed, as the prosecution merits—for I entertain the hope that no member of this court is satisfied that the case made out against me is by any means complete." He spoke easily, fluently, and calmly: a man supremely self-controlled. "It amounts, indeed, to throwing upon me the onus of proving myself innocent, and that is a burden which no British laws, civil or miliary, would ever commit the injustice of imposing upon an accused.

"That certain words of disagreement passed between Count Samoval and myself on the eve of the affair in which the Count met his death, as you have heard from various witnesses, I at once and freely admitted. Thereby I saved the court time and trouble, and some other witnesses who might have been caused the distress of having to testify against me. But that the dispute ever had any sequel, that the further subsequent discussion threatened at the time by Count Samoval ever took place, I most solemnly deny. From the moment that I left Sir Terence's luncheon-table on the Saturday I never set eyes on Count Samoval again until I discovered him dead or dying in the garden here at Monsanto on Sunday night. I can call no witnesses to support me in this, because it is not a matter susceptible to proof by evidence. Nor have I troubled to call the only witnesses I might have called—witnesses as to my character and my regard for discipline—who might have testified that any such encounter as that of which I am accused would be utterly foreign to my nature. There are officers in plenty in his Majesty's service who could bear witness that the practice of duelling is one that I hold in the utmost abhorrence, since I have frequently avowed it, and since in all my life I have never fought a single duel. My service in his Majesty's army has happily afforded me the means of dispensing with any such proof of courage as the duel is supposed to give. I say I might have called witnesses to that fact and I have not done so. This is because, fortunately, there are several among the members of this court to whom I have been known for many years, and who can themselves, when this court comes to consider its finding, support my present assertion.

"Let me ask you, then, gentlemen, whether it is conceivable that, entertaining such feelings as these towards single combat, I should have been led to depart from them under circumstances that might very well have afforded me an ample shield for refusing satisfaction to a too eager and pressing adversary? It was precisely because I hold the duel in such contempt that I spoke with such asperity to the deceased when he pronounced Lord Wellington's enactment a degrading one to men of birth. The very sentiments which I then expressed proclaimed my antipathy to the practice. How, then, should I have committed the inconsistency of accepting a challenge upon such grounds from Count Samoval? There is even more irony than Major Swan supposes in a situation which himself has called ironical.

"So much, then, for the motives that are alleged to have actuated me. I hope you will conclude that I have answered the prosecution upon that matter.

"Coming to the question of fact, I cannot find that there is anything to answer, for nothing has been proved against me. True, it has been proved that I arrived at Monsanto at half-past eleven or twenty minutes to twelve on the night of the 28th, and it has been further proved that half-an-hour later I was discovered kneeling beside the dead body of Count Samoval. But to say that this proves that I killed him is more, I think, if I understood him correctly, than Major Swan himself dares to assert.

"Major Swan is quite satisfied that Samoval came to Monsanto for the purpose of fighting a duel that had been prearranged; and I admit that the two swords found, which have been proven the property of Count Samoval, and which, therefore, he must have brought with him, are a prima-facie proof of such a contention. But if we assume, gentlemen, that I had accepted a challenge from the Count, let me ask you, can you think of any place less likely to have been appointed or agreed to by me for the encounter than the garden of the adjutant-general's quarters? Secrecy is urged as the reason for the irregularity of the meeting. What secrecy was ensured in such a place, where interruption and discovery might come at any moment, although the duel was held at

151

midnight? And what secrecy did I observe in my movements, considering that I drove openly to Monsanto in a curricle, which I left standing at the gates in full view of the guard, to await my return? Should I have acted thus if I had been upon such an errand as is alleged? Common sense, I think, should straightway acquit me on the grounds of the locality alone, and I cannot think that it should even be necessary for me, so as to complete my answer to an accusation entirely without support in fact or in logic, to account for my presence at Monsanto and my movements during the half-hour in question."

He paused. So far his clear reasoning had held and impressed the court. This he saw plainly written on the faces of all—with one single exception. Sir Terence alone the one man from whom he might have looked for the greatest relief—watched him ever malevolently, sardonically, with curling lip. It gave him pause now that he stood upon the threshold of falsehood; and because of that inexplicable but obvious hostility, that attitude of expectancy to ensnare and destroy him, Captain Tremayne hesitated to step from the solid ground of reason, upon which he had confidently walked thus far, on to the uncertain bogland of mendacity.

"I cannot think," he said, "that the court should consider it necessary for me to advance an alibi, to make a statement in proof of my innocence where I contend that no proof has been offered of my guilt."

"I think it will be better, sir, in your own interests, so that you may be the more completely cleared," the president replied, and so compelled him to continue.

"There was," he resumed, then, "a certain matter connected with the Commissary-General's department which was of the greatest urgency, yet which, under stress of work, had been postponed until the morrow. It was concerned with some tents for General Picton's division at Celorico. It occurred to me that night that it would be better dealt with at once, so that the documents relating to it could go forward early on Monday morning to the Commissary-General. Accordingly, I returned to Monsanto, entered the official quarters, and was engaged upon that task when a cry from the garden reached my ears. That cry in the dead of night was sufficiently alarming, and I ran out at once to see what might have occasioned it. I found Count Samoval either just dead or just dying, and I had scarcely made the discovery when Mullins, the butler, came out of the residential wing, as he has testified.

"That, sirs, is all that I know of the death of Count Samoval, and I will conclude with my solemn affirmation, on my honour as a soldier, that I am as innocent of having procured it as I am ignorant of how it came about.

"I leave myself with confidence in your hands, gentlemen," he ended, and resumed his seat.

That he had favourably impressed the court was clear. Miss Armytage whispered it to Lady O'Moy, exultation quivering in her whisper.

"He is safe!" And she added: "He was magnificent."

Lady O'Moy pressed her hand in return. "Thank God! Oh, thank God!" she murmured under her breath.

"I do," said Miss Armytage.

There was silence, broken only by the rustle of the president's notes as he briefly looked them over as a preliminary to addressing the court. And then suddenly, grating harshly upon that silence, came the voice of O'Moy.

"Might I suggest, Sir Harry, that before we hear you three of the witnesses be recalled? They are Sergeant Flynn, Private Bates and Mullins."

The president looked round in surprise, and Carruthers took advantage of the pause to interpose an objection.

"Is such a course regular, Sir Harry?" He too had become conscious at last of Sir Terence's relentless hostility to the accused. "The court has been given an opportunity of examining those witnesses, the accused has declined to call any on his own behalf, and the prosecution has already closed its case."

Sir Harry considered a moment. He had never been very clear upon matters of procedure, which he looked upon as none of a soldier's real business. Instinctively in this difficulty he looked at Lord Wellington as if for guidance; but his lordship's face told him absolutely nothing, the Commander-in-Chief remaining an impassive spectator. Then, whilst the president coughed and pondered, Major Swan came to the rescue.

"The court," said the judge-advocate, "is entitled at any time before the finding to call or recall any witnesses, provided that the prisoner is afforded an opportunity of answering anything further that may be elicited in re-examination of these witnesses."

"That is the rule," said Sir Terence, "and rightly so, for, as in the present instance, the prisoner's own statement may make it necessary."

The president gave way, thereby renewing Miss Armytage's terrors and shaking at last even the prisoner's calm.

Sergeant Flynn was the first of the witnesses recalled at Sir Terence's request, and it was Sir Terence who took up his re-examination.

"You said, I think, that you were standing in the guardroom doorway when Captain Tremayne passed you at twenty minutes to twelve on the night of the 28th?"

"Yes, sir. I had turned out upon hearing the curricle draw up. I had come to see who it was."

"Naturally. Well, now, did you observe which way Captain Tremayne went?—whether he went along the passage leading to the garden or up the stairs to the offices?"

The sergeant considered for a moment, and Captain Tremayne became conscious for the first time that morning that his pulses were throbbing. At last his dreadful suspense came to an end.

"No, sir. Captain Tremayne turned the corner, and was out of my sight, seeing that I didn't go beyond the guardroom doorway."

Sir Terence's lips parted with a snap of impatience. "But you must have heard," he insisted. "You must have heard his steps—whether they went upstairs or straight on."

"I am afraid I didn't take notice, sir."

"But even without taking notice it seems impossible that you should not have heard the direction of his steps. Steps going up stairs sound quite differently from steps walking along the level. Try to think."

The sergeant considered again. But the president interposed. The testiness which Sir Terence had been at no pains to conceal annoyed Sir Harry, and this insistence offended his sense of fair play.

"The witness has already said that the didn't take notice. I am afraid it can serve no good purpose to compel him to strain his memory. The court could hardly rely upon his answer after what he has said already."

"Very well," said Sir Terence curtly. "We will pass on. After the body of Count Samoval had been removed from the courtyard, did Mullins, my butler, come to you?"

"Yes, Sir Terence."

"What was his message? Please tell the court."

"He brought me a letter with instructions that it was to be forwarded first thing in the morning to the Commissary-General's office."

"Did he make any statement beyond that when he delivered that letter?"

The sergeant pondered a moment. "Only that he had been bringing it when he found Count Samoval's body."

"That is all I wish to ask, Sir Harry," O'Moy intimated, and looked round at his fellow-members of that court as if to inquire

154

whether they had drawn any inference from the sergeant's statements.

"Have you any questions to ask the witness, Captain Tremayne?" the president inquired.

"None, sir," replied the prisoner.

Came Private Bates next, and Sir Terence proceeded to question him..

"You said in your evidence that Captain Tremayne arrived at Monsanto between half-past eleven and twenty minutes to twelve?"

"Yes, sir."

"You told us, I think, that you determined this by the fact that you came on duty at eleven o'clock, and that it would be half-an-hour or a little more after that when Captain Tremayne arrived?"

"Yes, sir."

"That is quite in agreement with the evidence of your sergeant. Now tell the court where you were during the half-hour that followed—until you heard the guard being turned out by the sergeant."

"Pacing in front of quarters, sir."

"Did you notice the windows of the building at all during that time?"

"I can't say that I did, sir."

"Why not?"

"Why not?" echoed the private.

"Yes—why not? Don't repeat my words. How did it happen that you didn't notice the windows?"

"Because they were in darkness, sir."

O'Moy's eyes gleamed. "All of them?"

"Certainly, sir, all of them."

"You are quite certain of that?"

"Oh, quite certain, sir. If a light had shown from one of them I couldn't have failed to notice it."

"That will do."

"Captain Tremayne—" began the president.

"I have no questions for the witness, sir," Tremayne announced.

Sir Harry's face expressed surprise. "After the statement he has just made?" he exclaimed, and thereupon he again invited the prisoner, in a voice that was as grave as his countenance, to cross-examine he witness; he did more than invite—he seemed almost to plead. But Tremayne, preserving by a miracle his outward calm, for all that inwardly he was filled with despair and chagrin to see what a pit he had dug for himself by his falsehood, declined to ask any questions.

Private Bates retired, and Mullins was recalled. A gloom seemed to have settled now upon the court. A moment ago their way had seemed fairly clear to its members, and they had been inwardly congratulating themselves that they were relieved from the grim necessity of passing sentence upon a brother officer esteemed by all who knew him. But now a subtle change had crept in. The statement drawn by Sir Terence from the sentry appeared flatly to contradict Captain Tremayne's own account of his movements on the night in question.

"You told the court," O'Moy addressed the witness Mullins, consulting his notes as he did so, "that on the night on which Count Samoval met his death, I sent you at ten minutes past twelve to take a letter to the sergeant of the guard, an urgent letter which was to be forwarded to its destination first thing on the following morning. And it was in fact in the course of going upon this errand that you discovered the prisoner kneeling beside the body of Count Samoval. This is correct, is it not?"

"It is, sir."

"Will you now inform the court to whom that letter was addressed?"

"It was addressed to the Commissary-General."

"You read the superscription?"

"I am not sure whether I did that, but I clearly remember, sir, that you told me at the time that it was for the Commissary-General."

Sir Terence signified that he had no more to ask, and again the president invited the prisoner to question the witness, to receive again the prisoner's unvarying refusal.

And now O'Moy rose in his place to announce that he had himself a further statement to, make to the court, a statement which he had not conceived necessary until he had heard the prisoner's account of his movements during the half-hour he had spent at Monsanto on the night of the duel.

"You have heard from Sergeant Flynn and my butler Mullins that the letter carried from me by the latter to the former on the night of the 28th was a letter for the Commissary-General of an urgent character, to be forwarded first thing in the morning. If the prisoner insists upon it, the Commissary-General himself may be brought before this court to confirm my assertion that that communication concerned a complaint from headquarters on the subject of the tents supplied to the third division Sir Thomas Picton's—at Celorico. The documents concerning that complaint— that is to say, the documents upon which we are to presume that the prisoner was at work during tine half-hour in question—were at the time in my possession in my own private study and in another wing of the building altogether."

Sir Terence sat down amid a rustling stir that ran through the court, but was instantly summoned to his feet again by the president.

"A moment, Sir Terence. The prisoner will no doubt desire to question you on that statement." And he looked with serious eyes at Captain Tremayne.

"I have no questions for Sir Terence, sir," was his answer.

Indeed, what question could he have asked? The falsehoods he had uttered had woven themselves into a rope about his neck, and he stood before his brother officers now in an agony of shame, a man discredited, as he believed.

"But no doubt you will desire the presence of the Commissary-General?" This was from Colonel Fletcher his own colonel and a man who esteemed him—and it was asked in accents that were pleadingly insistent.

"What purpose could it serve, sir? Sir Terence's words are partly confirmed by the evidence he has just elicited from Sergeant Flynn and his butler Mullins. Since he spent the night writing a letter to the Commissary, it is not to be doubted that the subject would be such as he states, since from my own knowledge it was the most urgent matter in our hands. And, naturally, he would not have written without having the documents at his side. To summon the Commissary-General would be unnecessarily to waste the time of the court. It follows that I must have been mistaken, and this I admit."

"But how could you be mistaken?" broke from the president.

"I realise your difficulty in crediting, it. But there it is. Mistaken I was."

"Very well, sir." Sir Harry paused and then added "The court will be glad to hear you in answer to the further evidence adduced to refute your statement in your own defence."

"I have nothing further to say, sir," was Tremayne's answer.

"Nothing further?" The president seemed aghast. "Nothing, sir."

And now Colonel Fletcher leaned forward to exhort him. "Captain Tremayne," he said, "let me beg you to realise the serious position in which you are placed."

"I assure you, sir, that I realise it fully."

"Do you realise that the statements you have made to account for your movements during the half-hour that you were at Monsanto have been disproved? You have heard Private Bates's evidence to the effect that at the time when you say you were at

157

work in the offices, those offices remained in darkness. And you have heard Sir Terence's statement that the documents upon which you claim to have been at work were at the time in his own hands. Do you realise what inference the court will be compelled to draw from this?"

"The court must draw whatever inference it pleases," answered the captain without heat.

Sir Terence stirred. "Captain Tremayne," said he, "I wish to add my own exhortation to that of your colonel! Your position has become extremely perilous. If you are concealing anything that may extricate you from it, let me enjoin you to take the court frankly and fully into your confidence."

The words in themselves were kindly, but through them ran a note of bitterness, of cruel derision, that was faintly perceptible to Tremayne and to one or two others.

Lord Wellington's piercing eyes looked a moment at O'Moy, then turned upon the prisoner. Suddenly he spoke, his voice as calm and level as his glance.

"Captain Tremayne—if the president will permit me to address you in the interests of truth and justice—you bear, to my knowledge, the reputation of an upright, honourable man. You are a man so unaccustomed to falsehood that when you adventure upon it, as you have obviously just done, your performance is a clumsy one, its faults easily distinguished. That you are concealing something the court must have perceived. If you are not concealing something other than that Count Samoval fell by your hand, let me enjoin you to speak out. If you are shielding any one—perhaps the real perpetrator of this deed—let me assure you that your honour as a soldier demands, in the interests of truth and justice, that you should not continue silent."

Tremayne looked into the stern face of the great soldier, and his glance fell away. He made a little gesture of helplessness, then drew himself stiffly up.

"I have nothing more to say."

"Then, Captain Tremayne," said the president, "the court will pass to the consideration of its finding. And if you cannot account for the half-hour that you spent at Monsanto while Count Samoval was meeting his death, I am afraid that, in view of all the other evidences against you, your position is likely to be one of extremest gravity.

"For the last time, sir, before I order your removal, let me add my own to the exhortations already addressed to you, that you should speak. If still you elect to remain silent, the court, I fear, will be unable to draw any conclusion but one from your attitude."

For a long moment Captain Tremayne stood there in tense, expectant silence. Yet he was not considering; he was waiting. Lady O'Moy he knew to be in court, behind him. She had heard, even as he had heard, that his fate hung perhaps upon whether Richard Butler's presence were to be betrayed or not. Not for him to break faith with her. Let her decide. And, awaiting that decision, he stood there, silent, like a man considering. And then, because no woman's voice broke the silence to proclaim at once his innocence, and the alibi that must ensure his acquittal, he spoke at last.

"I thank you, sir. Indeed, I am very grateful to the court for the consideration it has shown me. I appreciate it deeply, but I have nothing more to say."

And then, when all seemed lost, a woman's voice rang out at last:

"But I have!"

Its sharp, almost strident note acted like an electric discharge upon the court; but no member of the assembly was more deeply stricken than Captain Tremayne. For though the voice was a woman's, yet it was not the voice for which he had been waiting.

In his excitement he turned, to see Miss Armytage standing there, straight and stiff, her white face stamped with purpose; and beside her, still seated, clutching her arm in an agony of fear, Lady O'Moy, murmuring for all to hear her:

"No, no, Sylvia. Be silent, for God's sake!"

But Sylvia had risen to speak, and speak she did, and though the words she uttered were such as a virgin might wish to whisper with veiled countenance and averted glance, yet her utterance of them was bold to the point of defiance.

"I can tell you why Captain Tremayne is silent. I can tell you whom he shields."

"Oh God!" gasped Lady O'Moy, wondering through her anguish how Sylvia could have become possessed of her secret.

"Miss Armytage—I implore you!" cried Tremayne, forgetting where he stood, his voice shaking at last, his hand flung out to silence her.

And then the heavy voice of O'Moy crashed in:

"Let her speak. Let us have the truth—the truth!" And he smote the table with his clenched fist.

"And you shall have it," answered Miss Armytage. "Captain Tremayne keeps silent to shield a woman—his mistress."

Sir Terence sucked in his breath with a whistling sound. Lady O'Moy desisted from her attempts to check the speaker and fell to staring at her in stony astonishment, whilst Tremayne was too

159

overcome by the same emotion to think of interrupting. The others preserved a watchful, unbroken silence.

"Captain Tremayne spent that half-hour at Monsanto in her room. He was with her when he heard the cry that took him to the window. Thence he saw the body in the courtyard, and in alarm went down at once—without considering the consequences to the woman. But because he has considered them since, he now keeps silent."

"Sir, sir," Captain Tremayne turned in wild appeal to the president, "this is not true." He conceived at once the terrible mistake that Miss Armytage had made. She must have seen him climb down from Lady O'Moy's balcony, and she had come to the only possible, horrible conclusion. "This lady is mistaken, I am ready to—"

"A moment, sir. You are interrupting," the president rebuked.

And then the voice of O'Moy on the note of terrible triumph sounded again like a trumpet through the long room.

"Ah, but it is the truth at last. We have it now. Her name! Her name!" he shouted. "Who was this wanton?"

Miss Armytage's answer was as a bludgeon-stroke to his ferocious exultation.

"Myself. Captain Tremayne was with me."

CHAPTER XVIII

FOOL'S MATE

Writing years afterwards of this event—in the rather tedious volume of reminiscences which he has left us—Major Carruthers ventures the opinion that the court should never have been deceived; that it should have perceived at once that Miss Armytage was lying. He argues this opinion upon psychological grounds, contending that the lady's deportment in that moment of self-accusation was the very last that in the circumstances she alleged would have been natural to such a character as her own.

"Had she indeed," he writes, "been Tremayne's mistress, as she represented herself, it was not in her nature to have announced it after the manner in which she did so. She bore herself before us with all the effrontery of a harlot; and it was well known to most of us that a more pure, chaste, and modest lady did not live. There was here a contradiction so flagrant that it should have rendered her falsehood immediately apparent."

Major Carruthers, of course, is writing in the light of later knowledge, and even, setting that aside, I am very far from agreeing with his psychological deduction. Just as a shy man will so overreach himself in his efforts to dissemble his shyness as to assume an air of positive arrogance, so might a pure lady who had succumbed as Miss Armytage pretended, upon finding herself forced to such self-accusation, bear herself with a boldness which was no more than a mask upon the shame and anguish of her mind.

And this, I think, was the view that was taken by those present. The court it was—being composed of honest gentlemen— that felt the shame which she dissembled. There were the eyes that fell away before the spurious effrontery of her own glance. They were disconcerted one and all by this turn of events, without precedent in the experience of any, and none more disconcerted— though not in the same sense—than Sir Terence. To him this was checkmate—fool's mate indeed. An unexpected yet ridiculously simple move had utterly routed him at the very outset of the deadly game that he was playing. He had sat there determined to have either Tremayne's life or the truth, publicly avowed, of Tremayne's dastardly betrayal. He could not have told you which he preferred. But one or the other he was fiercely determined to have, and now the springs of the snare in which he had so cunningly taken Tremayne had been forced apart by utterly unexpected hands.

"It's a lie!" he bellowed angrily. But he bellowed, it seemed, upon deaf ears. The court just sat and stared, utterly and hopelessly at a loss how to proceed. And then the dry voice of Wellington followed Sir Terence, cutting sharply upon the dismayed silence.

"How can you know that?" he asked the adjutant. "The matter is one upon which few would be qualified to contradict Miss Armytage. You will observe, Sir Harry, that even Captain Tremayne has not thought it worth his while to do so."

Those words pulled the captain from the spell of sheer horrified amazement in which he had stood, stricken dumb, ever since Miss Armytage had spoken.

"I—I—am so overwhelmed by the amazing falsehood with which Miss Armytage has attempted to save me from the predicament in which I stand. For it is that, gentlemen. On my oath as a soldier and a gentleman, there is not a word of truth in what Miss Armytage has said."

"But if there were," said Lord Wellington, who seemed the only person present to retain a cool command of his wits, "your honour as a soldier and a gentleman—and this lady's honour—must still demand of you the perjury."

"But, my lord, I protest—"

"You are interrupting me, I think," Lord Wellington rebuked him coldly, and under the habit of obedience and the magnetic eye of his lordship the captain lapsed into anguished silence.

"I am of opinion, gentlemen," his lordship addressed the court, "that this affair has gone quite far enough. Miss Armytage's testimony has saved a deal of trouble. It has shed light upon much that was obscure, and it has provided Captain Tremayne with an unanswerable alibi. In my view—and without wishing unduly to influence the court in its decision—it but remains to pronounce Captain Tremayne's acquittal, thereby enabling him to fulfil towards this lady a duty which the circumstances would seem to have rendered somewhat urgent."

They were words that lifted an intolerable burden from Sir Harry's shoulders.

In immense relief, eager now to make an end, he looked to right and left. Everywhere he met nodding heads and murmurs of "Yes, Yes." Everywhere with one exception. Sir Terence, white to the lips, gave no sign of assent, and yet dared give none of dissent. The eye of Lord Wellington was upon him, compelling him by its eagle glance.

"We are clearly agreed," the president began, but Captain Tremayne interrupted him.

"But you are wrongly agreed."

"Sir, sir!"

"You shall listen. It is infamous that I should owe my acquittal to the sacrifice of this lady's good name."

"Damme! That is a matter that any parson can put right," said his lordship.

"Your lordship is mistaken," Captain Tremayne insisted, greatly daring. "The honour of this lady is more dear to me than my life."

"So we perceive," was the dry rejoinder. "These outbursts do you a certain credit, Captain Tremayne. But they waste the time of the court."

And then the president made his announcement

"Captain Tremayne, you are acquitted of the charge of killing Count Samoval, and you are at liberty to depart and to resume your usual duties. The court congratulates you and congratulates itself upon having reached this conclusion in the case of an officer so estimable as yourself."

"Ah, but, gentlemen, hear me yet a moment. You, my lord—"

"The court has pronounced. The matter is at an end," said Wellington, with a shrug, and immediately upon the words he rose, and the court rose with him. Immediately, with rattle of sabres and sabretaches, the officers who had composed the board fell into groups and broke into conversation out of a spirit of consideration for Tremayne, and definitely to mark the conclusion of the proceedings.

Tremayne, white and trembling, turned in time to see Miss Armytage leaving the hall and assisting Colonel Grant to support Lady O'Moy, who was in a half-swooning condition.

He stood irresolute, prey to a torturing agony of mind, cursing himself now for his silence, for not having spoken the truth and taken the consequences together with Dick Butler. What was Dick Butler to him, what was his own life to him—if they should demand it for the grave breach of duty he had committed by his readiness to assist a proscribed offender to escape—compared with the honour of Sylvia Armytage? And she, why had she done this for him? Could it be possible that she cared, that she was concerned so much for his life as to immolate her honour to deliver him from peril? The event would seem to prove it. Yet the overmastering joy that at any other time, and in any other circumstances, such a revelation must have procured him, was stifled now by his agonised concern for the injustice to which she had submitted herself.

And then, as he stood there, a suffering, bewildered man, came Carruthers to grasp his hand and in terms of warm friendship to express satisfaction at his acquittal.

"Sooner than have such a price as that paid—" he said bitterly, and with a shrug left his sentence unfinished.

O'Moy came stalking past him, pale-faced, with eyes that looked neither to right nor left.

"O'Moy!" he cried.

Sir Terence checked, and stood stiffly as if to attention, his handsome blue eyes blazing into the captain's own. Thus a moment. Then:

"We will talk of this again, you and I," he said grimly, and passed on and out with clanking step, leaving Tremayne to reflect that the appearances certainly justified Sir Terence's resentment.

"My God, Carruthers! What must he think of me?" he ejaculated.

"If you ask me, I think that he has suspected this from the very beginning. Only that could account for the hostility of his attitude towards you, for the persistence with which he has sought either to convict or wring the truth from you."

Tremayne looked askance at the major. In such a tangle as this it was impossible to keep the attention fixed upon any single thread.

"His mind must be disabused at once," he answered. "I must go to him."

O'Moy had already vanished.

There were one or two others would have checked the adjutant's departure, but he had heeded none. In the quadrangle he nodded curtly to Colonel Grant, who would have detained him. But he passed on and went to shut himself up in his study with his mental anguish that was compounded of so many and so diverse emotions. He needed above all things to be alone and to think, if thought were possible to a mind so distraught as his own. There were now so many things to be faced, considered, and dealt with. First and foremost—and this was perhaps the product of inevitable reaction—was the consideration of his own duplicity, his villainous betrayal of trust undertaken deliberately, but with an aim very different from that which would appear. He perceived how men must assume now, when the truth of Samoval's death became known as become known it must—that he had deliberately fastened upon another his own crime. The fine edifice of vengeance he had been so skilfully erecting had toppled about his ears in obscene ruin, and he was a man not only broken, but dishonoured. Let him proclaim the truth now and none would believe it. Sylvia Armytage's mad and inexplicable self-accusation was a final bar to that. Men of honour would scorn him, his friends would turn from him in disgust, and Wellington, that great soldier whom he worshipped, and whose esteem he valued above all possessions, would be the first to cast him out. He would appear as a vulgar murderer who, having failed by falsehood to fasten the guilt upon an innocent man, sought now by falsehood still more damnable, at the cost of his wife's honour, to offer some mitigation of his unspeakable offence.

Conceive this terrible position in which his justifiable jealousy—his naturally vindictive rage—had so irretrievably ensnared him. He had been so intent upon the administration of poetic justice, so intent upon condignly punishing the false friend who had dishonoured him, upon finding a balm for his lacerated soul in the spectacle of Tremayne's own ignominy, that he had never paused to see whither all this might lead him.

He had been a fool to have adopted these subtle, tortuous ways; a fool not to have obeyed the earlier and honest impulse which had led him to take that case of pistols from the drawer. And he was served as a fool deserves to be served. His folly had recoiled upon him to destroy him. Fool's mate had checked his perfidious vengeance at a blow.

Why had Sylvia Armytage discarded her honour to make of it a cloak for the protection of Tremayne? Did she love Tremayne and take that desperate way to save a life she accounted lost, or was it that she knew the truth, and out of affection for Una had chosen to immolate herself?

Sir Terence was no psychologist. But he found it difficult to believe in so much of self-sacrifice from a woman for a woman's sake, however dear. Therefore he held to the first alternative. To confirm it came the memory of Sylvia's words to him on the night of Tremayne's arrest. And it was to such a man that she gave the priceless treasure of her love; for such a man, and in such a sordid cause, that she sacrificed the inestimable jewel of her honour? He laughed through clenched teeth at a situation so bitterly ironical. Presently he would talk to her. She should realise what she had done, and he would wish her joy of it. First, however, there was something else to do. He flung himself wearily into the chair at his writing-table, took up a pen and began to write.

CHAPTER XIX

THE TRUTH

To Captain Tremayne, fretted with impatience in the diningroom, came, at the end of a long hour of waiting, Sylvia Armytage. She entered unannounced, at a moment when for the third time he was on the point of ringing for Mullins, and for a moment they stood considering each other mutually ill at ease. Then Miss Armytage closed the door and came forward, moving with that grace peculiar to her, and carrying her head erect, facing Captain Tremayne now with some lingering signs of the defiance she had shown the members of the court-martial.

"Mullins tells me that you wish to see me," she said the merest conventionality to break the disconcerting, uneasy silence.

"After what has happened that should not surprise you," said Tremayne. His agitation was clear to behold, his usual imperturbability all departed. "Why," he burst out suddenly, "why did you do it?"

She looked at him with the faintest ghost of a smile on her lips, as if she found the question amusing. But before she could frame any answer he was speaking again, quickly and nervously.

"Could you suppose that I should wish to purchase my life at such a price? Could you suppose that your honour was not more precious to me than my life? It was infamous that you should have sacrificed yourself in this manner."

"Infamous of whom?" she asked him coolly.

The question gave him pause. "I don't know!" he cried desperately. "Infamous of the circumstances, I suppose."

She shrugged. "The circumstances were there, and they had to be met. I could think of no other way of meeting them."

Hastily he answered her out of his anger for her sake: "It should not have been your affair to meet them at all."

He saw the scarlet flush sweep over her face and leave it deathly white, and instantly he perceived how horribly he had blundered.

"I'm sorry to have been interfering," she answered stiffly, "but, after all, it is not a matter that need trouble you." And on the words she turned to depart again. "Good-day, Captain Tremayne."

"Ah, wait!" He flung himself between her and the door. "We must understand each other, Miss Armytage."

"I think we do, Captain Tremayne," she answered, fire dancing in her eyes. And she added: "You are detaining me."

"Intentionally." He was calm again; and he was masterful for the first time in all his dealings with her. "We are very far from any understanding. Indeed, we are overhead in a misunderstanding already. You misconstrue my words. I am very angry with you. I do not think that in all my life I have ever been so angry with anybody. But you are not to mistake the source of my anger. I am angry with you for the great wrong you have done yourself."

"That should not be your affair," she answered him, thus flinging back the offending phrase.

"But it is. I make it mine," he insisted.

"Then I do not give you the right. Please let me pass." She looked him steadily in the face, and her voice was calm to coldness. Only the heave of her bosom betrayed the agitation under which she was labouring.

"Whether you give me the right or not, I intend to take it," he insisted.

"You are very rude," she reproved him.

He laughed. "Even at the risk of being rude, then. I must make myself clear to you. I would suffer anything sooner than leave you under any misapprehension of the grounds upon which I should have preferred to face a firing party rather than have been rescued at the sacrifice of your good name."

"I hope," she said, with faint but cutting irony, "you do not intend to offer me the reparation of marriage."

It took his breath away for a moment. It was a solution that in his confused and irate state of mind he had never even paused to consider. Yet now that it was put to him in this scornfully reproachful manner he perceived not only that it was the only possible course, but also that on that very account it might be considered by her impossible.

Her testiness was suddenly plain to him. She feared that he was come to her with an offer of marriage out of a sense of duty, as an amende, to correct the false position into which, for his sake, she had placed herself. And he himself by his blundering phrase had given colour to that hideous fear of hers.

He considered a moment whilst he stood there meeting her defiant glance. Never had she been more desirable in his eyes; and hopeless as his love for her had always seemed, never had it been in such danger of hopelessness as at this present moment, unless he proceeded here with the utmost care. And so Ned Tremayne became subtle for the first time in his honest, straightforward, soldierly life. "No," he answered boldly, "I do not intend it."

"I am glad that you spare me that," she answered him, yet her pallor seemed to deepen under his glance.

"And that," he continued, "is the source of all my anger, against you, against myself, and against circumstances. If I had deemed myself remotely worthy of you," he continued, "I should have asked you weeks ago to be my wife. Oh, wait, and hear me out. I have more than once been upon the point of doing so—the last time was that night on the balcony at Count Redondo's. I would have spoken then; I would have taken my courage in my hands, confessed my unworthiness and my love. But I was restrained because, although I might confess, there was nothing I could ask. I am a poor man, Sylvia, you are the daughter of a wealthy one; men speak of you as an heiress. To ask you to marry me—" He broke off. "You realise that I could not; that I should have been deemed a fortune-hunter, not only by the world, which matters nothing, but perhaps by yourself, who matter everything. I—I—" he faltered, fumbling for words to express thoughts of an overwhelming intricacy. "It was not perhaps that so much as the thought that, if my suit should come to prosper, men would say you had thrown yourself away on a fortune-hunter. To myself I should have accounted the reproach well earned, but it seemed to me that it must contain something slighting to you, and to shield you from all slights must be the first concern of my deep worship for you. That," he ended fiercely, "is why I am so angry, so desperate at the slight you have put upon yourself for my sake—for me, who would have sacrificed life and honour and everything I hold of any account, to keep you up there, enthroned not only in my own eyes, but in the eyes of every man."

He paused, and looked at her and she at him. She was still very white, and one of her long, slender hands was pressed to her bosom as if to contain and repress tumult. But her eyes were smiling, and yet it was a smile he could not read; it was compassionate, wistful, and yet tinged, it seemed to him, with mockery.

"I suppose," he said, "it would be expected of me in the circumstances to seek words in which to thank you for what you have done. But I have no such words. I am not grateful. How could I be grateful? You have destroyed the thing that I most valued in this world."

"What have I destroyed?" she asked him.

"Your own good name; the respect that was your due from all men."

"Yet if I retain your own?"

"What is that worth?" he asked almost resentfully.

"Perhaps more than all the rest." She took a step forward and set her hand upon his arm. There was no mistaking now her smile. It was all tenderness, and her eyes were shining. "Ned, there is only one thing to be done."

He looked down at her who was only a little less tall than himself, and the colour faded from his own face now.

"You haven't understood me after all," he said. "I was afraid you would not. I have no clear gift of words, and if I had, I am trying to say something that would overtax any gift."

"On the contrary, Ned, I understand you perfectly. I don't think I have ever understood you until now. Certainly never until now could I be sure of what I hoped."

"Of what you hoped?" His voice sank as if in awe. "What?" he asked.

She looked away, and her persisting, yet ever-changing smile grew slightly arch.

"You do not then intend to ask me to marry you?" she said.

"How could I?" It was an explosion almost of anger. "You yourself suggested that it would be an insult; and so it would. It is to take advantage of the position into which your foolish generosity has betrayed you. Oh!" he clenched his fists and shook them a moment at his sides.

"Very well," she said. "In that case I must ask you to marry me."

"You?" He was thunderstruck.

"What alternative do you leave me? You say that I have destroyed my good name. You must provide me with a new one. At all costs I must become an honest woman. Isn't that the phrase?"

"Don't!" he cried, and pain quivered in his voice. "Don't jest upon it."

"My dear," she said, and now she held out both hands to him, "why trouble yourself with things of no account, when the only thing that matters to us is within our grasp? We love each other, and—"

Her glance fell away, her lip trembled, and her smile at last took flight. He caught her hands, holding them in a grip that hurt her; he bent his head, and his eyes sought her own, but sought in vain.

"Have you considered—" he was beginning, when she interrupted him. Her face flushed upward, surrendering to that questing glance of his, and its expression was now between tears and laughter.

"You will be for ever considering, Ned. You consider too much, where the issues are plain and simple. For the last time—will you marry me?"

169

The subtlety he had employed had been greater than he knew, and it had achieved something beyond his utmost hopes.

He murmured incoherently and took her to his arms. I really do not see that he could have done anything else. It was a plain and simple issue, and she herself had protested that the issue was plain and simple.

And then the door opened abruptly and Sir Terence came in. Nor did he discreetly withdraw as a man of feeling should have done before the intimate and touching spectacle that met his eyes. On the contrary, he remained like the infernal marplot that he intended to be.

"Very proper," he sneered. "Very fit and proper that he should put right in the eyes of the world the reputation you have damaged for his sake, Sylvia. I suppose you're to be married."

They moved apart, and each stared at O'Moy--Sylvia in cold anger, Tremayne in chagrin.

"You see, Sylvia," the captain cried, at this voicing of the world's opinion he feared so much on her behalf.

"Does she?" said Sir Terence, misunderstanding. "I wonder? Unless you've made all plain."

The captain frowned.

"Made what plain?" he asked. "There is something here I don't understand, O'Moy. Your attitude towards me ever since you ordered me under arrest has been entirely extraordinary. It has troubled me more than anything else in all this deplorable affair."

"I believe you," snorted O'Moy, as with his hands behind his back he strode forward into the room. He was pale, and there was a set, malignant sneer upon his lip, a malignant look in the blue eyes that were habitually so clear and honest.

"There have been moments," said Tremayne, "when I have almost felt you to be vindictive."

"D'ye wonder?" growled O'Moy. "Has no suspicion crossed your mind that I may know the whole truth?"

Tremayne was taken aback. "That startles you, eh?" cried O'Moy, and pointed a mocking finger at the captain's face, whose whole expression had changed to one of apprehension.

"What is it?" cried Sylvia. Instinctively she felt that under this troubled surface some evil thing was stirring, that the issues perhaps were not quite as simple as she had deemed them.

There was a pause. O'Moy, with his back to the window now, his hands still clasped behind him, looked mockingly at Tremayne and waited.

"Why don't you answer her?" he said at last. "You were confidential enough when I came in. Can it be that you are keeping something back, that you have secrets from the lady who has no doubt promised by now to become your wife as the shortest way to mending her recent folly?"

Tremayne was bewildered. His answer, apparently an irrelevance, was the mere enunciation of the thoughts O'Moy's announcement had provoked.

"Do you mean to say that you have known throughout that I did not kill Samoval?" he asked.

"Of course. How could I have supposed you killed him when I killed him myself?"

"You? You killed him!" cried Tremayne, more and more intrigued. And—

"You killed Count Samoval?" exclaimed Miss Armytage.

"To be sure I did," was the answer, cynically delivered, accompanied by a short, sharp laugh. "When I have settled other accounts, and put all my affairs in order, I shall save the provost-marshal the trouble of further seeking the slayer. And you didn't know then, Sylvia, when you lied so glibly to the court, that your future husband was innocent of that?"

"I was always sure of it," she answered, and looked at Tremayne for explanation.

O'Moy laughed again. "But he had not told you so. He preferred that you should think him guilty of bloodshed, of murder even, rather than tell you the real truth. Oh, I can understand. He is the very soul of honour, as you remarked yourself, I think, the other night. He knows how much to tell and how much to withhold. He is master of the art of discreet suppression. He will carry it to any lengths. You had an instance of that before the court this morning. You may come to regret, my dear, that you did not allow him to have his own obstinate way; that you should have dragged your own spotless purity in the mud to provide him with an alibi. But he had an alibi all the time, my child; an unanswerable alibi which he preferred to withhold. I wonder would you have been so ready to make a shield of your honour could you have known what you were really shielding?"

"Ned!" she cried. "Why don't you speak? Is he to go on in this fashion? Of what is he accusing you? If you were not with Samoval that night, where were you?"

"In a lady's room, as you correctly informed the court," came O'Moy's bitter mockery. "Your only mistake was in the identity of the lady. You imagined that the lady was yourself. A delusion purely. But you and I may comfort each other, for we are fellow-sufferers at the hands of this man of honour. My wife was the lady who entertained this gallant in her room that night."

171

"My God, O'Moy!" It was a strangled cry from Tremayne. At last he saw light; he understood, and, understanding, there entered his heart a great compassion for O'Moy, a conception that he must have suffered all the agonies of the damned in these last few days. "My God, you don't believe that I—"

"Do you deny it?"

"The imputation? Utterly."

"And if I tell you that myself with these eyes I saw you at the window of her room with her; if I tell you that I saw the rope ladder dangling from her balcony; if I tell you that crouching there after I had killed Samoval—killed him, mark me, for saying that you and my wife betrayed me; killed him for telling me the filthy truth—if I tell you that I heard her attempting to restrain you from going down to see what had happened—if I tell you all this, will you still deny it, will you still lie?"

"I will still say that all that you imply is false as hell and your own senseless jealousy can make it.

"All that I imply? But what I state—the facts themselves, are they true?"

"They are true. But—"

"True!" cried Miss Armytage in horror.

"Ah, wait," O'Moy bade her with his heavy sneer. "You interrupt him. He is about to construe those facts so that they shall wear an innocent appearance. He is about to prove himself worthy of the great sacrifice you made to save his life. Well?" And he looked expectantly at Tremayne.

Miss Armytage looked at him too, with eyes from which the dread passed almost at once. The captain was smiling, wistfully, tolerantly, confidently, almost scornfully. Had he been guilty of the thing imputed he could not have stood so in her presence.

"O'Moy," he said slowly, "I should tell you that you have played the knave in this were it not clear to me that you have played the fool." He spoke entirely without passion. He saw his way quite clearly. Things had reached a pass in which for the sake of all concerned, and perhaps for the sake of Miss Armytage more than any one, the whole truth must be spoken without regard to its consequences to Richard Butler.

"You dare to take that tone?" began O'Moy in a voice of thunder.

"Yourself shall be the first to justify it presently. I should be angry with you, O'Moy, for what you have done. But I find my anger vanishing in regret. I should scorn you for the lie you have acted, for your scant regard to your oath in the court-martial, for your attempt to combat an imagined villainy by a real villainy. But I realise what

172

you have suffered, and in that suffering lies the punishment you fully deserve for not having taken the straight course, for not having taxed me there and then with the thing that you suspected."

"The gentleman is about to lecture me upon morals, Sylvia." But Tremayne let pass the interruption.

"It is quite true that I was in Una's room while you were killing Samoval. But I was not alone with her, as you have so rashly assumed. Her brother Richard was there, and it was on his behalf that I was present. She had been hiding him for a fortnight. She begged me, as Dick's friend and her own, to save him; and I undertook to do so. I climbed to her room to assist him to descend by the rope ladder you saw, because he was wounded and could not climb without assistance. At the gates I had the curricle waiting in which I had driven up. In this I was to have taken him on board a ship that was leaving that night for England, having made arrangements with her captain. You should have seen, had you reflected, that—as I told the court—had I been coming to a clandestine meeting, I should hardly have driven up in so open a fashion, and left the curricle to wait for me at the gates.

"The death of Samoval and my own arrest thwarted our plans and prevented Dick's escape. That is the truth. Now that you have it I hope you like it, and I hope that you thoroughly relish your own behaviour in the matter."

There was a fluttering sigh of relief from Miss Armytage. Then silence followed, in which O'Moy stared at Tremayne, emotion after emotion sweeping across his mobile face.

"Dick Butler?" he said at last, and cried out: "I don't believe a word of it! Ye're lying, Tremayne."

"You have cause enough to hope so."

The captain was faintly scornful.

"If it were true, Una would not have kept it from me. It was to me she would have come."

"The trouble with you, O'Moy, is that jealousy seems to have robbed you of the power of coherent thought, or else you would remember that you were the last man to whom Una could confide Dick's presence here. I warned her against doing so. I told her of the promise you had been compelled to give the secretary, Forjas, and I was even at pains to justify you to her when she was indignant with you for that. It would perhaps be better," he concluded, "if you were to send for Una."

"It's what I intend," said Sir Terence in a voice that made a threat of the statement. He strode stiffly across the room and pulled open the door. There was no need to go farther. Lady O'Moy, white and tearful, was discovered on the threshold. Sir Terence stood aside, holding the door for her, his face very grim.

She came in slowly, looking from one to another with her troubled glance, and finally accepting the chair that Captain Tremayne made haste to offer her. She had so much to say to each person present that it was impossible to know where to begin. It remained for Sir Terence to give her the lead she needed, and this he did so soon as he had closed the door again. Planted before it like a sentry, he looked at her between anger and suspicion.

"How much did you overhear?" he asked her.

"All that you said about Dick," she answered without hesitation.

"Then you stood listening?"

"Of course. I wanted to know what you were saying."

"There are other ways of ascertaining that without stooping to keyholes," said her husband.

"I didn't stoop," she said, taking him literally. "I could hear what was said without that—especially what you said, Terence. You will raise your voice so on the slightest provocation."

"And the provocation in this instance was, of course, of the slightest. Since you have heard Captain Tremayne's story of course you'll have no difficulty in confirming it."

"If you still can doubt, O'Moy," said Tremayne, "it must be because you wish to doubt; because you are afraid to face the truth now that it has been placed before you. I think, Una, it will spare a deal of trouble, and save your husband from a great many expressions that he may afterwards regret, if you go and fetch Dick. God knows, Terence has enough to overwhelm him already."

At the suggestion of producing Dick, O'Moy's anger, which had begun to simmer again, was stilled. He looked at his wife almost in alarm, and she met his look with one of utter blankness.

"I can't," she said plaintively. "Dick's gone."

"Gone?" cried Tremayne.

"Gone?" said O'Moy, and then he began to laugh. "Are you quite sure that he was ever here?"

"But—" She was a little bewildered, and a frown puckered her perfect brow. "Hasn't Ned told you, then?"

"Oh, Ned has told me. Ned has told!" His face was terrible.

"And don't you believe him? Don't you believe me?" She was more plaintive than ever. It was almost as if she called heaven to witness what manner of husband she was forced to endure. "Then you had better call Mullins and ask him. He saw Dick leave."

"And no doubt," said Miss Armytage mercilessly, "Sir Terence will believe his butler where he can believe neither his wife nor his friend."

He looked at her in a sort of amazement. "Do you believe them, Sylvia?" he cried.

"I hope I am not a fool," said she impatiently.

"Meaning—" he began, but broke off. "How long do you say it is since Dick left the house?"

"Ten minutes at most," replied her ladyship.

He turned and pulled the door open again. "Mullins?" he called. "Mullins!"

"What a man to live with!" sighed her ladyship, appealing to Miss Armytage. "What a man!" And she applied a vinaigrette delicately to her nostrils.

Tremayne smiled, and sauntered to the window. And then at last came Mullins.

"Has any one left the house within the last ten minutes, Mullins?" asked Sir Terence.

Mullins looked ill at ease.

"Sure, sir, you'll not be after—"

"Will you answer my question, man?" roared Sir Terence.

"Sure, then, there's nobody left the house at all but Mr. Butler, sir."

"How long had he been here?" asked O'Moy, after a brief pause.

"'Tis what I can't tell ye, sir. I never set eyes on him until I saw him coming downstairs from her ladyship's room as it might be."

"You can go, Mullins."

"I hope, sir—"

"You can go." And Sir Terence slammed the door upon the amazed servant, who realised that some unhappy mystery was perturbing the adjutant's household.

Sir Terence stood facing them again. He was a changed man. The fire had all gone out of him. His head was bowed and his face looked haggard and suddenly old. His lip curled into a sneer.

"Pantaloon in the comedy," he said, remembering in that moment the bitter gibe that had cost Samoval his life.

"What did you say?" her ladyship asked him.

"I pronounced my own name," he answered lugubriously.

"It didn't sound like it, Terence."

"It's the name I ought to bear," he said. "And I killed that liar for it—the only truth he spoke."

He came forward to the table. The full sense of his position suddenly overwhelmed him, as Tremayne had said it would. A groan broke from him and he collapsed into a chair, a stricken, broken man.

175

CHAPTER XX

THE RESIGNATION

At once, as he sat there, his elbows on the table, his head in his hands, he found himself surrounded by those three, against each of whom he had sinned under the spell of the jealousy that had blinded him and led him by the nose.

His wife put an arm about his neck in mute comfort of a grief of which she only understood the half—for of the heavier and more desperate part of his guilt she was still in ignorance. Sylvia spoke to him kindly words of encouragement where no encouragement could avail. But what moved him most was the touch of Tremayne's hand upon his shoulder, and Tremayne's voice bidding him brace himself to face the situation and count upon them to stand by him to the end.

He looked up at his friend and secretary in an amazement that overcame his shame.

"You can forgive me, Ned?"

Ned looked across at Sylvia Armytage. "You have been the means of bringing me to such happiness as I should never have reached without these happenings," he said. "What resentment can I bear you, O'Moy? Besides, I understand, and who understands can never do anything but forgive. I realise how sorely you have been tried. No evidence more conclusive that you were being wronged could have been placed before you."

"But the court-martial," said O'Moy in horror. He covered his face with his hand. "Oh, my God! I am dishonoured. I—I—" He rose, shaking off the arm of his wife and the hand of the friend he had wronged so terribly. He broke away from them and strode to the window, his face set and white. "I think I was mad," he said. "I know I was mad. But to have done what I did—" He shuddered in very horror of himself now that he was bereft of the support of that evil jealousy that had fortified him against conscience itself and the very voice of honour. Lady O'Moy turned to them, pleading for explanation.

"What does he mean? What has he done?"

Himself he answered her: "I killed Samoval. It was I who fought that duel. And then believing what I did, I fastened the guilt upon Ned, and went the lengths of perjury in my blind effort to avenge myself. That is what I have done. Tell me, one of you, of your charity, what is there left for me to do?"

"Oh!" It was an outcry of horror and indignation from Una, instantly repressed by the tightening grip of Sylvia's hand upon her arm. Miss Armytage saw and understood, and sorrowed for Sir Terence. She must restrain his wife from adding to his present anguish. Yet, "How could you, Terence! Oh, how could you!" cried her ladyship, and so gave way to tears, easier than words to express such natures.

"Because I loved you, I suppose," he answered on a note of bitter self-mockery. "That was the justification I should have given had I been asked; that was the justification I accounted sufficient."

"But then," she cried, a new horror breaking on her mind—"if this is discovered—Terence, what will become of you?"

He turned and came slowly back until he stood beside her. Facing now the inevitable, he recovered some of his calm.

"It must be discovered," he said quietly. "For the sake of everybody concerned it must—"

"Oh, no, no!" She sprang up and clutched his arm in terror. "They may fail to discover the truth."

"They must not, my dear," he answered her; stroking the fair head that lay against his breast. "They must not fail. I must see to that."

"You? You?" Her eyes dilated as she looked at him. She caught her breath on a gasping sob. "Ah no, Terence," she cried wildly. "You must not; you must not. You must say nothing—for my sake, Terence, if you love me, oh, for my sake, Terence!"

"For honour's sake, I must," he answered her. "And for the sake of Sylvia and of Tremayne, whom I have wronged, and—"

"Not for my sake, Terence," Sylvia interrupted him.

He looked at her, and then at Tremayne.

"And you, Ned—what do you say?" he asked.

"Ned could not wish—" began her ladyship.

"Please let him speak for himself, my dear," her husband interrupted her.

"What can I say?" cried Tremayne, with a gesture that was almost of anger. "How can I advise? I scarcely know. You realise what you must face if you confess?"

"Fully, and the only part of it I shrink from is the shame and scorn I have deserved. Yet it is inevitable. You agree, Ned?"

"I am not sure. None who understands as I understand can feel anything but regret. Oh, I don't know. The evidence of what you suspected was overwhelming, and it betrayed you into this mistake. The punishment you would have to face is surely too heavy, and you have suffered far more already than you can ever be called upon to suffer again, no matter what is done to you. Oh, I don't know! The

177

problem is too deep for me. There is Una to be considered, too. You owe a duty to her, and if you keep silent it may be best for all. You can depend upon us to stand by you in this."

"Indeed, indeed," said Sylvia.

He looked at them and smiled very tenderly.

"Never was a man blessed with nobler friends who deserved so little of them," he said slowly. "You heap coals of fire upon my head. You shame me through and through. But have you considered, Ned, that all may not depend upon my silence? What if the provost-marshal, investigating now, were to come upon the real facts?"

"It is impossible that sufficient should be discovered to convict you."

"How can you be sure of that? And if it were possible, if it came to pass, what then would be my position? You see, Ned! I must accept the punishment I have incurred lest a worse overtake me—to put it at its lowest. I must voluntarily go forward and denounce myself before another denounces me. It is the only way to save some rag of honour."

There was a tap at the door, and Mullins came to announce that Lord Wellington was asking to see Sir Terence.

"He is waiting in the study, Sir Terence."

"Tell his lordship I will be with him at once."

Mullins departed, and Sir Terence prepared to follow. Gently he disengaged himself from the arms her ladyship now flung about him.

"Courage, my dear," he said. "Wellington may show me more mercy than I deserve."

"You are going to tell him?" she questioned brokenly.

"Of course, sweetheart. What else can I do? And since you and Tremayne find it in your hearts to forgive me, nothing else matters very much." He kissed her tenderly and put her from him. He looked at Sylvia standing beside her and at Tremayne beyond the table. "Comfort her," he implored them, and, turning, went out quickly.

Awaiting him in the study he found not only Lord Wellington, but Colonel Grant, and by the cold gravity of both their faces he had an inspiration that in some mysterious way the whole hideous truth was already known to them.

The slight figure of his lordship in its grey frock was stiff and erect, his booted leg firmly planted, his hands behind him clutching his riding-crop and cocked hat. His face was set and his voice as he greeted O'Moy sharp and staccato.

"Ah, O'Moy, there are one or two matters to be discussed before I leave Lisbon."

"I had written to you, sir," replied O'Moy. "Perhaps you will first read my letter." And he went to fetch it from the writing-table, where he had left it when completed an hour earlier.

His lordship took the letter in silence, and after one piercing glance at O'Moy broke the seal. In the background, near the window, the tall figure of Colquhoun Grant stood stiffly erect, his hawk face inscrutable.

"Ah! Your resignation, O'Moy. But you give no reasons." Again his keen glance stabbed into the adjutant's face. "Why this?" he asked sharply.

"Because," said Sir Terence, "I prefer to tender it before it is asked of me." He was very white, yet by an effort those deep blue eyes of his met the terrible gaze of his chief without flinching.

"Perhaps you'll explain," said his lordship coldly.

"In the first place," said O'Moy, "it was myself killed Samoval, and since your lordship was a witness of what followed, you will realise that that was the least part of my offence."

The great soldier jerked his head sharply backward, tilting forward his chin. "So!" he said. "Ha! I beg your pardon, Grant, for having disbelieved you." Then, turning to O'Moy again: "Well," he demanded, his voice hard, "have you nothing to add?"

"Nothing that can matter," said O'Moy, with a shrug, and they stood facing each other in silence for a long moment.

At last when Wellington spoke his voice had assumed a gentler note.

"O'Moy," he said, "I have known you these fifteen years, and we have been friends. Once you carried your friendship, appreciation, and understanding of me so far as nearly to ruin yourself on my behalf. You'll not have forgotten the affair of Sir Harry Burrard. In all these years I have known you for a man of shining honour, an honest, upright gentleman, whom I would have trusted when I should have distrusted every other living man. Yet you stand there and confess to me the basest, the most dishonest villainy that I have ever known a British officer to commit, and you tell me that you have no explanation to offer for your conduct. Either I have never known you, O'Moy, or I do not know you now. Which is it?"

O'Moy raised his arms, only to let them fall heavily to his sides again.

"What explanation can there be?" he asked. "How can a man who has been—as I hope I have—a man of honour in the past explain such an act of madness? It arose out of your order against

179

duelling," he went on. "Samoval offended me mortally. He said such things to me of my wife's honour that no man could suffer, and I least of any man. My temper betrayed me. I consented to a clandestine meeting without seconds. It took place here, and I killed him. And then I had, as I imagined—quite wrongly, as I know now—overwhelming evidence that what he had told me was true, and I went mad." Briefly he told the story of Tremayne's descent from Lady O'Moy's balcony and the rest.

"I scarcely know," he resumed, "what it was I hoped to accomplish in the end. I do not know—for I never stopped to consider—whether I should have allowed Captain Tremayne to have been shot if it had come to that. All that I was concerned to do was to submit him to the ordeal which I conceived he must undergo when he saw himself confronted with the choice of keeping silence and submitting to his fate, or saving himself by an avowal that could scarcely be less bitter than death itself."

"You fool, O'Moy-you damned, infernal fool!" his lordship swore at him. "Grant overheard more than you imagined that night outside the gates. His conclusions ran the truth very close indeed. But I could not believe him, could not believe this of you.'"

"Of course not," said O'Moy gloomily. "I can't believe it of myself."

"When Miss Armytage intervened to afford Tremayne an alibi, I believed her, in view of what Grant had told me; I concluded that hers was the window from which Tremayne had climbed down. Because of what I knew I was there to see that the case did not go to extremes against Tremayne. If necessary Grant must have given full evidence of all he knew, and there and then left you to your fate. Miss Armytage saved us from that, and left me convinced, but still not understanding your own attitude. And now comes Richard Butler to surrender to me and cast himself upon my mercy with another tale which completely gives the lie to Miss Armytage's, but confirms your own."

"Richard Butler!" cried O'Moy. "He has surrendered to you?"

"Half-an-hour ago."

Sir Terence turned aside with a weary shrug. A little laugh that was more a sob broke from him. "Poor Una!" he muttered.

"The tangle is a shocking one—lies, lies everywhere, and in the places where they were least to be expected." Wellington's anger flashed out. "Do you realise what awaits you as a result of all this damned insanity?"

"I do, sir. That is why I place my resignation in your hands. The disregard of a general order punishable in any officer is beyond pardon in your adjutant-general."

"But that is the least of it, you fool."

"Sure, don't I know? I assure you that I realise it all."

"And you are prepared to face it?" Wellington was almost savage in an anger proceeding from the conflict that went on within him. There was his duty as commander-in-chief, and there was his friendship for O'Moy and his memory of the past in which O'Moy's loyalty had almost been the ruin of him.

"What choice have I?"

His lordship turned away, and strode the length of the room, his head bent, his lips twitching. Suddenly he stopped and faced the silent intelligence officer.

"What is to be done, Grant?"

"That is a matter for your lordship. But if I might venture—"

"Venture and be damned," snapped Wellington.

"The signal service rendered the cause of the allies by the death of Samoval might perhaps be permitted to weigh against the offence committed by O'Moy."

"How could it?" snapped his lordship. "You don't know, O'Moy, that upon Samoval's body were found certain documents intended for Massena. Had they reached him, or had Samoval carried out the full intentions that dictated his quarrel with you, and no doubt sent him here depending upon his swordsmanship to kill you, all my plans for the undoing of the French would have been ruined. Ay, you may stare. That is another matter in which you have lacked discretion. You may be a fine engineer, O'Moy, but I don't think I could have found a less judicious adjutant-general if I had raked the ranks of the army on purpose to find an idiot. Samoval was a spy—the cleverest spy that we have ever had to deal with. Only his death revealed how dangerous he was. For killing him when you did you deserve the thanks of his Majesty's Government, as Grant suggests. But before you can receive those you will have to stand a court-martial for the manner in which you killed him, and you will probably be shot. I can't help you. I hope you don't expect it of me."

"The thought had not so much as occurred to me. Yet what you tell me, sir, lifts something of the load from my mind."

"Does it? Well, it lifts no load from mine," was the angry retort. He stood considering. Then with an impatient gesture he seemed to dismiss his thoughts. "I can do nothing," he said, "nothing without being false to my duty and becoming as bad as you have been, O'Moy, and without any of the sentimental justification that existed in your case. I can't allow the matter to be dropped, stifled. I have never been guilty of such a thing, and I refuse to become guilty of it now. I refuse—do you understand? O'Moy, you have acted; and you must take the consequences, and be damned to you."

"Faith, I've never asked you to help me, sir," Sir Terence protested.

"And you don't intend to, I suppose?"

"I do not."

"I am glad of that." He was in one of those rages which were as terrible as they were rare with him. "I wouldn't have you suppose that I make laws for the sake of rescuing people from the consequences of disobeying them. Here is this brother-in-law of yours, this fellow Butler, who has made enough mischief in the country to imperil our relations with our allies. And I am half pledged to condone his adventure at Tavora. There's nothing for it, O'Moy. As your friend, I am infernally angry with you for placing yourself in this position; as your commanding officer I can only order you under arrest and convene a court-martial to deal with you."

Sir Terence bowed his head. He was a little surprised by all this heat. "I never expected anything else," he said. "And it's altogether at a loss I am to understand why your lordship should be vexing yourself in this manner."

"Because I've a friendship for you, O'Moy. Because I remember that you've been a loyal friend to me. And because I must forget all this and remember only that my duty is absolutely rigid and inflexible. If I condoned your offence, if I suppressed inquiry, I should be in duty and honour bound to offer my own resignation to his Majesty's Government. And I have to think of other things besides my personal feelings, when at any moment now the French may be over the Agueda and into Portugal."

Sir Terence's face flushed, and his glance brightened.

"From my heart I thank you that you can even think of such things at such a time and after what I have done."

"Oh, as to what you have done—I understand that you are a fool, O'Moy. There's no more to be said. You are to consider yourself under arrest. I must do it if you were my own brother, which, thank God, you're not. Come, Grant. Good-bye, O'Moy." And he held out his hand to him.

Sir Terence hesitated, staring.

"It's the hand of your friend, Arthur Wellesley, I'm offering you, not the hand of your commanding officer," said his lordship savagely.

Sir Terence took it, and wrung it in silence, perhaps more deeply moved than he had yet been by anything that had happened to him that morning.

There was a knock at the door, and Mullins opened it to admit the adjutant's orderly, who came stiffly to attention.

"Major Carruthers's compliments, sir," he said to O'Moy, "and his Excellency the Secretary of the Council of Regency wishes to see you very urgently."

There was a pause. O'Moy shrugged and spread his hands. This message was for the adjutant-general and he no longer filled the office.

"Pray tell Major Carruthers that I—" he was beginning, when Lord Wellington intervened.

"Desire his Excellency to step across here. I will see him myself."

CHAPTER XXI

SANCTUARY

"I will withdraw, sir," said Terence.

But Wellington detained him. "Since Dom Miguel asked for you, you had better remain, perhaps."

"It is the adjutant-general Dom Miguel desires to see, and I am adjutant-general no longer."

"Still, the matter may concern you. I have a notion that it may be concerned with the death of Count Samoval, since I have acquainted the Council of Regency with the treason practised by the Count. You had better remain."

Gloomy and downcast, Sir Terence remained as he was bidden.

The sleek and supple Secretary of State was ushered in. He came forward quickly, clicked his heels together and bowed to the three men present.

"Sirs, your obedient servant," he announced himself, with a courtliness almost out of fashion, speaking in his extraordinarily fluent English. His sallow countenance was extremely grave. He seemed even a little ill at ease.

"I am fortunate to find you here, my lord. The matter upon which I seek your adjutant-general is of considerable gravity—so much that of himself he might be unable to resolve it. I feared you might already have departed for the north."

"Since you suggest that my presence may be of service to you, I am happy that circumstances should have delayed my departure," was his lordship's courteous answer. "A chair, Dom Miguel."

Dom Miguel Forjas accepted the proffered chair, whilst Wellington seated himself at Sir Terence's desk. Sir Terence himself remained standing with his shoulders to the overmantel, whence he faced them both as well as Grant, who, according to his self-effacing habit, remained in the background by the window.

"I have sought you," began Dom Miguel, stroking his square chin, "on a matter concerned with the late Count Samoval, immediately upon hearing that the court-martial pronounced the acquittal of Captain Tremayne."

His lordship frowned, and his eagle glance fastened upon the Secretary's face.

"I trust, sir, you have not come to question the finding of the court-martial."

"Oh, on the contrary—on the contrary!" Dom Miguel was emphatic. "I represent not only the Council, but the Samoval family as well. Both realise that it is perhaps fortunate for all concerned that in arresting Captain Tremayne the military authorities arrested the wrong man, and both have reason to dread the arrest of the right one."

He paused, and the frown deepened between Wellington's brows.

"I am afraid," he said slowly, "that I do not quite perceive their concern in this matter."

"But is it not clear?" cried Dom Miguel.

"If it were I should perceive it," said his lordship dryly.

"Ah, but let me explain, then. A further investigation of the manner in which Count Samoval met his death can hardly fail to bring to light the deplorable practices in which he was engaged; for no doubt Colonel Grant, here, would consider it his duty in the interests of justice to place before the court the documents found upon the Count's dead body. If I may permit myself an observation," he continued, looking round at Colonel Grant, "it is that I do not quite understand how this has not already happened."

There was a pause in which Grant looked at Wellington as if for direction. But his lordship himself assumed the burden of the answer.

"It was not considered expedient in the public interest to do so at present," he said. "And the circumstances did not place us under the necessity of divulging the matter."

"There, my lord, if you will allow me to say so, you acted with a delicacy and wisdom which the circumstances may not again permit. Indeed any further investigation must almost inevitably bring these matters to light, and the effect of such revelation would be deplorable."

"Deplorable to whom?" asked his lordship.

"To the Count's family and to the Council of Regency."

"I can sympathise with the Count's family, but not with the Council."

"Surely, my lord, the Council as a body deserves your sympathy in that it is in danger of being utterly discredited by the treason of one or two of its members."

Wellington manifested impatience. "The Council has been warned time and again. I am weary of warning, and even of threatening, the Council with the consequences of resisting my policy. I think that exposure is not only what it deserves, but the surest means of providing a healthier government in the future. I am weary of picking my way through the web of intrigue with which the Council entangles my movements and my dispositions. Public sympathy has enabled it to hamper me in this fashion. That sympathy will be lost to it by the disclosures which you fear."

"My lord, I must confess that there is much reason in what you say." He was smoothly conciliatory. "I understand your exasperation. But may I be permitted to assure you that it is not the Council as a body that has withstood you, but certain self-seeking members, one or two friends of Principal Souza, in whose interests the unfortunate and misguided Count Samoval was acting. Your lordship will perceive that the moment is not one in which to stir up public indignation against the Portuguese Government. Once the passions of the mob are inflamed, who can say to what lengths they may not go, who can say what disastrous consequences may not follow? It is desirable to apply the cautery, but not to burn up the whole body."

Lord Wellington considered a moment, fingering an ivory paper-knife. He was partly convinced.

"When I last suggested the cautery, to use your own very apt figure, the Council did not keep faith with me."

"My lord!"

"It did not, sir. It removed Antonio de Souza, but it did not take the trouble to go further and remove his friends at the same time. They remained to carry on his subversive treacherous intrigues. What guarantees have I that the Council will behave better on this occasion?"

"You have our solemn assurances, my lord, that all those members suspected of complicity in this business or of attachment to the Souza faction, shall be compelled to resign, and you may depend upon the reconstituted Council loyally to support your measures."

"You give me assurances, sir, and I ask for guarantees."

"Your lordship is in possession of the documents found upon Count Samoval. The Council knows this, and this knowledge will compel it to guard against further intrigues on the part of any of its members which might naturally exasperate you into publishing those documents. Is not that some guarantee?"

His lordship considered, and nodded slowly. "I admit that it is. Yet I do not see how this publicity is to be avoided in the course of the further investigations into the manner in which Count Samoval came by his death."

"My lord, that is the pivot of the whole matter. All further investigation must be suspended."

Sir Terence trembled, and his eyes turned in eager anxiety upon the inscrutable, stern face of Lord Wellington.

"Must!" cried his lordship sharply.

"What else, my lord, in all our interests?" exclaimed the Secretary, and he rose in his agitation.

"And what of British justice, sir?" demanded his lordship in a forbidding tone.

"British justice has reason to consider itself satisfied. British justice may assume that Count Samoval met his death in the pursuit of his treachery. He was a spy caught in the act, and there and then destroyed—a very proper fate. Had he been taken, British justice would have demanded no less. It has been anticipated. Cannot British justice, for the sake of British interests as well as Portuguese interests, be content to leave the matter there?"

"An argument of expediency, eh?" said Wellington. "Why not, my lord! Does not expediency govern politicians?"

"I am not a politician."

"But a wise soldier, my lord, does not lose sight of the political consequences of his acts." And he sat down again.

"Your Excellency may be right," said his lordship. "Let us be quite clear, then. You suggest, speaking in the name of the Council of Regency, that I should suppress all further investigations into the manner in which Count Samoval met his death, so as to save his family the shame and the Council of Regency the discredit which must overtake one and the other if the facts are disclosed—as disclosed they would be that Samoval was a traitor and a spy in the pay of the French. That is what you ask me to do. In return your Council undertakes that there shall be no further opposition to my plans for the military defence of Portugal, and that all my measures however harsh and however heavily they may weigh upon the landowners, shall be punctually and faithfully carried out. That is your Excellency's proposal, is it not?"

"Not so much my proposal, my lord, as my most earnest intercession. We desire to spare the innocent the consequences of the sins of a man who is dead, and well dead." He turned to O'Moy, standing there tense and anxious. It was not for Dom Miguel to know that it was the adjutant's fate that was being decided. "Sir Terence," he cried, "you have been here for a year, and all matters connected with the Council have been treated through you. You cannot fail to see the wisdom of my recommendation."

His lordship's eyes flashed round upon O'Moy. "Ah yes!" he said. "What is your feeling in this matter, 'O'Moy?" he inquired, his tone and manner void of all expression.

Sir Terence faltered; then stiffened. "I—The matter is one that only your lordship can decide. I have no wish to influence your decision."

187

"I see. Ha! And you, Grant? No doubt you agree with Dom Miguel?"

"Most emphatically—upon every count, sir," replied the intelligence officer without hesitation. "I think Dom Miguel offers an excellent bargain. And, as he says, we hold a guarantee of its fulfilment."

"The bargain might be improved," said Wellington slowly.

"If your lordship will tell me how, the Council, I am sure, will be ready to do all that lies in its power to satisfy you."

Wellington shifted his chair round a little, and crossed his legs. He brought his finger-tips together, and over the top of them his eyes considered the Secretary of State.

"Your Excellency has spoken of expediency—political expediency. Sometimes political expediency can overreach itself and perpetrate the most grave injustices. Individuals at times are unnecessarily called upon to suffer in the interests of a cause. Your Excellency will remember a certain affair at Tavora some two months ago—the invasion of a convent by a British officer with rather disastrous consequences and the loss of some lives."

"I remember it perfectly, my lord. I had the honour of entertaining Sir Terence upon that subject on the occasion of my last visit here."

"Quite so," said his lordship. "And on the grounds of political expediency you made a bargain then with Sir Terence, I understand, a bargain which entailed the perpetration of an injustice."

"I am not aware of it, my lord."

"Then let me refresh your Excellency's memory upon the facts. To appease the Council of Regency, or rather to enable me to have my way with the Council and remove the Principal Souza, you stipulated for the assurance—so that you might lay it before your Council—that the offending officer should be shot when taken."

"I could not help myself in the matter, and—"

"A moment, sir. That is not the way of British justice, and Sir Terence was wrong to have permitted himself to consent; though I profoundly appreciate the loyalty to me, the earnest desire to assist me, which led him into an act the cost of which to himself your Excellency can hardly appreciate. But the wrong lay in that by virtue of this bargain a British officer was prejudged. He was to be made a scapegoat. He was to be sent to his death when taken, as a peace-offering to the people, demanded by the Council of Regency.

"Since all this happened I have had the facts of the case placed before me. I will go so far as to tell you, sir, that the officer in question has been in my hands for the past hour, that I have closely questioned him, and that I am satisfied that whilst he has been guilty of conduct which might compel me to deprive him of his Majesty's commission and dismiss him from the army, yet that conduct is not such as to merit death. He has chiefly sinned in folly and want of judgment. I reprove it in the sternest terms, and I deplore the consequences it had. But for those consequences the nuns of Tavora are almost as much to blame as he is himself. His invasion of their convent was a pure error, committed in the belief that it was a monastery and as a result of the porter's foolish conduct.

"Now, Sir Terence's word, given in response to your absolute demands, has committed us to an unjust course, which I have no intention of following. I will stipulate, sir, that your Council, in addition to the matters undertaken, shall relieve us of all obligation in this matter, leaving it to our discretion to punish Mr. Butler in such manner as we may consider condign. In return, your Excellency, I will undertake that there shall be no further investigation into the manner in which Count Samoval came by his death, and consequently, no disclosures of the shameful trade in which he was engaged. If your Excellency will give yourself the trouble of taking the sense of your Council upon this, we may then reach a settlement."

The grave anxiety of Dom Miguel's countenance was instantly dispelled. In his relief he permitted himself a smile.

"My lord, there is not the need to take the sense of the Council. The Council has given me carte blanche to obtain your consent to a suppression of the Samoval affair. And without hesitation I accept the further condition that you make. Sir Terence may consider himself relieved of his parole in the matter of Lieutenant Butler."

"Then we may look upon the matter as concluded."

"As happily concluded, my lord." Dom Miguel rose to make his valedictory oration. "It remains for me only to thank your lordship in the name of the Council for the courtesy and consideration with which you have received my proposal and granted our petition. Acquainted as I am with the crystalline course of British justice, knowing as I do how it seeks ever to act in the full light of day, I am profoundly sensible of the cost to your lordship of the concession you make to the feelings of the Samoval family and the Portuguese Government, and I can assure you that they will be accordingly grateful."

"That is very gracefully said, Dom Miguel," replied his lordship, rising also.

The Secretary placed a hand upon his heart, bowing. "It is but the poor expression of what I think and feel." And so he took his leave of them, escorted by Colonel Grant, who discreetly volunteered for the office.

Left alone with Wellington, Sir Terence heaved a great sigh of supreme relief.

"In my wife's name, sir, I should like to thank you. But she shall thank you herself for what you have done for me."

"What I have done for you, O'Moy?" Wellington's slight figure stiffened perceptibly, his face and glance were cold and haughty. "You mistake, I think, or else you did not hear. What I have done, I have done solely upon grounds of political expediency. I had no choice in the matter, and it was not to favour you, or out of disregard for my duty, as you seem to imagine, that I acted as I did."

O'Moy bowed his head, crushed under that rebuff. He clasped and unclasped his hands a moment in his desperate anguish.

"I understand," he muttered in a broken voice, "I—I beg your pardon, sir."

And then Wellington's slender, firm fingers took him by the arm.

"But I am glad, O'Moy, that I had no choice," he added more gently. "As a man, I suppose I may be glad that my duty as Commander-in-Chief placed me under the necessity of acting as I have done."

Sir Terence clutched the hand in both his own and wrung it fiercely, obeying an overmastering impulse.

"Thank you," he cried. "Thank you for that!"

"Tush!" said Wellington, and then abruptly: "What are you going to do, O'Moy?" he asked.

"Do?" said O'Moy, and his blue eyes looked pleadingly down into the sternly handsome face of his chief, "I am in your hands, sir."

"Your resignation is, and there it must remain, O'Moy. You understand?"

"Of course, sir. Naturally you could not after this—" He shrugged and broke off. "But must I go home?" he pleaded.

"What else? And, by God, sir, you should be thankful, I think."

"Very well," was the dull answer, and then he flared out. "Faith, it's your own fault for giving me a job of this kind. You knew me. You know that I am just a blunt, simple soldier—that my place is at the head of a regiment, not at the head of an administration. You should have known that by putting me out of my proper element I was bound to get into trouble sooner or later."

"Perhaps I do," said Wellington. "But what am I to do with you now?" He shrugged, and strode towards the window. "You had better go home, O'Moy. Your health has suffered out here, and you are not equal to the heat of summer that is now increasing. That is the reason of this resignation. You understand?"

"I shall be shamed for ever," said O'Moy. "To go home when the army is about to take the field!"

But Wellington did not hear him, or did not seem to hear him. He had reached the window and his eye was caught by something that he saw in the courtyard.

"What the devil's this now?" he rapped out. "That is one of Sir Robert Craufurd's aides."

He turned and went quickly to the door. He opened it as rapid steps approached along the passage, accompanied by the jingle of spurs and the clatter of sabretache and trailing sabre. Colonel Grant appeared, followed by a young officer of Light Dragoons who was powdered from head to foot with dust. The youth—he was little more—lurched forward wearily, yet at sight of Wellington he braced himself to attention and saluted.

"You appear to have ridden hard, sir," the Commander greeted him.

"From Almeida in forty-seven hours, my lord," was the answer. "With these from Sir Robert." And he proffered a sealed letter.

"What is your name?" Wellington inquired, as he took the package.

"Hamilton, my lord," was the answer; "Hamilton of the Sixteenth, aide-de-camp to Sir Robert Craufurd."

Wellington nodded. "That was great horsemanship, Mr. Hamilton," he commended him; and a faint tinge in the lad's haggard cheeks responded to that rare praise.

"The urgency was great, my lord," replied Mr. Hamilton.

"The French columns are in movement. Ney and Junot advanced to the investment of Ciudad Rodrigo on the first of the month."

"Already!" exclaimed Wellington, and his countenance set.

"The commander, General Herrasti, has sent an urgent appeal to Sir Robert for assistance."

"And Sir Robert?" The question came on a sharp note of apprehension, for his lordship was fully aware that valour was the better part of Sir Robert Craufurd's discretion.

"Sir Robert asks for orders in this dispatch, and refuses to stir from Almeida without instructions from your lordship."

"Ah!!" It was a sigh of relief. He broke the seal and spread the dispatch. He read swiftly. "Very well," was all he said, when he had reached the end of Sir Robert's letter. "I shall reply to this in person and at, once. You will be in need of rest, Mr. Hamilton. You had best take a day to recuperate, then follow me to Almeida. Sir Terence no doubt will see to your immediate needs."

"With pleasure, Mr. Hamilton," replied Sir Terence mechanically—for his own concerns weighed upon him at this moment more heavily than the French advance. He pulled the bell-rope, and into the fatherly hands of Mullins, who came in response to the summons, the young officer was delivered.

Lord Wellington took up his hat and riding-crop from Sir Terence's desk. "I shall leave for the frontier at once," he announced. "Sir Robert will need the encouragement of my presence to keep him within the prudent bounds I have imposed. And I do not know how long Ciudad Rodrigo may be able to hold out. At any moment we may have the French upon the Agueda, and the invasion may begin. As for you, O'Moy, this has changed everything. The French and the needs of the case have decided. For the present no change is possible in the administration here in Lisbon. You hold the threads of your office and the moment is not one in which to appoint another adjutant to take them over. Such a thing might be fatal to the success of the British arms. You must withdraw this resignation." And he proffered the document.

Sir Terence recoiled. He went deathly white.

"I cannot," he stammered. "After what has happened, I—"

Lord Wellington's face became set and stern. His eyes blazed upon the adjutant.

"O'Moy," he said, and the concentrated anger of his voice was terrifying, "if you suggest that any considerations but those of this campaign have the least weight with me in what I now do, you insult me. I yield to no man in my sense of duty, and I allow no private considerations to override it. You are saved from going home in disgrace by the urgency of the circumstances, as I have told you. By that and by nothing else. Be thankful, then; and in loyally remaining at your post efface what is past. You know what is doing at Torres Vedras. The works have been under your direction from the commencement. See that they are vigorously pushed forward and that the lines are ready to receive the army in a month's time from now if necessary. I depend upon you—the army and England's honour depend upon you. I bow to the inevitable and so shall you." Then his sternness relaxed. "So much as your commanding officer. Now as your friend," and he held out his hand, "I congratulate you upon your luck. After this morning's manifestations of it, it should pass into a proverb. Goodbye, O'Moy. I trust you, remember."

"And I shall not fail you," gulped O'Moy, who, strong man that he was, found himself almost on the verge of tears. He clutched the extended hand.

"I shall fix my headquarters for the present at Celorico. Communicate with me there. And now one other matter: the Council of Regency will no doubt pester you with representations that I should—if time still remains—advance to the relief of Ciudad Rodrigo. Understand, that is no part of my plan of campaign. I do not stir across the frontier of Portugal. Here let the French come and find me, and I shall be ready to receive them. Let the Portuguese Government have no illusions on that point, and stimulate the Council into doing all possible to carry out the destruction of mills and the laying waste of the country in the valley of the Mondego and wherever else I have required.

"Oh, and by the way, you will find your brother-in-law, Mr. Butler, in the guard-room yonder, awaiting my orders. Provide him with a uniform and bid him rejoin his regiment at once. Recommend him to be more prudent in future if he wishes me to forget his escapade at Tavora. And in future, O'Moy, trust your wife. Again, good-bye. Come, Grant!—I have instructions for you too. But you must take them as we ride."

And thus Sir Terence O'Moy found sanctuary at the altar of his country's need. They left him incredulously to marvel at the luck which had so enlisted circumstances to save him where all had seemed so surely lost an hour ago.

He sent a servant to fetch Mr. Butler, the prime cause of all this pother—for all of it can be traced to Mr. Butler's invasion of the Tavora nunnery—and with him went to bear the incredible tidings of their joint absolution to the three who waited so anxiously in the dining-room.

POSTSCRIPTUM

The particular story which I have set myself to relate, of how Sir Terence O'Moy was taken in the snare of his own jealousy, may very properly be concluded here. But the greater story in which it is enshrined and with which it is interwoven, the story of that other snare in which my Lord Viscount Wellington took the French, goes on. This story is the history of the war in the Peninsula. There you may pursue it to its very end and realise the iron will and inflexibility of purpose which caused men ultimately to bestow upon him who guided that campaign the singularly felicitous and fitting sobriquet of the Iron Duke.

Ciudad Rodrigo's Spanish garrison capitulated on the 10th of July of that year 1810, and a wave of indignation such as must have overwhelmed any but a man of almost superhuman mettle swept up against Lord Wellington for having stood inactive within the frontiers of Portugal and never stirred a hand to aid the Spaniards. It was not only from Spain that bitter invective was hurled upon him; British journalism poured scorn and rage upon his incompetence, French journalism held his pusillanimity up to the ridicule of the world. His own officers took shame in their general, and expressed it. Parliament demanded to know how long British honour was to be imperilled by such a man. And finally the Emperor's great marshal, Massena, gathering his hosts to overwhelm the kingdom of Portugal, availed himself of all this to appeal to the Portuguese nation in terms which the facts would seem to corroborate.

He issued his proclamation denouncing the British for the disturbers and mischief-makers of Europe, warning the Portuguese that they were the cat's-paw of a perfidious nation that was concerned solely with the serving of its own interests and the gratification of its predatory ambitions, and finally summoning them to receive the French as their true friends and saviours.

The nation stirred uneasily. So far no good had come to them of their alliance with the British. Indeed Wellington's policy of devastation had seemed to those upon whom it fell more horrible than any French invasion could have been.

But Wellington held the reins, and his grip never relaxed or slackened. And here let it be recorded that he was nobly and stoutly served in Lisbon by Sir Terence O'Moy. Pressure upon the Council resulted in the measures demanded being carried out. But much time had been lost through the intrigues of the Souza faction, with

194

the result that those measures, although prosecuted now more vigorously, never reached the full extent which Wellington had desired. Treachery, too, stepped in to shorten the time still further. Almeida, garrisoned by Portuguese and commanded by Colonel Cox and a British staff, should have held a month. But no sooner had the French appeared before it, on the 26th August, than a powder magazine traitorously fired exploded and breached the wall, rendering the place untenable.

To Wellington this was perhaps the most vexatious of all things in that vexatious time. He had hoped to detain Massena before Almeida until the rains should have set in, when the French would have found themselves struggling through a sodden, water-logged country, through bridgeless floods and a land bereft of all that could sustain the troops. Still, what could be done Wellington did, and did it nobly. Fighting a rearguard action, he fell back upon the grim and naked ridges of Busaco, where at the end of September he delivered battle and a murderous detaining wound upon the advancing hosts of France. That done, he continued the retreat through Coimbra. And now as he went he saw to it that the devastation was completed along the line of march. What corn and provisions could not be carried off were burnt or buried, and the people forced to quit their dwellings and march with the army—a pathetic, southward exodus of men and women, old and young, flocks of sheep, and herds of cattle, creaking bullock-carts laden with provender and household goods, leaving behind them a country bare as the Sahara, where hunger before long should grip the French army too far committed now to pause. In advancing and overtaking must lie Massena's hope. Eventually in Lisbon he must bring the British to bay, and, breaking them, open out at last his way into a land of plenty.

Thus thought Massena, knowing nothing of the lines of Torres Vedras; and thus, too, thought the British Government at home, itself declaring that Wellington was ruining the country to no purpose, since in the end the British must be driven out with terrible loss and infamy that must make their name an opprobrium in the world.

But Wellington went his relentless way, and at the end of the first week of October brought his army and the multitude of refugees safely within the amazing lines. The French, pressing hard upon their heels and confident that the end was near, were brought up sharply before those stupendous, unsuspected, impregnable fortifications.

After spending best part of a month in vain reconnoitering, Massena took up his quarters at Santarem, and thence the country was scoured for what scraps of victuals had been left to relieve the dire straits of the famished host of France. How the great marshal contrived to hold out so long in Santarem against the onslaught of famine and concomitant disease remains something of a mystery. An appeal to the Emperor for succour eventually brought Drouet with provisions, but these were no more than would keep his men alive on a retreat into Spain, and that retreat he commenced early in the following March, by when no less than ten thousand of his army had fallen sick.

Instantly Wellington was up and after him. The French retreat became a flight. They threw away baggage and ammunition that they might travel the lighter. Thus they fled towards Spain, harassed by the British cavalry and scarcely less by the resentful peasantry of Portugal, their line of march defined by an unbroken trail of carcasses, until the tattered remnants of that once splendid army found shelter across the Coira. Beyond this Wellington could not continue the pursuit for lack of means to cross the swollen river and also because provisions were running short.

But there for the moment he might rest content, his immediate object achieved and his stern strategy supremely vindicated.

On the heights above the yellow, turgid flood rode Wellington with a glittering staff that included O'Moy and Murray, the quartermaster-general. Through his telescope he surveyed with silent satisfaction the straggling columns of the French that were being absorbed by the evening mists from the sodden ground.

O'Moy, at his side, looked on without satisfaction. To him the close of this phase of the campaign which had justified his remaining in office meant the reopening of that painful matter that had been left in suspense by circumstances since that June day of last year at Monsanto. The resignation then refused from motives of expediency must again be tendered and must now be accepted.

Abruptly upon the general stillness came a sharply humming sound. Within a yard of the spot where Wellington sat his horse a handful of soil heaved itself up and fell in a tiny scattered shower. Immediately elsewhere in a dozen places was the phenomenon repeated. There was too much glitter about the staff uniforms and vindictive French sharpshooters were finding them an attractive mark.

"They are firing on us, sir!" cried O'Moy on a note of sharp alarm.

"So I perceive," Lord Wellington answered calmly, and leisurely he closed his glass, so leisurely that O'Moy, in impatient fear of his chief, spurred forward and placed himself as a screen between him and the line of fire.

Lord Wellington looked at him with a faint smile. He was about to speak when O'Moy pitched forward and rolled headlong from the saddle.

They picked him up unconscious but alive, and for once Lord Wellington was seen to blench as he flung down from his horse to inquire the nature of O'Moy's hurt. It was not fatal, but, as it afterwards proved, it was grave enough. He had been shot through the body, the right lung had been grazed and one of his ribs broken.

Two days later, after the bullet had been extracted, Lord Wellington went to visit him in the house where he was quartered. Bending over him and speaking quietly, his lordship said that which brought a moisture to the eyes of Sir Terence and a smile to his pale lips. What actually were his lordship's words may be gathered from the answer he received.

"Ye're entirely wrong, then, and it's mighty glad I am. For now I need no longer hand you my resignation. I can be invalided home."

So he was; and thus it happens that not until now—when this chronicle makes the matter public—does the knowledge of Sir Terence's single but grievous departure from the path of honour go beyond the few who were immediately concerned with it. They kept faith with him because they loved him; and because they had understood all that went to the making of his sin, they condoned it.

If I have done my duty as a faithful chronicler, you who read, understanding too, will take satisfaction in that it was so.